JOHN BAE

A KILLER'S TEARS

ISBN 978-1-66783-497-9 eBook 978-1-66783-498-6

1.

Hope Kane stood and stared into the distance – too lost to bring herself to scream. The thought that he was gone forever froze her mind and body. She heard the sirens echoing through the streets. A tear drop found its path down her cheek. Two men in uniform pointed their weapons at her. She didn't move, her mind refusing to accept the reality that had unfolded in front of her. Then, after a long while, she gave up. There was no point in trying to fight it. She was stuck in a different world that she could not escape. He had given her no choice. Nothing could pull her from the darkness that engulfed her. There was no longer a right or wrong. There were no more choices to be made. The path for the rest of her life had been paved. She would walk down that road because she had nowhere else to go. They shouted at her to drop the gun. She stood with it pointing down, still warm in her hand. The thud echoed through the room as the black pistol fell to the oak floor. The two officers rushed her. They said things to her, but none of it much mattered. She finally looked at him, lying in the pool of his own blood. His eyes were still open, with the indescribable look of a man who knew it was all going to end. He laid on the floor as the blood poured out of the back of his head. His white shirt had turned crimson red as it soaked up the blood from the bullet hole in his heart. She tried to imagine that he was just resting, but there was nothing peaceful about the stillness that surrounded him.

She turned to the two officers and focused on the younger one. His eyes were large. His hands shook. She remembered seeing him in town. He wiped the sweat from his brows. "You are being arrested for the murder of your husband, Ms. Kane," he said. He then locked her wrists in cuffs. They walked her out of the house. The tranquil tree-lined street of her

Westchester home was now a crime scene, with lights red and blue that lit up the neighborhood in rhythmic flashes. The neighbors that had gathered stood behind the crime scene tape that separated their world from hers. Hope Kane closed her eyes and allowed the officers to pull her into her new world – a world she could never leave.

2.

The slight woman behind the bar slid the glass of whisky toward him. Dom noticed she avoided making eye contact. He wondered if it was because of his towering size, or that he was staring at her. He reached for the glass with his calloused left hand and downed it. He slid the glass back to the bartender. She refilled it without saying a word. The voices of the two women sitting at a table behind him caught his ear.

"I can't believe it's been over a year," said the woman with the tightly pulled back blond hair. "She takes a gun to her husband and daughter and she still hasn't been convicted. What crap justice system."

The pretty one with brown hair shook her head. "She's sitting in prison waiting for her trial, so who cares. So long as she's not walking the streets, let them take their time."

"I guess," said the blond. "But, I just want her to be sent away for good. We don't need people like her. I'm tired of all this waiting."

It had been a while since he heard anyone make mention of Hope Kane. Dom turned toward the women. They saw him and lowered their voices. He smiled at them and turned back to the bartender. "How much?" he asked.

"Sixteen even," she said.

Dom pulled out a twenty and dropped it on the bar. He got up and pulled on his coat and opened the heavy wooden door. It had gotten colder, and he saw snow flurries against the street lamps.

"Hey mister," said a man behind him. Dom turned to see two men standing a few feet away from the door. They looked to be in their twenties. He nodded at them and started walking. He could hear them following him.

"Hey mister," said the man again. "I'm talking to you."

Dom kept on walking. He saw a dark alley and walked into it and quickened his pace until he was about thirty feet in. There was a single lightbulb burning from the entry of a building down the street that shed enough light for Dom to see the two men walking toward him. Dom stood in the middle of the street with his hands in his coat pockets. The two men stopped about ten feet away from Dom.

"The mother fucker's big," said one of the guys. The other one chuckled as he pulled out a gun and aimed it at Dom's head.

"You can make this easy," said the guy with the gun. "Give us your wallet and you can walk."

Dom stared into his eyes. "What's your name?" he asked. Dom could see the surprise in their faces, obviously startled that the gun aimed at their victim had no effect.

"Name," Dom said again.

"What the fuck you wanna know my name for. Give me your fucking wallet!" the man with the gun said.

"I like to know who I'm dealing with."

The man cocked his gun. "Hey dickhead, either gimme your fucking wallet, or die right here."

Before he could say another word, Dom pulled out his Sig Sauer and put three bullets in the man's chest. He then pointed the gun at the other man's head. He could see the man physically shaking. He held up his two hands in surrender.

"Turn around and walk," said Dom.

The man nodded and started to turn. Dom fired another shot at the back of his head and saw him go down. He heard sirens in the distance. He shoved his pistol in his pocket and walked away.

Dom parked his car in front of the small white house he was renting. He walked to the kitchen and pulled out the bottle of whisky. He downed the glass and refilled it. He made a fire in the living room and sat down on the couch. The conversation of the two women he overheard was still fresh in his mind. He pulled out his phone and dialed the number for Jacob Milstein. He answered right away.

"Hello?"

"It's me."

"Hi."

"Anything new for me?"

"No. All I know is the Artists Legal Network is trying to find a replacement lawyer. I'll let you know as soon as I hear anything more."

Dom ended the call and sat in the dark room for a few minutes. He reached for the remote and turned on the television. Broncos were playing the Jets. Dom leaned back in his couch and took a sip of his whisky.

3.

Dr. Klingman seemed afraid to look into Tom Rose's eyes. His eyes looked swollen. He had been crying. Doctors usually don't get too emotional about giving bad news, especially experienced, older ones who had given the unfortunate news once too many. But not Dr. Klingman this morning. He had known Tom for too long. The doctor and his father had grown up together, got married the same year and had kids around the same time. They had grown to be like family – two men who chose each other because of the bond of their friendship and not out of obligation that comes with blood siblings. "The blood tests came back with irregularities, elevated level of platelets," the doctor finally said. "You need to see a specialist to rule it out."

"Same as my father?" Tom asked.

Dr. Klingman looked down at the test results and shook his head. "Uh, yes, but that doesn't mean you have the same thing. We shouldn't guess. There are a lot more accurate tests that have to be run. Don't assume the worst."

Tom's heartbeat quickened as he saw the doctor's dejected expression. He didn't need to hear any more. Tom closed his eyes and thought about Melanie. He remembered the way she smiled last night as she brought the wineglass to her lips; the way her black hair fell to her shoulders like silk and the sparkle of her blue eyes.

Tom felt his throat tightening and the tears welling up in his eyes.

"I'm sorry if I'm worrying you, Tom," said the doctor. "The tests are not conclusive at all. You'll need to get it checked by an oncologist, someone who specializes in this area." The doctor wrote down a name and a phone number on his notepad. "Here," he said, as he ripped off the sheet of paper and handed it to Tom. "This is the number for Doctor Sylvia Monroe. She's the best there is. I'll give her a call and let her know you'll be calling. Make an appointment with her and let's get this thing check out. You still have the pain killers I prescribed last week?"

Tom nodded. "Yea. I have it."

"Continue to take them until you see Dr. Monroe, OK?"

"OK," said Tom. He stood and walked out of Dr. Klingman's office and onto 117th Street. He looked up toward Columbus Avenue. It was the path he used to take every day for a month last year to go to Green Oaks Assisted Living. It had become his father's last home after the hopeless surgeries and treatments couldn't rid him of the cancer eating away at his stomach. His father would wait for Tom, lying in his bed with tubes connecting him to a life he no longer wanted. Tom refused to believe the doctors who said he was too far gone to recognize anyone. Although he never opened his eyes, Tom believed his father knew when he was there. That gave him reason to go see him every day.

Tom stared at the frozen sidewalk. He couldn't shake the memories of his father. Tom took in a deep breath and took a few steps. He felt as if he had no control over his six-foot body. It seemed like yesterday when he was finishing the New York City marathon. Now, he had no strength in his long legs, and feared they would give out from under him. Tom stopped and leaned against the cold black lamp post. Tom closed his eyes and remembered the morning of his last visit to Green Oaks. He remembered pressing the intercom and walking down the long hallway to his father's room. Next to the wooden door was a small plastic sign that read, "Earnest Rose." Tom opened the door slowly, "Hi dad," he said. He saw his father lying on the inclined bed. Tom pulled up a chair and sat down next to him. His father slowly opened his eyes and turned to him. Tom couldn't remember the last time he saw his father's eyes.

"How'd you sleep?" Tom asked. His father didn't answer. He just stared at Tom and then smiled. Tom took his father's hand and felt his fingers tighten around his hand. "Hi dad," he said again.

His father slowly closed his eyes. At that moment, the grip loosened and Tom knew his father was finally at peace. Tom leaned over his bed and hugged his father. "Dad, I love you," he said as the tears streamed down his face.

The sound of a truck passing by brought him back to the moment. Tom opened his eyes and turned away from Columbus Avenue. He looked down at the piece of paper with Sylvia Monroe's phone number. A gust of wind took the paper from his hand, and Tom watched it drift down the block and fall to the icy pavement.

He pulled up his collar and started walking, not caring where he wound up.

4.

Tom sat on the windowsill, staring out at the 59th Street Bridge hovering over the East River. He thought about the night before, when he sat across from Melanie at the kitchen table with the open bottle of Scotch. She didn't know he had gone to see his doctor, but there was a sadness in her eyes he had not seen before. She smiled often as she talked about her new job, the friends she had made, her cute boss, Lance Ark. Tom nodded along as he stared into those sad, beautiful eyes. He couldn't hear her words. His mind was too caught up in the meeting with the doctor, the memories of his father. He wanted to see her eyes sparkle, but all he saw was sadness filling them. His heart ached as he sat and stared at her. Tom turned away from the window when he heard her voice.

"Good morning," she said as she stood in her bathrobe.

Tom stared at his fiancé for a few seconds and then turned back to the window. In the years he had been with her, he never stopped loving her – her warm heart, the smile that lit up the room, her lips and her delicate voice. But this morning, he didn't want to notice any of it.

"You have a big day today. Are you excited?" she asked.

Tom nodded. "Yea, I guess."

"You've been waiting for this for eight years. You have to be at least a little excited."

Tom looked down. "I'm not sure why I bothered."

"What's wrong?" Melanie asked, furrowing her eyebrows.

Tom put down his cup. "I don't know what's wrong," he muttered under his breath as he briefly looked up at her. "I wish I knew. I don't know what I want."

9

Melanie stood, frozen, seemingly afraid to respond to what Tom said.

"I'm sorry," he finally said. "I don't know what I'm saying."

Melanie put on a smile. "Let's talk tonight. I have to get ready for work," she said and kissed his cheek.

Tom watched her as she walked down the hallway. He knew he was unfair to her. All she wanted was to share the excitement of the day ahead, yet he threw all that crap at her about not knowing what he wanted. It wasn't her fault that she was excited for him to be elected to the partnership at Stern and Hobbs. He's the one who made her believe that this was his ultimate goal. It meant going from a comfortable life to the life of the privileged. It meant instant repositioning in their stature in society. They'd rub elbows with important people, dine at the best of restaurants, and put away millions of dollars for a rainy day that would never come. Tom didn't blame her for wanting that life. He's the one who convinced her that that was the life they deserved.

He thought back to the time when they first met at Harvard University. She was a freshman when he was in his final year. He saw her at Harvard Square and fell for her flawless beauty the moment their eyes met. She was perfect in every way – a smile that'll make a man weak at the knees, thin and strong five-foot six-inch body of an athlete, yet with curves that exuded femininity. She turned to him and smiled, and he felt his heart melt. He asked her if she'd have dinner with him. She declined, but the way she smiled at him, he knew she'd say yes eventually. They began dating days later, and things got serious fast.

All she wanted was to be with him; to talk about things, to experience things together. But he wanted more than to just go through life with her. He had a goal. He told her he wanted to become a lawyer. He told her he wanted to marry her. He promised her he'd find success and give her a life she deserved. With those promises, he started at Harvard Law School with the goal of becoming a partner at a major New York City law firm. She graduated college the same year he graduated law school, and they moved to Manhattan when he accepted the first year associate position at Stern. They rented a one-bedroom apartment – the same apartment he was standing in. She got a job as an analyst at an investment bank. Their two incomes were more than enough to pay the bills, but not enough for Tom's liking. Last fall, she joined a hedge fund, Ark Capital, as an analyst. Only after four months, she was about to be promoted to a portfolio manager. He was proud of her and all that she had accomplished. But, that didn't change the goals he had set for himself. It had been eight years since he graduated from law school, and today, he was going to be told whether or not the firm would put him up for a vote to become a partner. But, this morning, he didn't much care what they told him – not after his meeting with Dr. Klingman. After making her wait with him for eight long years for this day, he celebrated the moment by drinking too much the night before, and telling her he didn't know what he wanted.

Tom's eyes began to well up. For the first time in a very long time, he began rethinking what he wanted to do with his life. Becoming a partner at Stern and making a lot of money were no longer goals that mattered. The conversation with Dr. Klingman had changed everything; made him open his eyes to the life he had led. Memories of his father made him want to do more with whatever was left of his life. What did it really mean to become a partner at Stern? Who really gives a shit? Tom knew being drunk wouldn't change what the doctor told him, but he wanted to be numb to it. That was about the only thing that made any sense to him.

Tom wiped his eyes and put down his coffee cup on the window-sill. He put on his black overcoat and wrapped the purple scarf around his neck. The briefcase his father gave him when he graduated law school waited for him by the door. The black finish on the leather had worn to show streaks of gray from the years it had been exposed to the elements. Tom picked it up and headed out of the apartment and onto York Avenue. The cold January air helped to clear his head a little. He stepped carefully onto the icy pavement and headed toward Third Avenue. He thought about Melanie. It bothered him that he treated her the way he did. But his love for her told him he had no choice. He had made up his mind. He couldn't see those sad eyes again.

"Good morning, Tom," he heard Helena say as he walked past her station.

"Hi," said Tom and opened his office door.

"Edward just called," she said. "He said to meet him at Wolfgang's at 12:30. He said he had a meeting out of the office, so he'll just meet you at the restaurant."

Tom nodded and walked into his office. He saw the red message light blinking on his phone. He punched in his PIN and heard the mechanical voice say he had three new messages. The first was from a legal recruiter. He pressed delete and moved to the second. It was Melanie. "Hi, it's me. I just wanted to say hi and wish you luck today." Tom closed his eyes. He listened to her voice again, and then pressed delete. The third message was from Scott King, a senior partner at Stern who headed up pro bono projects. "Tom, we have a new pro bono matter that I was hoping you might be able to take on. Can you give me a call this morning?"

Tom dialed King's number.

"Hey Tom, how're you doing?"

"I'm OK. I'm returning your call."

"I'll walk down to your office. It's an intriguing situation."

"Oh, I'm not so sure I'm the right person . . ."

King cut in before Tom could finish. "You're going to want to hear me out on this, Tom. I'll be right down," King said and hung up.

Tom felt slight nausea coming on. He stepped to the office pantry and poured a cup of coffee and returned to his office. He stared at the piles of documents on his desk and floor. He had spent the past year defending a breach of contract lawsuit against an important client of the firm. The case settled days before, and he no longer needed the files that engulfed his office. He knew he'd have to organize the files to have them shipped to the records department, but he had no motivation. Tom heard a knock on his door and looked up to see King.

"I hear you settled the Armor Peak litigation," said King as he took a seat on the chair facing Tom's desk. He looked around at the piles of file folders all over the office. "Looks like you need a larger office. This associate office is getting too small for you."

Tom nodded and took his chair. "Like I tried to tell you. I'm not so sure I'm the right person for this project."

"Of course you are," said King. "As I said, it's an intriguing situation. The matter was sent to us by the Artists Legal Network, which is one of the not-for-profits we work with on a pro bono basis. The defendant is Hope Kane, who's being prosecuted for the murder of her husband, Mark Kane, and her daughter, Mila. I'm sure you read about the case in the papers."

Tom nodded. He recalled reading the stories about the "mute murderer" – a woman kills her husband and daughter and then refuses to speak. It had captivated the nation a year ago when she was arrested.

"The neighbors called the Scarsdale police when they heard gunshots. The arresting officers found her standing in their living room, standing over her dead husband. She was holding the murder weapon when the police arrived."

"Yea, I remember reading about it," said Tom. "She'll do her twenty-five to life, and then everyone'll move on to some other sensational story. Why would we want to take on a sure loser like this one?"

King nodded. "Yes, it's a sure loser, but as you may recall, what makes this case so intriguing is that she's not uttered a word since she's been arrested. She just won't speak to anyone. The prosecutors, legal aid attorneys, the police, no one's been able to get her to say whether she'll even plead guilty or innocent."

"Yes, I remember the stories about her refusing to speak, but that doesn't change the fact that she murdered her family. What possible defense could she put up?"

"That's for you to figure out."

Tom shook his head. "Scott, as much as I would love to help, I'm not sure what I possibly can do for her. If she won't talk to anyone, why would she talk to me?"

"There's one other thing," said King. "Let's talk about Mila, Hope Kane's three-year old daughter who went missing on the night of the murder. The prosecution is going after her for the murder of both the husband and the daughter. Of course, no one's seen the daughter's body, so theoretically, she could be alive."

Tom shook his head. "What a mess."

"That it is. So, this engagement is more than just trying to help Hope. We all know the case will turn into a plea deal at some point. The greater question is can we get her to help us find her daughter, dead or alive? If she's lying dead somewhere, we'd like to find her body. We want to show the world that we've done everything we can to locate her."

Tom furrowed his eyebrows. "What do you mean 'we' have to show the world? We haven't even taken on this engagement."

King stood to close Tom's door and then sat back down. "Tom, the firm's already committed to take on the assignment. It's a good case politically. You're going to be a partner here soon, so I may as well be straight up with you. The firm's been under attack for making too much money." King chuckled. "Imagine that. We're being crucified for being good at what we do. We're depicted as an overly aggressive law firm that's only motivated by money. You taking on this high profile case will send the right message that we care about public interest and that we'll do our part."

"Why me?"

"You're the rising star. You were written up in every legal publication out there as someone to keep an eye on. This is the year you'll be considered for partnership. To have you take on this project will send the right message that we care about things other than making money. The message we want to send is that we're willing to commit our brightest stars and the firm's future for the good of the public."

"So, you want me to spend the year that I'm up for partner, babysitting an impossible case? I don't see how this helps the firm. There's no good that can come of this case. She'll wind up in prison and we'll never find her daughter. It'll be a complete failure."

King shook his head. "To the contrary. It's a no-lose case for us. Everyone knows that she won't talk, so defending her will be impossible. The circumstantial evidence of her killing her husband is insurmountable. Without her talking, there's no defense. Plus, we can't find her daughter without her help. As you say, the expectation is that she'll wind up in prison and we'll never find her daughter. So, failure is what everyone expects, and no one will think any less of you or the firm. But, if we get lucky and get any information from her to solve the mystery of her daughter, then we're all heroes. Also, this is a quick in and out. Trial is scheduled for two weeks from now. I know you'll get an extension as new counsel, but all you have to do is baby sit this case for a few weeks, see if you can make any progress on Mila, and then Hope will be sent to prison, and you'll be done."

Tom shook his head. "So, you want me to take this case as a PR stunt?"

King smiled. "No. Not just me. This is coming from the Management Committee. This is Timothy Ryan's baby. He came up with the idea."

"Are you saying I don't have a choice?" asked Tom, staring into King's eyes.

King pulled out a business card and set it down on Tom's desk and smiled. "You always have a choice, Tom, but it's probably not a good idea to turn down an assignment that was hand-picked by the Management

Committee, particularly when you'll be considered for the partnership this year."

Tom picked up the card and looked at it. "Artists Legal Network," said Tom, reading the business card out loud.

"That's the contact information for Janet Gold. She's with the Artists Legal Network who's responsible for this file. Give her a call for all the details."

"Why are they involved?"

"Hope apparently tried her hand at art at some point and befriended some people in the art world here in the city, which is how the Artists Legal Network got involved."

Tom nodded and stared at the business card. King stood to leave. "She's expecting your call."

Tom watched King walk out. He remembered the extensive coverage of the Hope Kane story. From everything he had read, she was a lost cause. But whether or not she was guilty, she was entitled to a lawyer who could devote his efforts for her defense. Tom knew he was not that person. He closed his eyes and thought about Dr. Klingman, his father, Melanie. He shook his head. He needed to run from those thoughts. He reached for the phone.

5.

"Stern and Hobbs took the case," said Jacob Milstein as Linda Starr walked past him. She stopped short and turned back to him. "Hey, you finally acknowledged me," Milstein said with a grin.

"What did you say?" asked Linda, taking a step toward him.

"The Kane case. Heather told me Stern and Hobbs took it on pro bono. You're going to have your hands full."

Linda shook her head. "Why are you so fixated on my case?"

Milstein laughed. "I'm fixated on everything about you."

"It doesn't matter who represents her. She was caught with the murder weapon in her hand, and with her refusal to speak, she won't be able to explain her way out of a conviction." Linda smiled. "No one can save her," she said as she turned to walk to her office.

"I like your confidence," she heard him say. "Dinner tonight?"

Linda didn't answer. She was tired of having to turn down his advances. It was just easier to ignore him. She saw a message slip on her desk that Heather Palmer had called. Linda picked up a notepad and walked to Palmer's office and saw her speaking on the phone. She motioned for Linda to come in. Linda sat down and waited until Palmer hung up.

"Hope Kane's finally got counsel," Palmer said. "Thomas Hunter Rose with Stern and Hobbs will be representing her."

"How do we know this?"

"I got a call from Janet Gold with the Artists Legal Network. She told me that Stern committed to take on the case. I separately got a call from

Timothy Ryan. It's not official yet, but Timothy told me that it's a done deal."

Linda nodded. "Good. Now that she's got counsel, maybe we can finally get to trial."

"I wouldn't bet on it," said Palmer. "They're going to want an extension to learn the file."

"There isn't anything to learn. She was caught red handed, and she hasn't said anything to anyone to even try and deny it. The file's empty other than irrelevant garbage the police gathered from their interviews."

Palmer nodded. "I know, but Rose is supposed to be good. He'll find a way to muck this up. He's at least going to want some time to investigate what happened."

Linda rolled her eyes. "He can investigate all he wants. He's not going to find anything that's going to help her. No one else was able to come up with a theory for the defense."

"I suppose you're right, but let's not assume anything. If you want to hold on to the February trial date, you may want to pull together whatever we're planning on using at trial and send it to them. We may as well give them everything. There's nothing there to help Kane, and we don't want any more delay."

"Got it. Anything else?" asked Linda as she stood.

"Nope. Speak with me if you run into any trouble. These guys are aggressive. If they take Kane's defense seriously, they're pretty good at screwing things up."

Linda headed back to her office and booted up her computer. She launched the browser and went to Stern and Hobbs' webpage. The home page opened with an impressive list of recent litigation victories and multibillion dollar corporate deals. She typed in Thomas Rose in the "professionals" section. His biography popped up with his picture. Linda stared at the chiseled face, the deep set eyes, the perfectly parted dark hair. She made her way down to the long list of his accomplishments and shook her head. "They put their star Harvard boy on the case," she muttered to herself. She scrolled back up to his picture. As much as she dreaded having a formidable opponent, she couldn't help but be drawn to his good looks. "You are so fucking shallow," Linda said under her breath as she chuckled in embarrassment.

Milstein dialed the number. He heard the same voice. "Hi Mick, it's Jacob."

"What do you have?"

"Hope's got a new lawyer. It's the firm, Stern and Hobbs. We were told that a lawyer by the name of Tom Rose will be handling the case."

"What do you mean 'you were told?' Is he or is he not her lawyer?"

"Until he actually appears in the case, we won't know for sure, but we did get a call from Timothy Ryan who's with Stern. He knows the DA and told her that he'll assign Tom Rose to the case. We got the same information from the Artists Legal Network."

"When did you find this out?"

"Earlier today."

"I want everything real time, understand?"

"Yes."

Jacob ended the call. There was something about Mick's voice that unnerved him. He was tired of having to phrase every sentence just perfectly to avoid upsetting the man. He shook his head and wondered if he had made a mistake in agreeing to be Mick's informer. But none of that mattered at the moment. He had taken the money, and there was no going back.

6.

Janet Gold's assistant announced that Tom Rose was on the line. This was one call she wasn't going to miss.

"Janet Gold speaking," she said into the phone.

"This is Tom Rose with Stern and Hobbs. I'm calling about the Hope Kane matter."

"Yes, yes. Thank you for calling. I've been waiting for your call. I think the best way to do this is for me to come up to your offices and I can give you the background and hand over the file. Would you have time to meet today, around 1 pm?"

"I have a meeting at 12:30. Can we do it later in the day?"

"Let me check." Gold clicked on her Outlook calendar and saw that she had a closing for a client's contract for an art exhibition. "Tom, I can shuffle things around. What time would be good for you?"

"I should free up around 2 or 3."

"Let's shoot for 3. I'll see you then," said Gold. She was about to hang up when she heard him call out her name.

"Janet?"

"Yes."

"Just out of curiosity, why isn't the Artists Legal Network handling this case directly? I thought you handled these types of matters in house?"

"The Artists Legal Network had never before handled a matter like this. We're much more comfortable handling transactions like real estate closings, setting up corporations for not for profits and occasional contract disputes. The Kane case is a little too much for us to handle."

"I had thought you handled criminal matters, but I guess it really doesn't matter. I'll see you at 3," said Tom as he hung up.

Gold dialed the number for Brian Kushner, the director of the Artists Legal Network.

"Yes, Janet."

"Tom Rose will be handling it."

"Good."

"I'm sorry I put us in this mess," said Gold.

"Look, it was wrong of me to raise my voice at you, but you really should've spoken to me before taking this case from Legal Aid."

"I had no idea the facts were this bad."

"If you had read the media coverage, you would've known. With charitable contributions as low as they are, we have to be much more careful and selective in the cases we take on. The last thing our supporters would want is to see us representing a woman who murdered her own husband and her baby."

"Understood," said Gold.

"When will you be transferring the file to him?"

"This afternoon. I'm meeting him at his office."

"Make sure it gets done. Just make sure he doesn't figure out how bad the facts are. He may run for the hills."

"I don't think you'll have to worry about that. I have a commitment from Timothy Ryan that Stern will take this on, and that Tom Rose will handle the matter himself."

"Good."

7.

Melanie stared out of the window of her thirty fifth floor office at Ark Capital, but the grand view of Central Park didn't grab her interest. She looked out into the distance, lost in the conversation she had with Tom that morning. He wasn't himself last night or this morning. She couldn't remember ever spending an evening with him when they didn't speak. He had come home and just opened a bottle of Scotch. He wouldn't look her in the eyes. She wondered if something had happened that upset him. She wondered if this was his way of dealing with the stress of not knowing whether Stern would make him a partner. All of this will pass, she said to herself. He'll achieve his dream of becoming a partner, and life would go on just the way he planned it. The plan was to wait until he had been elected to the partnership before getting married. He had their entire future planned out, and she was happy to run by his side. But the words, "I don't know what I want," repeatedly echoed through her mind. Her heart ached, not knowing what he meant.

A knock on her door made her look up. "Sorry, I didn't' mean to startle you," said Lance Ark, the forty-two year old wunderkind who founded Ark Capital.

Melanie put on a smile. "Hi."

"I've scheduled a lunch with some new investors. Can you join me at 12?"

Melanie nodded, "Yes, of course."

"Good," he said and walked off.

Melanie saw her assistant Pamela sitting at her station, following Lance with her eyes. She turned back to Melanie and looked at her with a coy smile. Melanie rolled her eyes and looked down at the document sitting on her desk. When Melanie first joined Ark Capital, Pamela made tremendous efforts to befriend her. Their relationship quickly evolved from a working relationship into a friendship, and that meant Pamela felt she had a license to inject herself into Melanie's personal life. Melanie regretted allowing Pamela to break down the professional barrier, though she wondered if she even had an option to keep her out. For whatever reason, Pamela was convinced that Lance had a thing for Melanie. She'd point out all the little things he'd do, like always inviting Melanie to investor lunches, hovering around her during office parties just a minute longer than he needed to, and the way he'd just stare at her for short stretches. Pamela called him the perfect man; slightly long blond hair, deep blue eyes, a girlish pretty face that most women would envy, six feet two with a perfect body, and most importantly, rich. She'd say she'd leave her husband Tony in a heartbeat if she thought she had a chance with Lance. Pamela would say that no woman should say no to a man like Lance, and Tony would just have to suck it up and let her go.

Melanie was in no mood to let Pamela engage her in another discussion about Lance. "I saw the way you looked at him," she heard Pamela say from her desk.

Melanie didn't look up. "You have to stop this, Pamela," said Melanie. "I didn't look at him in any way." Melanie could hear Pamela getting up out of her chair. There was no polite way to make Pamela stop. She would just have to suffer through another conversation and hope that Pamela would lose interest and get back to work.

"And I saw the way he looked at you too," said Pamela.

Melanie looked up at her. "You were sitting behind him. You couldn't have seen the way he looked at me."

"I saw him as he was turning to leave. His eyes were glued to you. He nearly walked into the plant outside your office."

Melanie shook her head. "Pamela, you need to listen to me, okay? I am not interested. I am engaged to be married to a man I love. So it really doesn't matter how he may have looked at me."

Pamela smiled. "You aren't married yet. And besides, does your fiancé look at you the way Lance does? And on that note, when will you two be married?"

"We don't have a date yet," said Melanie. "But why are you so down on Tom?"

"Because I don't like Tom. He's too serious."

"You've only met him once. You have no idea what he's like."

Pamela's phone started ringing. She jumped out of Melanie's office and ran to her station to pick up the headset. Melanie breathed a sigh of relief, grateful the conversation had ended. She was startled as she saw Lance stick his head into her office.

"Melanie, the lunch got pushed back to 12:30. Let's leave here at 12:15. We're just going down the street to Amanda's." Lance smiled at her and then walked off.

Melanie sat, frozen. Her face turned beet red as she wondered if he heard her conversation with Pamela. She could see Pamela sitting at her station with her arms crossed, nodding her head slowly up and down with an evil grin. Melanie stepped out to Pamela and then looked around to make sure no one could hear her.

"Pamela, I'm engaged to be married," Melanie said in a hushed voice. "I know you're not crazy about Tom, but he will be my husband. You have to stop this fantasy about me and Lance. Will you promise me you'll stop?"

Pamela nodded. "I will, but remember. You're not married yet."

Melanie shook her head. There was no getting through to her. She walked back to her office and closed the door.

8.

Tom leaned back in his chair and closed his eyes. He felt his head pounding. The Scotch he downed last night wanted payback, and the headache was the price. It was near Noon. He wrapped his scarf tightly around his neck and put on his coat. He stepped out onto Third Avenue. Temperature had dropped from earlier and it started to snow. The thin leather gloves Melanie gave him for Christmas did nothing to warm his hands. He shoved his hands in his coat pockets and walked west on 62nd Street toward Park Avenue, looking for a cab.

The restaurant was humming, with every table filled. The host led him to his table, and he saw Edward, who stood to shake his hand. For no apparent reason, Tom noticed how old Edward looked. His full head of hair had turned silver. He still had that mature good looks to him, but Tom hadn't before noticed the way the skin around his eyes drooped, and the pronounced lines around the edges of his mouth. His eyes lacked the sparkle they once had. There was a time when Edward stood a few inches taller than Tom, but now, with his poor posture and older bones, Edward looked a lot smaller than Tom. Tom wondered if Edward's deterioration was just the human body giving way to age, or the result of too many late nights with alcohol and paid companions. Tom had known Edward since he was a first year associate. Edward took Tom under his wings right away, and they had grown close. They had worked on every case together until Edward's work slowed down.

"Hey Tom, I hope you brought your appetite. I ordered for the both of us. Porterhouse for two, some creamed spinach, mashed potatoes, and the seafood platter to start. I have to run to a meeting by 2:30."

"Sounds good, Edward," said Tom as he sat down.

A man with long hair tied in a ponytail walked over to the table. "Good afternoon. I'm Ron, and I'll be serving you. What can I get you to drink?"

"What're you drinking?" Tom asked Edward.

"Vodka martini."

"I thought you had a meeting," said Tom.

Edward laughed. "I didn't say with whom," he said, winking.

Tom shook his head and looked up at the server. "I'll have the same."

Tom turned back to Edward. "I'm not sure I want to hear any more about your meeting, Edward."

"Then you won't," said Edward smiling.

Ron returned with two bottles of water. "Your drinks will be out shortly. Would you like sparkling or still?" he asked, looking at Tom.

"Sparkling."

He poured the water and refilled Edward's half empty water glass. Tom downed the water, hoping it'll help clear his head.

"I heard you settled the Armor case. What're you going to work on next?" Edward asked, breaking a breadstick in half.

"I'll be taking on a new project."

"Good. What is it?"

"A pro bono project. I'll be representing that woman from Westchester who's accused of killing her husband. Hope Kane. Remember that story?"

Edward looked down and shook his head. "Did you commit already?"

Tom furrowed his eyebrows, "Sort of. I told Scott I'd take it on. Why are you shaking your head?"

"I wish you had talked to me first."

"Why?"

The server returned and placed two martini glasses down on the table. He shook the stainless steel mixer and poured the clear vodka. "Your appetizers will be out shortly," he said before walking off.

"We're going to put you up to become a partner this year. You know that," said Edward.

"Well, I actually didn't know that for sure."

"Come on Tom, cut the crap. You know this is your year. It's just not good timing to take on a time-consuming pro bono project."

"I'm not following you, Edward. This was given to me by the Management Committee. It came directly from Timothy Ryan."

"Ryan? That fuck? Who told you that?"

"Scott told me," said Tom, picking up his martini.

Edward picked up his glass and held it out toward Tom. "Cheers," he said as he tapped it against Tom's glass. Tom took a long sip. He felt the vodka dull the pounding in his head.

"It takes three things to become a partner at Stern and Hobbs," Edward said. "This pro bono woman will just get in the way."

Tom sat quietly and watched Edward take a long sip out of his martini glass, waiting for him to continue.

"First, you have to be a great lawyer. You are a great lawyer. I've always told you that. But, being a great lawyer isn't enough. You also need economics to back you. Stern and Hobbs is all about making money. We can't make a new partner, if doing so will make the pie smaller and all partners have to take home less money. So, in order to make a new partner, the partnership has to believe that you'll help make the pie larger. Can you accomplish that?"

Edward stared at Tom for a few seconds, but didn't wait for a response. "You have two different ways to show that you'll add to the bottom line. Generating your own clients and billable hours. Can you generate your own clients? Most eighth-year associates don't have very many clients that can afford to hire Stern and Hobbs. So, the question is do you have potential to build a client base? I think the answer's yes, but there are some who aren't so convinced. So, that factor is neutral. The more practical way you can show that you'll make money for the firm is to jack up your billable hours. Associates who are up for partner usually bill twenty-five hundred to three thousand hours in their eighth year to show that they're profitable to the firm. You taking on the Hope Kane case will kill you there."

Tom nodded as he stared at Edward.

"Now, let's talk about politics, the third factor. The most powerful partners at the firm are the biggest rainmakers. You know that. That means, their point of view matters the most in influencing other partners on how they should vote. In my heyday, this would've been a done deal. The trouble is, you know what's happened to my practice. But, I still have old friends whose backs I've scratched who'll support me. Whether that's enough, I don't know. So, that piece is a serious question mark.

"Let's now introduce the Hope Kane case to this equation. You've read the papers about her. Everyone's read the papers about her. She's accused of killing her husband and her daughter, and she doesn't speak. From what I remember, she was caught with the murder weapon in her hand. It's a sure bet loser. And, to make matters worse, she's public enemy number one. You're playing with fire taking on a hot button case like this one. If things go south and the firm's reputation gets tarnished, it won't matter how many clients you or I have. They *will* skewer you. Tom, the bottom line is you being put up for partner is a sure thing. Whether or not you get elected is another matter, and I have concerns. You can't be taking risks you don't need to take."

Tom took another sip of his martini. The second sip had less of an effect on his headache than the first. He put down the glass and looked up at Edward. "I don't see it as a risk," said Tom.

Edward downed his martini. "Well, it is, and you sound like a man who wants to take a risk for the sake of taking it, Tom."

"I don't see it that way."

Edward looked into Tom's eyes. "Listen to me. This is plain stupid. Find an excuse to pass the case onto someone else. This is the last thing you need."

"I'm meeting with the lawyer from the Artists Legal Network at 3 today. Who am I going to pass this onto?"

"Call what's her face, the assignment partner. Blame it on me. Tell her I have an exhaustive marketing trip planned for us. We'll be traveling all over the country, meeting with everyone we know. You'll have no time for the Kane case. She'll understand that."

Tom looked down at his half empty glass. The pounding in his head felt more pronounced now. The truth was, becoming a partner at Stern no longer mattered. Representing Hope Kane didn't much matter to him either, but it would've been something to do, something to distract him. "I'll think about it," he finally said, hoping to change subjects.

Edward nodded. "I'm just trying to look out for you, kid."

The server returned with a large metal plate filled with cold lobsters, crab meat, and clams and oysters."

"Let's eat," said Edward as he reached for an oyster. Tom stared at the plate for a moment and then turned to the server. "I'll take another martini."

9.

Tom walked out of the restaurant and looked at the falling snow. The sidewalks were beginning to turn white. He looked around for a cab when he remembered he hadn't called Melanie. Tom pulled out his phone and dialed her cell phone.

"Hi," he heard her say.

"Sorry I didn't call you earlier," Tom said.

"It's OK. Tom, I'm at a lunch meeting, so can't talk, but how was your lunch with Edward?"

"It went fine."

"Is it good news?" she asked.

Tom closed his eyes. "Yes," he said.

"That's wonderful. I love you."

"I'll see you later," he said and ended the call. Nausea set in as he felt a deep pain in his stomach. Deep breaths did nothing to ease the pain. Tom took a few steps and saw a trash can. He hunched over it and felt the food and alcohol come up. The taste of the vodka mixed with his stomach acids made him feel even more sick. When there was nothing left in his stomach, he felt his mind clearing a bit. He wiped his mouth with his hand and looked up. Two women stared at him with a disgusted look as they walked past. Tom closed his eyes and shook his head. He felt a rush of emotion overwhelm him as the tears welled up in his eyes. Tom braced himself against a lamp post. "Fuck," he said under his breath. After a few minutes, he started to walk back to his office. Janet Gold was going to be there in an hour. He'd hear her out and then decline the representation, he thought. He just had to hold it together until he got though the meeting.

10.

Dom checked his watch. It was almost 3 o'clock. He walked up Bleeker Street and stopped in front of the small restaurant. He turned around and scanned the street. Ortega was nowhere in sight. Dom walked down the half flight of stairs and opened the wooden door. He saw a handful of people hanging around the bar, but the place was otherwise empty. A woman walked up to him.

"Would you like to sit at the bar?" she asked.

"No. Can you get me a table? Something in the back?" he asked. She led him past the bar to a small room with a half dozen tables. "This is good," he said.

"What can I get you?" she asked.

"Glass of Jack Daniels," he said and sat down. She returned a minute later and set down a glass of whisky in front of him. Dom downed it before she could walk away. "Bring me the bottle," he said.

"Yes sir," she said and hurried off. Dom saw Ortega walking toward him. "Bring me another glass," Dom shouted to the waitress.

"About time you got here," said Dom.

"Couldn't find a taxi. And the subway was delayed," said Ortega as he took off his coat.

The waitress returned with a bottle and an empty glass.

"Just shout if you need anything else," she said as she walked off.

Dom refilled his glass. "You shouldn't be riding in taxis here anyway, especially in this weather."

"What are you a fucking New Yorker now?"

Dom chuckled and filled Ortega's glass. "You get me what I need?"

"Yea," said Ortega and handed him a cell phone. "This is all you need. Just turn it on, and you're good to go."

Dom shoved the phone in his pocket. "Where's the rest of it?"

"Where's my money?" Ortega asked.

Dom pulled out an envelope from his coat pocket and slid it across the table. Ortega opened it and looked inside and smiled. He reached into his breast pocket and pulled out a large envelope folded in half. "It's all in there."

Ortega took a sip of his drink and set the glass down. "Gotta run," he said. "Let me know if you need anything else."

Dom nodded and watched Ortega walk out of the restaurant. Dom refilled his glass and opened the envelope. He saw a dozen pages of notes. But he focused on the picture. He wanted to make sure he remember the face – the face of Thomas Hunter Rose.

11.

Tom splashed cold water on his face, hoping it'll help him out of the fog. He cupped his hands to catch the water, and then poured it into his mouth. He wiped his face with paper towels and then saw his image in the mirror. Nothing looked different. He was the same man as the day before and the days before that. But he knew so much had changed. Everything would be different from now on. The sadness began to creep back into his thoughts. Tom closed his eyes and took in a deep breath. He hated this feeling. No more, he said to himself. I can't live like this.

Tom made his way back to the conference room. He sat across the table from Janet Gold as she opened her briefcase and pulled out a thin stack of manila folders. She rambled on about the snow, the chill in the air, her long commute home to Long Island, and on and on. She pulled out a notepad and a pen and then looked up at Tom.

"Let me tell you what we know about Hope Kane," she said as she opened one of the files. "Hope Kane is a complete mystery to us. What we know about her is that she lived in Scarsdale with her husband, Mark, and daughter, Mila. But, we don't have any records of her or her husband before they moved to Scarsdale about four and a half years ago. They both have a New York driver's license with their Scarsdale address. They have one bank account that was filled every once in a while with cash. Neither of them worked, so we don't know where they got their money. They began renting the house in Scarsdale when Hope was pregnant with Mila. The baby girl was born at the Northern Westchester Hospital about six months after they moved to Scarsdale, and she's the only one with a record of her life. Neither Hope nor Mark seem to have even existed before they moved to Scarsdale right before Mila was born."

Tom stood to pour a cup of coffee. "Do they have any family?" he asked.

"No one that anyone's been able to track down. They did have some friends in the neighborhood, but they couldn't offer much help. They knew nothing about Hope or Mark's background. But, they all said Hope and Mark were lovely people, seemed madly in love. They were completely shocked that she would kill her own husband. No one really believes that she could have done any of this."

Tom sat back down with his coffee. "That's not what I recall reading in the papers."

"What, what do you mean?" asked Gold.

Tom could see the feigned surprise in Gold's expression. "I mean, I remember reading the papers a year ago when all this happened. She was caught with the gun in her hand. My recollection is that people were shocked because she came across as such a gentle person, and no one saw it coming, but I don't think anyone was doubting that she was the murderer."

Gold looked pale and lost for words. It was obvious she wanted to hand this file off to Stern and move on.

"I'm not saying Stern won't represent her," Tom reassured her, "But I also don't like to start on a false premise."

Gold nodded and color returned to her face.

"I didn't mean to interrupt you," Tom said. "So, let's get back to her background. She just appeared in Scarsdale some time ago. No one knew anything about her background. People she knew in the neighborhood thought she and Mark had a good relationship, and then she just suddenly shot her husband. Doesn't make much sense."

Gold nodded. "Yes, that's pretty much what we know."

"Maybe he was having an affair? Crime of passion?" asked Tom.

Gold shrugged. "We saw no evidence of that, but that doesn't mean it didn't happen."

"Did anyone look?" asked Tom.

Gold shook her head. "I, uh, I don't think so."

"I don't get it," said Tom shaking his head. "Has anyone done anything to formulate a defense?"

"Uh, we didn't have a chance to conduct our own analysis, so you'll have to speak with Legal Aid about that. An obvious difficulty with this case is that Hope won't speak. She won't speak to anyone. She just sits without saying a word when people ask her questions. All she does is just cry once in a while, but no words."

"So strange," muttered Tom.

"Yes. It is very strange," said Gold, seemingly happy to take the discussion in a different direction. "And what's even more strange is her daughter's missing. People who knew them were convinced that Hope loved her daughter. The fact that she's missing has people in shock. And the prosecution's trying to pin Mila on Hope also."

"Has the prosecution said anything about a plea deal?" Tom asked.

Gold shook her head. "No, because there isn't any point. The prosecution knows the difficulties of this case for the defense, so they won't offer anything even worth discussing. Also, Hope won't speak or respond to questions. No one's been able to engage her to even have the discussion of whether she'd plead guilty or innocent, or agree to a deal."

"Let's get back to her defense," said Tom. "What investigation was done by Legal Aid and the Artists Legal Network?"

Gold looked uneasy again. "Uh, the police and the prosecutors conducted a thorough investigation and prepared reports, which they turned over to the attorney assigned to her from the Legal Aid Society."

"What investigation did Legal Aid do?" Tom asked again.

"Well, we really don't know. All we have are these files."

"Why did they drop the case?"

"They didn't just drop the case," said Gold with a hint of annoyance. "With all the cuts in funding, the attorneys there are overwhelmed. They contacted us to see if we can help."

Tom nodded. "And what investigation have you done?"

Gold slid the files across the table to Tom. "It's all here. I need to get back downtown for a meeting. Review the files and call me if you would like to discuss further."

Gold stood and picked up her briefcase. "Oh, I almost forgot the most important piece of information. There is a trial date of February 8."

Tom nodded. "Yes, I'm aware of that."

Gold smiled. "Good. I'm sure the judge will give you an adjournment. After all, you are new counsel."

Gold took another step toward the door. "And, Hope is being held at the Bedford Hills Women's Prison. The prison's contact information is in the files. The prosecutor assigned to the case is Linda Starr. She's been with the DA's office for about six years. That's everything," she said as she quickly left the conference room.

Tom sat staring at the files. He shook his head. It was obvious the defense lawyers assigned to Hope Kane had conducted no investigation to formulate a defense. He wasn't surprised. With all of the bad facts surrounding the murder, it would have been easy to lose interest fast. Why waste energy on a lost cause? So now, his firm was stuck with the file and a trial date in two weeks. He didn't have any desire to handle the case. Someone else can do it, he thought. He picked up the phone and dialed the number for Joann Creed, the assignment partner for the litigation department. Her assistant said she was in a meeting. Tom didn't leave a message and hung up. He stood and walked to the window. The tops of the nearby buildings had all turned white from the snow that wasn't in the forecast. "Partner," he said to himself, and then he chuckled. He turned and looked at the stack of files sitting on the table. Tom sat down and reached for them. He read them, one by one. Most of the files included notes from meetings with Hope's acquaintances. All of the interview notes were virtually identical – Hope and Mark were a happy couple who loved their daughter Mila. They largely kept to themselves. No one had any information about their background, motive or anything else that would provide a clue as to how to defend the case. He saw a report prepared by the medical examiner, Dr. Tanya Rego. He next read the report of the forensics expert, Malachy O'Neal. He closed the files and pushed them aside. With a sure-bet conviction in their hands, the prosecution had no incentive to offer an acceptable plea deal. This case was going to go to trial – a trial where everyone already knew the outcome. Tom stared at the medical examiner's report he had just pushed aside. He reached for it and opened it again. He read about the two gunshots. Why would she shoot her husband twice? Two weeks, he muttered to himself. How could he in good conscience dump this case on another associate? Tom ran through the files once again. The woman had been sitting in prison for over a year, and there wasn't a single piece of paper to show that a lawyer was looking out for her interests. Maybe she killed her husband, but she was entitled to be represented. Everybody dumped her to the next lawyer in line, until she landed in front of him. If he were to take on the case, he would have to raise a reasonable doubt to buy her freedom. There was nothing here to make him believe he could do it. He turned to the forensics report and started to read about the angles in which the bullets entered Mark Kane's body.

12.

"Edward's assistant called and wants you to meet him in his office tomorrow morning at nine," said Helena on the intercom.

"OK," said Tom. "Is my car here yet?"

"Yes. It's waiting for you on 63rd Street," said Helena.

Tom picked up his briefcase and headed out to the waiting Town Car.

"Anyone else joining you?" asked the driver.

"No. Just me. We can go."

The driver nodded. Tom heard his cell phone ringing. He saw Melanie on the caller ID.

"Hi," he said into the phone.

"I'm sorry I couldn't speak before," said Melanie.

"It's Okay."

"So what happened at lunch with Edward?"

"He said I'll be put up for a vote this year."

"That's wonderful news, Tom."

"The partnership still has to vote."

"I'm sure you'll get the vote," said Melanie.

"No," said Tom in a firmer voice than he had intended. "I mean, we can't assume anything. There are a lot of things that can go wrong."

"Oh," said Melanie, seemingly perplexed at Tom's tone.

"I'm sorry," said Tom. "I just have a lot on my mind. We'll speak later when I get home."

"Okay," she said.

Tom shoved his phone in his pocket. He stared out of the window as the car drove up the Saw Mill River Parkway. She has been sitting in prison for over a year. She'll likely spend the rest of her life there. What about Mila? Where is she? Could Hope really have harmed her own daughter? The black Town Car pulled into the parking lot in front of the large grey structure surrounded by tall fences trimmed with barbed wire on top.

"Maximum security prison," said the driver.

"Yep," said Tom as he opened the door.

"Amy Fisher was held here and there were a bunch of stories about this prison," the driver said.

Tom nodded. "Please wait for me. I shouldn't be more than an hour."

Tom walked through the entrance and up to the reception counter. A woman in a uniform looked up at him.

"Can I help you?"

"I'm Thomas Rose with the law firm of Stern and Hobbs. I'm here to see my client, Hope Kane. I called earlier."

The woman punched in Tom's name into a computer and stared at the screen. "Here you are. Just a minute. A corrections officer will take you to the meeting room."

A man stepped up to Tom. "Follow me."

He guided Tom to the elevators. "You here to see the mute?" asked the officer.

"If you mean Hope Kane, yea."

"Good luck," he said. "She's said nothing to anyone. You'll just waste your time."

He opened the door to a room with a metal table and chairs around it. "Wait in here."

Tom stepped in and took a seat. A few moments later, he heard the door open. The officer stood behind a woman in an orange jumpsuit. He guided her to the table and sat her down across from Tom. "Knock on the door when you're done," he said and left the room.

Tom saw the woman looking down and couldn't see her face. He waited a minute, hoping she'd look up. She didn't move.

"My name is Tom Rose. I'm a lawyer with the law firm of Stern and Hobbs. Can I call you Hope?"

Still no response.

"I know you haven't spoken since the arrest, and you don't have to speak now. No matter what you think, I'm here to try and help you. You don't have to respond to anything I say, but I do want you to know what I think. And then, I'm going to leave you, and you'll have to decide whether or not you want me to represent you."

Hope didn't move. Tom continued. "I was assigned to this case earlier today, so my knowledge of this case is minimal to none. I frankly should not even take on this case for a whole host of reasons, and I was planning on passing this off to another lawyer. But, then I had to consider the fact that you are up for trial in two weeks and you need a lawyer. So here we are."

Tom paused, hoping to get a reaction. Nothing.

"What jumped out at me when I read your files is not a single lawyer took any steps to formulate a defense for you. Every single one of them was focused on trying to figure out who you are, and trying to solve the mystery of why you would murder the man you seemed to be in love with, but not one of them bothered to think about a possible defense for you. Don't get me wrong, the evidence here is pretty damning, and everyone has assumed you're guilty of murdering him. But, I'm not going to assume anything. I'm going to start from a clean canvas. If there is more to your story, I plan on finding out what that story is."

Hope slowly lifted her head and looked into Tom's eyes. Tom was taken by her angelic face that had been blemished by a single tear that flowed down her cheek. Her disheveled brown hair only accentuated her delicate nose, the sparkling blue eyes and the porcelain like complexion of her skin. She stared into his eyes with an honesty that reached his soul. Tom sat in silence for a moment, wondering how this woman could have killed anyone, much less her husband and daughter.

"So, I reviewed the forensics report," Tom said, looking down at the file folder.

Hope sat staring, without speaking.

"According to this report, your husband was killed when a bullet hit his forehead. I think that bullet was shot from a distance. I say that because the police found a bullet casing near the front door. The shot to his chest was fired a lot closer, and the bullet entered his heart at an angle beneath his heart that went through the heart and got lodged in his left shoulder blade."

Hope continued to look into Tom's eyes. Tom pushed the forensics report in front of her.

"What this report tells me is that your husband was shot in his head by someone from a distance. After he fell onto his back, a second shot was fired from near his feet that caused the bullet to hit his heart at an upward angle. I don't know what happened that night, but I do know that if you are the killer, you would have had no reason to shoot a man lying dead on your floor."

Hope didn't respond.

"In my profession, we have a rule that you should never ask your client if she committed the crime. The reason for the rule is an attorney has an ethical duty to not let his client lie on the witness stand. It's a silly rule. It's a stupid loophole that allows the attorney to have his client lie on the stand, but comply with the ethical rules by ensuring that he is ignorant of the truth." Tom stared into her eyes. "Everyone already assumes you are guilty, Hope. If I'm going to help you, I need a little help from you. You don't have to tell me if you killed Mark. But, telling me who you are, where you came from. That'll at least help me get started."

At that moment, Hope looked away. She was crying. Hope turned her body to the side of the chair and looked away. Tom could see a small tattoo on her left arm. It was a red heart with the letters "SD" in its center.

"If you don't want me as your lawyer, just say so. Otherwise, I'll take your silence as a yes."

Hope sat still, staring into the distance.

"I'm going to take that as a yes," Tom said as he got up. Hope slowly turned and looked into his eyes and refused to release them. There wasn't any anger or fear in her eyes. He just saw sorrow; disappointed eyes of a woman who believes no one can help her. Tom smiled at her and nodded. He walked to the door and knocked. The corrections officer opened the door to guide Tom out while another officer walked toward Hope.

Tom walked out of the building and noticed that it had already turned dark. He checked his watch and saw that it was 6:30. The driver closed the door after he climbed in and drove off toward the parkway. Tom turned on his phone and saw that Melanie had tried to call him. He closed his eyes and leaned his head back against the headrest. Memories of all the time he had spent with her flooded his thoughts. Tom lowered his head and covered his face with his two hands. There was nothing he could do to contain the emotions pouring out of him. "You OK, sir?" asked the driver, staring into his rearview mirror. Tom didn't answer. He wiped his face with his sleeve and looked out of the window. He wanted to run from the life he had to face. But he knew there was nowhere to hide, just as he knew he could not outrun the full moon that shined through the leafless tree branches, coming at him with a full head of steam.

Tom unlocked the door to his apartment and walked in. "Tom?" he heard Melanie's voice coming from the bedroom. He didn't answer. He took off his coat and walked to the kitchen. He poured a glass of Scotch.

"Hi," said Melanie. Tom turned and saw her standing by the kitchen.

"Hey," said Tom and took a sip of the Scotch. He stared at the glass.

"Is everything OK?" she asked. Tom didn't answer.

"Tom?" she said.

He turned to her without saying anything.

"What's going on?" she asked. "Why aren't you speaking to me? Is everything OK?"

Tom downed what was left of the Scotch in his glass and refilled it. "No, everything's not OK."

Melanie stood frozen, waiting for Tom to continue.

"Nothing's right. Nothing's OK with my life."

Melanie stared at Tom, lost for words. Tom put down his glass. "Melanie, I want to talk to you about us," he said.

Melanie stood with an expressionless face. "What about?"

"This isn't working."

"What do you mean?"

"Us. You and me."

"I, I don't understand," she said as the her eyes welled up.

"There's nothing to understand. I no longer want to marry you."

"Tom, what are you saying? What's making you say this?"

"It doesn't matter. We both need to move on with our lives."

Melanie's voice shook as she tried to speak through her tears. "After all these years, I have a right to know. You can't throw our lives away in a thirty second conversation. I deserve more."

Tom refilled his glass. "You do deserve more," he said in a low voice. "But I can't tell you now. I'll sleep on the couch until I can find a new place."

Tom walked past her and over to the couch. He leaned his head back. He could hear Melanie walking to the room. He could hear her crying

43

through the closed door. Tom buried his face in his hands. He felt the deep cut of the words that he unleashed on Melanie. It had to be done, but he couldn't numb the pain in his heart. Tom downed the Scotch. He hated the taste, the smell and everything else about it. But the pain was too much to handle. The Scotch would help him run from it. He knew he loved her, and that meant he had to let her go. Tom closed his eyes, hoping sleep will find him.

13.

Melanie spent the day, staring out of her window, confused as to what had happened the night before. It was so sudden. Everything was wonderful, then without warning, everything fell apart. They had been together for so long; had planned to spend the rest of their lives together. What had she done wrong? What made him no longer want to be with her? They were in love at one point. What had she done to change all of that? Melanie shut down her computer. She had a right to know, she said to herself again. She would go home and make him tell her. She would demand an answer.

"I thought you handled yourself really well yesterday," she heard Lance say. She looked up and saw him at her door.

"They agreed to make a significant new investment," he said.

"That's wonderful news, Lance. Congratulations."

Lance smiled. "And congratulations to you. This was all you. You answered their questions about our investment strategy. They were completely taken by you. In fact, one of them called me today to say how much he appreciated you joining us at lunch."

Melanie smiled. "Really?"

"The older gentleman, Arthur. He actually told me that he was debating between Ark Capital and Pine Row Investments. He said you tipped him toward us."

"That's very nice of him to say," she said.

"Anyway, I thought you might want to hear that. Let's talk tomorrow about some investment ideas. Enjoy the night," he said and walked off.

Melanie stepped out of her office and watched him walk down the hall and into his corner office. She appreciated that he took the time to come see her. After the conversation with Tom last night, she needed something, anything to make her feel like something more than a ragdoll tossed to the gutter. Lance's kind words calmed her and made her feel wanted.

Melanie packed up her things for the evening. As she started for the glass doors, she heard music coming from his office. She took a few steps closer and recognized the melody of the Moonlight Sonata. It was her favorite song when she was learning to play the piano as a child. She walked to Lance's office and saw him, leaning back on his chair with his eyes closed. The beautiful music played out of speakers hidden in the cabinetry behind his desk. She was about to turn to leave when she heard him.

"Come in," he said.

"I didn't mean to interrupt you," she said, turning back to Lance. "I just heard the music."

He sat up on his chair and smiled. "It's my little escape time. After a long day, when I'm sure everyone's gone for the evening, I turn up the music and just try and get away from the day."

"You do this every night?"

Lance smiled.

"Well, it must be nice to have a place to run to," said Melanie.

Lance turned to open a cabinet behind him. He pulled open a drawer and Melanie could see that it was a refrigerator. "This is the other thing I do," he said. He pulled out a bottle of Grey Goose and a frosted martini glass. "Would you like a glass?"

Melanie shook her head. "Oh no, I should get going."

Lance smiled. "Okay. But let me tell you, a sip of cold vodka with this music is a wonderful combination. A grand escape from whatever is haunting you."

Melanie furrowed her eyebrows. "What do you mean haunting me?"

"Just something in your eyes tells me you're troubled. But that's none of my business. And even if I'm wrong, take a sip and let the music take you. No harm in trying, right?"

Melanie stared at him for a few seconds, and then put on a smile. "Well, OK," she said as she walked to his desk.

Lance poured a half glass for Melanie and handed it to her. He pointed at the loveseat on the other side of his office. "Now, take off your coat, sit back on that couch. Sip the vodka and close your eyes. Listen to the melody and forget about everything else. Let your mind go blank."

A part of her wondered if this was Lance's way of trying to seduce her, but the innocence and honesty with which he offered her the drink made her want to trust him. She took her drink and sat down on the couch. She looked over at Lance, expecting him to join her, but he remained behind his desk.

"Aren't you going to join me?" she asked, almost surprising herself.

Lance smiled and shook his head. "No. This is a time for you and your escape. Take me out of your mind and just try and enjoy the next couple of minutes."

Melanie took a sip of the ice cold vodka and then closed her eyes as Lance said. She leaned back against the couch and embraced the melody. She allowed her mind to get lost in that moment. A short while later, the song came to an end. Melanie opened her eyes and turned to Lance. He was at his desk, putting the vodka away. Melanie walked over to him and handed him the martini glass. "Thank you," she said.

"You're welcome, but you have to promise me you won't tell anyone about this," he said.

"Why do you want to keep it a secret?" she asked.

Lance's smile vanished. "Because I need these few moments for myself. I would need to keep it that way."

Melanie nodded. "Okay."

Lance's smile returned. "Good. Get home safely. I'll see you tomorrow."

Melanie nodded and headed for the door. She walked out onto Madison Avenue. It had stopped snowing. Her mind wandered back to the few minutes she spent in Lance's office. That he needed those few minutes of escape made him seem more human to her. Lance Ark had made hundreds of millions from his hedge fund. But the few minutes he spent with Melanie told her that he wasn't afraid to admit he had a vulnerability. That he shared that moment with her warmed her. She saw a taxi and waved it down. As she closed the door, her mind drifted to Tom. What would she say to him? What could she ask him that'll make him open up to her – like the way he used to just a few days ago? She wondered if this is what happens if people stay together for too long. She wanted to go back to the way things used to be, but the way he spoke to her last night, she knew that life was gone forever.

14.

The small one bedroom apartment was dark. Melanie wasn't home. Tom took off his coat and hung it in the closet. The vents cranked out heat, and the room felt like a sauna. Tom walked over to the window and opened it a few inches to let the cold air in to cool the room. He poured a glass of Scotch and sat down on the couch. His mind drifted off to his parents. Tom remembered the day his mother died when he was in college. He took the next flight out of Boston to get back to New York. She was a victim of a drunken driver. By the time the ambulance came, she had already died. His father wouldn't leave her side at the funeral. He stood by the open casket and just cried. It wasn't fair, he kept repeating. Tom put his head against the couch and wiped the tears with the back of his hand. It's not fair, he whispered as he closed his eyes. But it doesn't matter, he thought as he gritted his teeth. He remembered back to his mother's death. His father was angry that she was taken from him. No one gets to negotiate with death, he had said then. It just comes when it's good and ready, and you have no say on how or why it happens. That's what his father told him at the funeral. Years later, his father came down with stomach cancer that claimed his life. Now the same monster had come back for him. Tom took in a deep breath. "I'm not going to let you take me on your terms," he said. "I'm going to go the way I want to go."

Tom thought about his meeting with Hope. He remembered her face and the tears. He thought through the investigation he would have to start. There was nothing in the files that gave him a starting point. He would have to start from nothing. He didn't know what strategy to pursue, but he believed the answers would come. Though she said nothing to him, something about her made him want to save her. He was not interested in just raising a reasonable doubt of her guilt. Something in the way she looked into his eyes made him believe she wasn't interested in playing a legal game of survival. Her silence, her tears and the way she grabbed his eyes all made him believe the story about her pulling the trigger that December night was far more complicated than what everyone thought.

Tom heard someone at the door. He looked up and saw Melanie.

"Hi," she said.

Tom stood. "Hi." He could see the tears welling up in her eyes.

"I'll get some of my things. I'm moving in with Rachel until I can find a place," she said.

"You don't have to leave, Melanie. I told you I'd find a place."

"No, Tom. If this is really the end, I have no desire to be in this place."

Tom nodded. He wanted to say something, but he couldn't find the words. He held his breath, trying to suppress the emotions filling his heart.

"Before I go, I need to know. What happened to us?" she asked.

Tom swallowed hard. "Why does it matter?" he finally said.

"How can you say that? After all these years together, you don't think I'm entitled to an explanation?"

Tom shook his head. "I'm no good for you," he said in a low voice.

"What?"

Tom looked up. "Melanie, it's over. You and me. You need to move on. I want you to be with someone who can make you happy. I'm not that guy."

Melanie shook her head. "I don't understand. You do make me happy. What's changed that's making you do this?"

Tom turned his back to her. "I can't explain. It just happened. I'm sorry," he said as he sat down on the couch and picked up his glass. He could hear her walking to the bedroom. Tom stared out of the window at the lights of the 59th Street Bridge. "Good bye," he heard her say. Tom sat frozen as the door closed. He could no longer contain the pain in his heart or the uncontrollable emotions filling his mind. After a long while, there were no more tears left to shed. His mind went blank. Tom sat on the couch staring at the lights of the bridge knowing full well that this was not a nightmare from which he could ever open his eyes.

15.

Timothy Ryan carefully examined the burl wood cabinetry. He slid his fingers gently against the glass-like finish, protecting the mother of pearl inlay along the edges of the doors. Then, he saw it. He opened the cabinet door and closed it. The gap in the bottom was wider than the top. He pressed his intercom.

"Maria, come in my office."

He heard a knock and saw her standing in the doorway. "Yes, Mr. Ryan."

"Come over here."

She walked over and stood next to him.

"Look. See the gap?"

"Yes, I see it."

"Call that moron and tell him to get this fixed immediately, and make sure we don't pay the last installment until this gets fixed."

"Yes sir," she said and walked out.

Ryan walked back to his desk and picked up his coffee. He turned toward his corner office windows that looked out toward downtown and the East River. His focus returned to the gap in his cabinet door. "Dumb fuck," he muttered.

His intercom buzzed. "Mr. Mobley is here to see you."

"Send him in."

Ryan leaned back in his chair and watched Bob Mobley step into his office.

"Bob, you're early," said Ryan.

"I thought we should chat before we spoke with Edward."

Ryan chuckled. "What's there to talk about?"

"You know he's gonna want an explanation about Hope Kane."

"And we'll tell him how things will be."

"Look, I just want to be prepared for some pushback. You worked for him. You know how he can get."

Ryan stopped smiling. "Bob, you like being the managing partner here?"

Mobley nodded with a perplexed look.

"Don't you ever fucking say that I worked for anybody! Got it?"

"Sorry. I, uh, I didn't mean it the way it came out."

"You are a fucking lawyer. Think before you talk!"

Ryan's intercom buzzed again. "Yea!" he shouted into the phone.

"Mr. Miller's here."

"Send him in."

Edward stepped in. Ryan smiled and pointed to the empty chair next to Mobley. "Have a seat, Edward."

Edward nodded at Ryan and then patted Mobley's back before sitting.

"Thank you for seeing me."

"What can we do for you, Edward?" asked Ryan.

"I wanted to talk to you about Tom Rose."

"What about?"

"I understand the Management Committee asked him to work on the Hope Kane case."

"Yes, we did," said Ryan as he carefully placed his coffee mug on a coaster resting on his leather top desk.

"I don't think that's such a great idea," said Edward.

"I didn't think the Management Committee was looking for a performance evaluation on its decisions," said Ryan, glaring at Edward.

"I'm not evaluating its performance. I'm just trying to look out for Tom. This is the year he's up for partner, and I don't think it's fair for him to spend the year working on a pro bono case, particularly a case that's as politically charged as this one. He'll become public enemy number one for representing Hope Kane, who everyone wants to see rot in jail. We have 400 associates at this firm who are not up for partner this year. Why can't we assign the case to one of them?"

Ryan laughed.

"What's so funny?"

"You."

Edward stared at him with a confused look.

"Edward, do you really think Tom has a shot of being elected?"

"Yes, I do."

"On what basis?"

"He's a brilliant lawyer. He's won every case that was thrown at him. Every client who's ever worked with him love him. He's developing a number of loyal clients."

"They're not his clients," said Ryan. "They're the firm's clients."

"The in-house lawyers who've worked with Tom are very loyal to him. If he leaves the firm, they'll go with him. That makes them Tom's clients."

Ryan rolled his eyes. "All you've done is tell me that Tom's a good lawyer, Stern's filled with good lawyers."

"The kid's got talent. He's pulled shit out of his ass to win cases that the rest of us could never have concocted in our dreams. Other lawyers here, including partners, don't come close to him in terms of his ability to formulate a strategy or think on his feet. He's got great instincts."

"Please Edward, I think you're overstating this a little bit," said Ryan as he picked up his mug.

"I'm not overstating anything."

"Look, if he's as good as you say, then you don't have anything to worry about. The partnership is more than capable of recognizing talent."

"Then why are you prejudging him and telling me he won't get elected."

Ryan sat up in his chair and leaned in close to Edward. "How many new clients have you brought into the firm the past few years?"

Edward sat quietly.

"You are sixty eight years old, and got probably a year, maybe two, before you retire. You haven't had a major matter for the firm in five years. You've got enough work to barely keep yourself and an associate busy. That's fine for now, but you know that's not sustainable. Everyone knows you are a drunk and you spend any available moment you have screwing whores. Not only do you not have any juice to make Tom a partner, you are a fucking embarrassment. If you didn't have as many friends as you have in the partnership, we would have thrown you out years ago."

Edward didn't respond. Ryan continued. "Good lawyers are a dime a dozen, Edward. You know damn well that that alone isn't enough to be elected to the partnership at Stern and Hobbs. We are the premier firm in the country. Not every Tom, Dick and Harry can become a partner here. One of the reasons we are where we are is because we can attract the most talented lawyers from other law firms to join our firm. And do you know why we can attract the best? It's because we can pay them a shit load of money. Tom Rose? Yea, he's good, but his rabbi's got no more juice. You haven't done shit in years. There's no basis for the partnership to believe he can generate serious revenue for the firm, and that gives us no economic basis to make him a partner. I don't give a shit how talented he is."

Edward shook his head. "Then why are we bothering to put him up?"

Ryan chuckled. "You've been in this business a long time, and you know how it works. Don't sound so naïve, Edward. We have to put him up to give credibility to the partnership process for the other associates. We have to give them hope. It's the carrot that keeps them billing hours."

"At least give him a chance," pleaded Edward. "The kid's done everything we've asked him to do. He earned his right to be considered fairly. We've made partners in the past based on potential."

"And we'll continue to make partners based on potential," said Mobley.

"Then why are you pulling the rug from underneath him by tying him up with Hope Kane? It's not a winnable case. And his numbers will be shit at the end of the year."

"We have to look out for Stern and Hobbs," said Ryan. "We've been battered in the legal press as a firm with no heart. Our clients don't give a shit about that reputation, but it does get in the way of recruiting top law students. That's where Tom can help us. Hope Kane is a lost cause, but has gotten a lot of the public's attention. It's a great little mystery. A perfectly happy family faces tragedy. She kills her husband and her daughter's dead body is missing. And, she won't utter a word. It's a fascinating case. Everyone knows she's guilty as hell, but it's fascinating nevertheless. She's even got the attention of our favorite celebrity mobster, Ian Ramsey. The guy's gone on public television to express his horror at what she's done. Not one firm has volunteered to take this case on pro bono, because no one wants to walk into a case that's a sure bet loser. That's where we come in. And, we put our star associate on the case. That'll go a long way to restoring our reputation as a firm that gives a shit."

"And what does Tom get out of this?" asked Edward.

"He gets to practice law for a paycheck."

"And what are we going to do if his numbers suffer because of this case?"

Ryan chuckled. "Edward, why are you being so damned stubborn. This isn't about Tom's numbers. He's forever tied to you. The reason he'll never be elected to the partnership is because you fucked up. There's no credible case that you can make that'll prove to the partnership that Tom will generate revenue for the firm. We all know this case will not consume that much of his time. It's a quick kill. Trial is scheduled to start in two weeks. She'll get convicted and Tom will be back to work for your paying clients. The trouble is, you have no paying clients."

"That is such bullshit!"

Ryan smiled and picked up his coffee. "It's not bullshit, Edward. We all know Tom will never be elected to the partnership based on your performance. But that doesn't mean we should ignore what he can do for the firm."

"I'm going to make Tom hand the case off to someone else, and he's going to make a run at making partner."

Ryan closed his eyes and shook his head as if in deep thought. A few seconds later, he opened his eyes and spoke in a low voice. "I'll say it again. This isn't about Tom or Hope Kane, Edward. This is about Stern and Hobbs. Tom dropping the case won't change a thing. We make partners here based on money. Tom may be a good lawyer, but we have no basis to believe he'll make the pie bigger. We are in business to make money. And that means we need to stockpile associate talent. That's where Tom can help the firm. It won't help him make partner, but it will help the firm. I can't force Tom to represent Hope Kane, but the Management Committee won't be very happy with you, Edward, if you make him drop the case."

"As you've said, I still have friends in the partnership. I'll take that risk."

16.

White Plains had grown to such a big city, Linda Starr thought as she stared out of the large window, overlooking the hills beyond the skyline. When she was growing up in Armonk, White Plains was nothing more than a small wannabe city, and its only claim to fame was the Galleria Mall. Now, it was a real city, with restaurants, bars, a singles scene. Linda sipped her coffee, hoping the caffeine will help clear her head. Her friends insisted on taking her out the night before for her thirtieth birthday. She couldn't say no. A drink with dinner at the restaurant turned into several, and then more drinks at the bar. The cute guy who came over to hit on her bought her drinks into the night – probably one too many. Linda finished her coffee and then stepped into the shower, hoping the cool water will soothe her dull headache. She dried herself off and stared into the mirror. She could see the bags under her blue eyes. A little makeup will cover that up, she thought. Her blond hair was a wet mess, but she had no energy to play with it. Linda stared at her breasts and wondered if she should have invited the cute guy home. But then she'd have to deal with him afterwards, and find a way to dump him. Linda smiled into the mirror. The hangover was bad, but not enough to diminish the satisfaction she felt over herself. Men desired her beautiful face and body. She was a rock star prosecutor with a clear path to the district attorney's office. She just needed for Heather Palmer to move onto something else in a few years, then the job would be hers for the taking. Life was pretty damned good. Linda dressed in a black pant suit and put on her 3 inch heels. She was far from being short at 5 feet 9 inches, but she liked towering over her adversaries and work colleagues alike. It gave her a sense of power; an intimidating presence. She downed two Advils and then headed to the garage to get in her new BMW 335i – her thirtieth birthday gift from her parents. She pulled into the employee parking lot and took the elevator to her office. The red message light was blinking on her phone. She pressed the message button.

"Good morning. My name is Tom Rose with Stern and Hobbs. I represent Hope Kane, and I wanted to introduce myself. I also wanted to discuss pushing back the pretrial conference for a week. Please give me a call this morning."

Linda wrote down Tom's number. She pulled out Hope Kane's file and read her notes. The Court had scheduled a pretrial conference for January 28, just three days away, and trial was to start on February 8. There was no way she was going to agree to an adjournment of the trial. She had waited over a year while Hope's lawyers were playing hot potato. This was going to be a simple case. Her witnesses were already lined up. The officers who arrested Hope would testify that they caught her hovering over her dead husband's body with the murder weapon. The forensics expert would provide testimony that the bullets that killed Mark Kane came from the gun she was holding. He would testify that the residue from the discharged bullet was all over her hand and arm. This was a slam dunk case, and she wanted to get the conviction and get the file off of her desk. Linda picked up the phone and dialed the number for Tom Rose.

"Tom Rose speaking," she heard him say.

"Hi, this is Linda Starr with the Westchester DA's office. I'm returning your call."

"Thank you for calling me back," he said.

"You're welcome. What can I do for you?"

"As I said in my message, I just got involved with this case. I would like to ask you for a short adjournment of the pretrial conference. I'll need the time to conduct my investigation."

"Tom, normally I would extend the courtesy and adjourn the conference, which necessarily will mean adjourning the trial, but frankly, there really isn't anything to investigate. This is about a simple a case as there is.

You should have her entire file already. She was caught with the murder weapon, standing over her dead husband. I don't see any point to adjourning the conference or trial. I know you recently took on this case, so I had a package of documents sent to you yesterday. You should've received them this morning."

"I got those files, but they are the documents the prosecution gathered. I'm entitled to conduct my own investigation to formulate my defense. We still do live in a system that allows criminal defendants to have representation."

"She's had representation," snapped Linda.

"In name only," said Tom. "She had lawyers assigned to her, but as far as I can tell, they haven't done anything to represent her interests."

"I'm sorry. I can't help you," said Linda.

"You're really not going to extend this courtesy? You're going to make me take this to the court?"

"I'm not making you do anything. She's guilty, Tom, and no amount of time or investigation's going to change anything. If you want to run to the judge, that's your choice, but I warn you, this trial's been adjourned twice already and it's been sitting on the judge's docket collecting dust. This judge doesn't like to have a backlog. Your request will fall on deaf ears," said Linda.

"I'll take my chances," he said before hanging up. Linda closed Hope's file and pushed it aside. She shook her head and pulled out the file for the next defendant.

17.

The ice cold rain fell gently as Tom walked down the gravel path. He moved past the gravestones of people he had never known, but ones he remembered from each of his many prior visits. The two gravestones stood side by side. One for his father, and another for his mother, Sharon Rose. Tom stared at them for a long while as the rain fell onto his shoulders. "They're at peace," said a voice. Tom turned to see Edward standing behind him with an umbrella.

"Helena told me you were here."

Tom nodded and turned back toward the graves.

"You OK?" Edward asked.

"Yea," said Tom and started to walk away. Edward called out to Tom, but he didn't stop. He kept on walking toward the parking lot. He could hear Edward's footsteps behind him. "Hey," said Edward, touching his arm. "What's going on?"

"I just wanted to see them," said Tom as the rain dripped down the strands of his wet hair.

"They're both at peace now. They're with God," said Edward.

Tom turned to him. "There is no God."

Edward stood with a surprised look. Tom continued. "There's life and then there's death, and death always wins in the end."

A black Town Car pulled into the lot. "Tom, let's have dinner tonight," said Edward.

Tom shook his head. "I have work to do."

"You can take a break. Maybe you and I should go away together. Take a little time off. I'll find someone else to handle the Kane matter."

"I don't have time," said Tom as he opened the car door.

"Come on Tom, I need to talk to you. Maybe the girls can join us. We haven't gotten together in a while."

Tom turned back toward Edward. "Melanie and I broke up."

"What?"

"It's better this way," said Tom. "One other thing, Edward. I'm going to represent Hope Kane. Don't try to change my mind."

The rain got heavier. Tom got in the car and closed the door. He could see Edward staring at him with a dejected look. Tom turned away from him. "Let's go," he told the driver.

18.

"Call him on his cell. Where the hell is he?" asked Edward.

"I don't know," said Monica. "I'll try his assistant again." A few moments later his intercom buzzed. "I got a hold of Helena. She said he came in this morning but left right away. He didn't take a car service, so Helena has no idea where he went."

"Alright, let me know if she hears from him," said Edward and ended the call. He thought back to the cemetery and his conversation with Tom. Why would he suddenly break off his engagement with Melanie? They were so much in love as far as he could tell. Edward leaned back in his chair and closed his eyes. He thought about his lunch with Tom. He wondered if he had made a mistake, unloading on the kid all the shit about firm politics. Edward shook his head. No. Tom had a right to know how the game is played. His conversation with Ryan and Mobley didn't change anything. Tom deserved to become a partner at Stern, and there was nothing that anyone could do to convince him otherwise. His mind drifted to Melanie again. Why Tom? Why did you do it?

Edward's intercom buzzed. "Yea?"

"Tom's on line two."

Edward pressed the blinking button on his phone. "Tom, where are you? I've been trying to reach you all morning."

"I'm sorry about what I said yesterday," said Tom.

"Hey, forget it. Where are you?"

"I'm in Scarsdale."

"I guess you decided to ignore my advice."

"I want to do this," said Tom.

"Tom, you are going through a lot right now. This is not something you need. I can find someone else to take over the case. Take a break. You can come back fresh and then we can sit down and come up with a marketing plan. I have some thoughts on which clients to visit."

"I'm not interested in a marketing plan," said Tom.

"This is your career we're talking about. What's going on with you? First you tell me you broke off your wedding with a woman you're madly in love with, and now you're telling me you don't give a shit about your job. Whatever it is you're going through, there's no reason for you to sabotage everything that's important to you."

"I need to run, Edward. I appreciate you thinking of me, but I know what I'm doing."

"Tom, just tell me what's going on. Why are you pushing everyone away?"

"There comes a time when we have to do what we believe in. When it's all said and done, that's all you have – memories of what you did with the life you had."

"What? What the hell are you talking about?" said Edward. He didn't hear a response. "Tom?" said Edward into the phone, but Tom had already hung up.

19.

Tom sat in his rented Nissan on Mulberry Street, in front of the home Hope Kane was renting at the time of the murder. There was no activity at the house. In light of the publicity the Kane murder received, he wasn't surprised that the homeowner would have had difficulty selling the house or finding a new tenant. Tom noticed the house across the street was under construction, with men nailing down the asphalt shingles to the bare roof. One of the men noticed Tom staring and waved. Tom waved back, and watched the man go back to his nail gun. Hope Kane's files from the DA's office were filled with useless interview notes of Hope's acquaintances, and people she interacted with on the days leading up to the murder. He skimmed through them, hoping to find something that may give him a clue as to where to start. The interview notes were remarkably consistent and useless – loving family, didn't say much, very pleasant to everyone, kept to themselves, completely shocked that she could murder her husband. Tom closed the file with the interview notes and turned to the copy of the receipt from the Capri Restaurant. That was where they dined on the night of the murder. Tom dialed the number to the restaurant and heard a recording that the restaurant will open at 5 pm. He checked his watch and it was nearing Noon. He started the engine and drove toward town. He pulled into the parking lot of the first restaurant he saw – 15 minutes away from Hope's house. Tom parked the car and stepped into the small diner.

"Sit anywhere you like," said a woman behind the counter.

"OK if I take a booth?" asked Tom.

"Go right ahead," she said. "Coffee?"

"Sure."

Tom slid into the booth and opened the files again. He pulled out a notepad and began jotting down the steps he would take. There was no point in speaking with the people who had already been interviewed, so he began making a list of people who may have interacted with Hope or Mark on or before December 26. Tom pulled out his iPhone and did a search for gas stations in the area. He looked for the Toyota dealership in Mamaroneck, where Mark Kane had purchased a used Camry.

"Here you go. Anything to eat?" asked the waitress as she set down a cup of coffee on the table.

Tom looked up and saw a petite blond with deep green eyes. "Yea. Just a bowl of soup please."

"We have chicken noodle and chick pea. Which would you like?"

"Chicken."

She smiled. "Coming right up. My name's Annie if you need anything else." She turned to walk away, then turned back. "I haven't seen you here before."

"I'm here on business," said Tom. Annie smiled and walked to the kitchen. Tom opened his notepad and wrote down, "Mel's Diner – Annie."

Annie came back a short while later with a bowl of soup. "The crackers are next to the ketchup," she said as she turned to leave.

"Annie, can I ask you something?"

She turned back and smiled. "Of course."

"How long have you worked here?"

"Oh, about five years."

"Do you get regulars here?"

Annie nodded. "For the most part. People have their routine, you know."

"Did Hope Kane ever dine here? Do you know who she is?"

The smile on Annie's face vanished as she took a step back. "Why, why do you ask?"

"Her house is just fifteen minutes up the road. I thought she might've dined here on occasion."

"She did, but I don't feel comfortable talking about her."

"Why?"

"After all that's happened with her family," said Annie as she shook her head. "You do know what happened to her, right? I just don't feel it's right to gossip about her."

"Annie, I'm a lawyer and I represent Hope Kane. That's the reason I'm asking about her."

Annie's eyes widened. "Oh. I thought she had gone to jail already. Why are you asking about her now?"

"I was just recently retained to represent her, and I'm trying to see if I can figure out what happened the night of Mark Kane's death."

Annie shook her head. "I don't know what there is to figure out. Everyone knows what happened." Annie looked away. "She was such a lovely lady," she said in a low voice.

"So, you knew her?" asked Tom.

Annie turned back to Tom. "Yes. They used to come here every Sunday morning. They'd be nicely dressed, the three of them. They'd go to Sunday mass and then come here for a late breakfast. That little girl, Mila, she was so adorable. They would order the silver dollar pancakes, and she would eat like a little lady, with a fork in one hand and a butter knife in the other. They were such a lovely family." Annie shook her head as she leaned against the side of the booth.

Two men walked into the restaurant. "Hey Frank, Tony, anywhere you like," said Annie. "I'll be with you in a minute."

"Is there anything else I can get for you?" she asked Tom.

67

"I know you're busy working, but will you meet with me for a few minutes later today when you have more time?"

Annie looked down. "I don't know what I could tell you to help you. From what I remember, the papers said she was caught red handed."

"Maybe, but she is entitled to have a lawyer represent her. Even if she committed the murder."

"Annie," said a man behind the register, pointing toward the booth where the two men were seated. Annie turned back to Tom. "I'll meet you for a few minutes after my shift. I get done at five when the dinner shift takes over."

Tom smiled. "Thank you, Annie. I'll come back here at five."

Annie nodded and walked off to the table with the two men to take their orders. Tom stared at his uneaten soup. Annie's description of Hope and her family was consistent with the interview notes in Hope's file. Could she really have killed her own family? Tom shook his head. What if she were innocent, he wondered. She would be sitting in prison, accused of killing the two people she loved. Tom shook his head. If she's innocent, why is she not speaking? If someone else had committed the murders, why isn't Hope telling the world about her innocence? The answers to those questions led him to only one place – that she is guilty as hell. But still, the thought that an innocent woman could be sitting in prison made his heart race.

20.

The Mobile sign hovered over the small white structure. The gas station was a five-minute drive from the diner. He didn't see any other gas station in the area. It was only 2 o'clock, and he still had three hours to kill. Tom parked by the entrance to the station and stepped in. He saw a man behind the register in a blue shirt with a Mobile patch above his breast pocket. His name, Vincent Larkin, was written in script below the patch.

"Good afternoon," Tom said.

The man looked up. "What can I do for you?"

"Can I get a cup of coffee?" asked Tom.

Larkin pointed to the back of the small store, with three long aisles filled with chips, candy and other junk food. "There's coffee in the back. Help yourself."

Tom walked to the back and poured a cup of French Roast into a paper cup and returned to the counter.

"How much do I owe you?"

"Dollar twenty five."

Tom pulled out two singles and handed them to Larkin. "Would you mind if I asked you a question?"

Larkin looked up at Tom as he handed him his change. "What about?"

"Do you know who Hope Kane is?"

Larkin closed the register drawer and stared into Tom's eyes. "Yea, I know who she is. What do you want to know?" he asked.

"I'm Hope Kane's lawyer, and I'm trying to get some information. Have you interacted with her at all before the night of the murder?"

Larkin studied Tom's face for a few seconds. "I dealt with her and her husband. This is a small community, so you get to know people over time. They used to swing by in the mornings to fill up."

"Did you ever speak with them?"

"Just your routine hello and good-bye. Unlike most customers who buy gas with a credit card at the pump, they typically paid with cash, so they would have to come in to pay. They'd say hi, pay and then leave."

"Have you seen any sign of problems in their relationship?"

Larkin chuckled. "I pump gas and I do oil changes. I have no idea what was happening in their relationship. They seemed perfectly fine, but what do I know?"

"You said they only paid with cash?"

Larkin nodded. "Yea, I did think that was a little odd. Most people who live around here don't want to be bothered with handling cash. They pay for everything with their credit cards. It's a lot faster. They slide their card into the card reader by the pump, and then they're on their way."

"Do you know why they paid with cash?"

"I have no idea, and it wasn't my place to ask."

Tom nodded. "I understand. Thank you. Is there anything you can think of that you didn't tell me about Mark or Hope?"

Larkin thought for a few seconds, then looked up. "There is one thing."

Tom waited for him to continue.

"About a week before Christmas, Ms. Kane came in to pay for gas. She had her daughter in the back seat. I noticed a guy pumping gas on the other side of them, staring into her car. I got a little worried, because I hadn't seen the guy before, and he was just staring at the little girl and at Ms. Kane when she returned to her car. Hope Kane was a beautiful woman, and it wasn't so strange to see a guy staring at her, but the way he stared at the little girl was a little creepy. I kept my eye on him and wrote down his license plate number, just in case."

"Do you still have that number?" asked Tom.

"Nah, I threw it out the next day when she came in to get coffee, and knew she was alright."

"You can't remember?"

"Look, it was over a year ago. I can't remember what I had for dinner last night."

"What did the man look like? What kind of car was it?"

Larkin chuckled as he pointed out the window. "That your car?"

Tom followed Larkin's finger and saw him pointing at the rented Altima.

"Yea, I rented it in the city."

"Same car, but black."

"How about the man? You remember anything about him?"

"I wish I could help you, but like I said, it was more than a year ago, and a lot of people come through here, and I just can't remember a complete stranger that I saw for less than a minute. Besides, from what I read, Hope's guilty as hell."

Tom shook his head. "She hasn't been convicted yet."

Larkin chuckled. "You think she's innocent?"

"I don't know. That's what I'm trying to figure out."

"Look, it was a long time ago. I'm trying to picture the guy, but I can't. I do remember him being pretty big. Maybe six three. Other than that, I really don't remember."

"Hair?"

Larkin looked away, thinking. "I think he had reddish hair. It was short, like a crew cut."

"You said you were concerned because he was staring at Hope's baby. Do you know if he followed Hope after she got back in her car?"

"I don't think he did. I can sort of picture him staring out at Hope's car as she drove away, but it's pretty fuzzy for me."

Tom nodded. "Thank you, Vincent." Tom handed Larkin his business card. "Here. If you remember anything else, will you call me? My cell phone is written on the back of the card there."

Larkin nodded. Tom returned to his car and pulled out a notepad to write down everything Larkin had told him. Tom checked his watch. It was only 2:30. He still had a couple of hours before his meeting with Annie. He dialed the number for the Bedford Hills Women's Prison. "I would like to meet with my client Hope Kane in thirty minutes."

21.

Edward slowly poured the Scotch into the small shot glass resting on his desk. He picked up the glass and stared at it for a while. He tilted his head back and allowed the alcohol to rest on his tongue, before slowly letting it flow down his throat. His mind drifted back to his conversation with Ryan and Mobley. He wasn't angry at the way Ryan spoke to him. It was more disappointment at himself that he had fallen so far. There was a time when he had power, and the likes of Timothy Ryan kissed the ground he walked on. Edward was the lead outside counsel for virtually every major financial institution in New York and Charlotte. He had a team of twenty lawyers working round the clock putting together documentation for mortgage back securitization deals, while he and another team of lawyers represented the banks in complex lawsuits where hundreds of millions of dollars were at stake. He had been grooming Tom Rose to take over that practice, and it was just a matter of time. Edward never had any kids, and Tom had grown to be more than just a friend and a colleague. Everything was turned on its head when the real estate market crashed a few years ago. His securitization practice evaporated into thin air. His close contacts at the banks lost their jobs, and almost in an instant, his $45 million annual practice eroded to nothing. Now, he was a nobody at the firm. Stern and Hobbs was all about money, and a partner who couldn't generate revenues was worthless to the firm. What he had delivered to the firm in the past meant nothing. There were many before him who had brought in money by the truckload, but were nevertheless escorted out the door when their star ceased to shine. Edward managed to hang on, because the partnership agreement required that a minimum of 75% of the voting partners must vote to remove a partner. Edward still had friends at the firm, and he was safe for now. He had plenty of money saved to walk away, but, he had to finish one more task. He wanted to deliver the partnership to Tom. It was a promise he had made to himself, an unspoken promise he had made to Tom.

Edward stared at the large mirror hanging on the other side of his office. He saw the reflection of himself, his graying hair, the deep wrinkles in his face, and his shaking hand as he poured another glass. Deep inside he knew he couldn't deliver on the promise he had made to Tom. His cell phone rang. The caller ID said "Marie." She always called at this time, he remembered. There would be another young beauty waiting for him at the hotel. All he had to do was answer the phone, and he would find his escape from his existence for an hour, maybe two. Edward stared at the mirror again longing for the days past. He threw the shot glass against the large mirror and watched it crumble to the floor. He closed his eyes and answered the phone.

22.

Tom saw her being escorted into the meeting room. He sat and stared at her until the prison guard left.

"Hi," he finally said. "I don't expect for you to respond, but I do believe you hear me when I speak."

Hope sat, staring down at the floor.

"I went by your house today," he said. "Looks like they're doing a lot of work on the house across the street from your house. It looks like it's going to be beautiful whenever they finish."

Hope looked up at Tom with a confused look.

"I thought you might be curious. I'll tell you more as the construction gets completed. So, let me tell you what I did today, and what I'm going to do later. I swung by the Mobile gas station by your house. I spoke to Vincent. Do you remember Vincent?"

Hope stared at Tom for a second, and then her eyes drifted off, as if she was trying to remember Vincent.

"Well, Vincent told me about an incident at the gas station that got me thinking. He said a big guy was staring at Mila and then at you about a week before Christmas. Do you remember that man?"

Hope turned back to Tom, and then looked away into the distance. Tom knew he struck a nerve. He wanted to stay on the man at the gas station.

"So, this guy had red hair. With a crew cut. You know the guy I'm talking about?"

Hope didn't turn back to Tom. He could see the tears running down her cheeks.

"Well, Hope, I'm going to see if I can follow that trail. Maybe I'll find nothing, and you'll wind up in jail for a very long time. But, maybe there's something there. Maybe there's more to what happened that night? Everyone thinks you did it. If you did, you'll pay the price. They'll make you pay, and there isn't a whole lot that I can do about it. But, if you didn't kill your husband, I won't stop until I find a way to get you out."

Hope slowly turned back to Tom.

"Later, after I leave here, I'm going to meet Annie from the diner. Then, I'm going to take a ride over to Capri. Do you remember Annie from the diner? Capri? Well, that's all I have today. I'll come back and talk to you when I get more, but I thought you should know what I was up to."

He stood and then walked to the door. The guard opened the door and let Tom out. Tom turned back to watch another guard escort Hope away. She turned back to him as she was taken down the hallway. He saw her holding onto his eyes and not letting go. Something he said had gotten her attention. He needed to know what it was. Tom took a step toward her, wondering whether she might tell him something. The metal door slammed closed, shutting him out of whatever thoughts she might have held at that moment.

23.

Tom pulled into the parking lot, and saw Annie standing by the door to the restaurant, holding the lapels of her coat closed to keep warm. He pulled up next to her and she jumped in the passenger seat.

"Thank you for agreeing to meet me," said Tom.

Annie nodded. "What would you like to know about Hope? As I said, other than what I've seen at the diner, I really don't have a lot more to tell you."

Tom smiled. "Did you have dinner yet?"

"Excuse me?"

"We need a place to talk. I thought maybe we can take a ride over to Capri and get a bite to eat. I have to go there anyway, since that's where Hope and her family dined on the night of the murder."

Annie smiled coyly. "Is this your way of trying to ask me out?"

Tom chuckled. "You are a beautiful woman Annie, but that's the furthest thing from my mind. I'm just trying to kill two birds with one stone."

Annie smiled. "Alright. I've never been there, but I hear food's good."

Tom pulled out of the parking lot. "What did you do today after you left the diner?" Annie asked.

"I met Vincent at the Mobile station. Do you know him?"

Annie nodded. "Yea. He's a sweetie. He comes to the diner for breakfast after the morning rush. Nice man."

"He told me about a large man who was staring at Hope about a week before the incident."

"And?"

"He didn't remember much, but I'm hoping he'll remember more details."

"How does this man relate to Hope?"

"That's what I'm trying to figure out."

"I don't want to be a downer, but you can't go around town assuming anyone who may have looked at Hope is the murderer of her husband."

Tom nodded. "Tell me what you remember about the Kane family."

"There really isn't that much I could tell you. Like I said before, they came in on Sundays. They were very quiet, but seemed like a very happy family. It was a complete shock when we read the news about the murder."

"Did you ever see them arguing?"

Annie shook her head. "Never."

"Did they come to the diner the Sunday before Christmas?"

"Yes."

"Did you notice anything different about their behavior?"

"No. Nothing. I'm sorry. I'm not being very helpful."

Tom shook his head. "Don't be sorry," he said as he fell silent.

"We don't have to go to Capri, if you'd prefer not to. I told you everything I know," said Annie.

Tom turned to her and smiled. "We both have to eat."

They pulled up in front of the restaurant. A man stood with a green jacket in front of a large sign that read "Valet."

Tom and Annie got out of the car and headed into the restaurant. The room was dark with lots of thick drapes separating the reception area from the dining room. He noticed the large wooden bar to the left of the restaurant with a dark haired man setting up glasses on the empty bar. A heavyset, balding man greeted them.

"Good evening. May I have your name please?"

"We don't have a reservation," said Tom. "Do you have a table for two?"

The man looked up in surprise. "I'm sorry sir, but we have no tables. All of our tables are reserved."

Tom nodded. "Would you mind if we ate at the bar?"

The man smiled. "Of course. There are two seats at the far end of the bar. I'll ask Missy to set you up," he said as he nodded toward a young woman in a black dress.

"Please, follow me," she said as she picked up two leather bound menus. "Danny, two place settings please," she said, smiling at the bartender.

"How're you folks doing this evening?" asked the bartender as he spread open two white napkins on the bar to serve as placemats. He put down two plates and utensils. "Anything to drink?"

Tom looked over at Annie. "A glass of white wine would be nice," she said.

"Chardonnay? Pinot grigio?" asked the bartender.

"Chardonnay, please."

"Certainly. And for you, sir?"

"That sounds good. The same," said Tom.

"Coming right up."

Tom leaned toward Annie. "Is it always this hard to get a table?"

"This is where all the rich people come, and it has the best food. I've never eaten here before. People like me couldn't afford to eat here."

The bartender came back with two glasses of wine. "Have you had a chance to look over the menu? We have a couple of specials tonight. We have the bronzino. It's prepared with olive oil with cherry tomatoes with lemon. Just like the way they prepare it in the Amalfi Coast. For the pasta, we have the seafood pasta. It's black pasta served with lobster, scallops and shrimp. It's served with a light marinara sauce blended with truffle oil. It is delicious."

Tom looked over at Annie. "Have you decided?"

"I'll have the penne a la vodka," she said. "Does it come with salad?"

"No. Would you like a house salad or something else to start?"

"I guess just a house salad."

The bartender looked over at Tom. "And you, sir?"

"I'll try the pasta special and a house salad."

"Very good," the bartender said as he walked to the other end of the bar to hand the order to a waitress.

Tom thought back to the files he reviewed. A waitress at the restaurant by the name of Louisa Faher was interviewed extensively by the prosecution. She had said the Kane family was at the restaurant on the night of the murder; that she saw them leave the restaurant together. The prosecution did not interview anyone else at the restaurant.

Tom picked up his wine glass and took a sip. He saw Annie do the same. She looked over at him and smiled.

"Do you know if the Kane family came here a lot?" asked Tom.

"I have no idea."

The bartender came back with two salads. "Are you folks OK on your wine?" he asked pointing at Tom's half empty glass.

"Why don't you bring us a refill," said Tom.

The bartender returned with the uncorked bottle and refilled the two glasses.

"Can I ask you something, Danny?" asked Tom.

"Sure."

"Did you know Mark and Hope Kane?"

The bartender looked up and his smile vanished. He shook his head. "Yes. They used to come here. What a tragedy."

"How often did they come here?"

The bartender furrowed his eyebrows. "Why do you want to know? You know their situation, right?"

Tom nodded. "Yes. I'm Hope Kane's lawyer. I'm trying to gather some information about her."

"I thought she didn't have a lawyer. The last I read, she wasn't speaking to anyone, and no lawyer wanted to take on her case."

Tom took out a business card and handed it to the bartender. "I work at Stern and Hobbs. It's a large law firm in New York City. I agreed to take this on a few days ago."

The bartender looked at the business card and then looked up at Tom. "I don't know very much about them. They did come here pretty regularly."

"How often?"

"I'd say about once a month. They'd come, sit at the bar for a drink and then have dinner. Never really spoke very much. I remembered them when I read the news."

"Do you remember anything peculiar about them?" asked Tom.

"Nothing really comes to mind. They looked like a pretty ordinary couple with a daughter."

Tom thought back to his conversation with Vincent Larkin at the Mobile station. "Do you remember how they paid their bill after their meal?"

"Yea. They always paid with cash. The servers liked them, because they prefer to receive their tips in cash and not on the credit card."

"Do most people who dine here pay with credit cards?"

The bartender nodded. "Yea, but some business owners who deal in cash would sometimes pay with cash, but I'd say most pay with credit cards."

"Do you know why they paid with cash?"

81

"Nah. It's not something you'd ask a customer. It's just something we've noticed."

Tom noticed a waitress bringing over their dinner. The bartender picked up the two plates and placed them down in front of Annie and Tom.

"Enjoy," he said.

"Were you here the night Mark Kane was murdered?" asked Tom, not looking at his food.

"Yea, I was here."

"Was it crowded that night?"

"It's almost never crowded the day after Christmas. People around here don't usually go out to eat the day after Christmas, and the place was pretty empty. Even though the Kane family had a reservation, they probably could've walked in and gotten a table. I'd say the bar was only about half full."

"Were the people at the bar regulars that night?"

The bartender looked up, thinking. "I really can't remember. I do remember the Smiths and the Reinhards, because they come almost every week. We also get random walk-ins who grab a drink and then take off."

"Do you remember any men drinking at the bar that night?"

"I'm sure there were men here who I don't know, but I can't remember for sure."

A crowd of people walked into the restaurant and headed over to the bar. "Enjoy your dinner," said the bartender as he walked over toward the new customers.

Tom closed his eyes, trying to digest everything he had heard. "Are you going to eat?" asked Annie. Tom turned to her and nodded, but his conversation with the bartender swirled around in his head. They paid with cash. How did they afford to eat at Capri when Hope doesn't have money to pay for a lawyer? He wondered if these were clues to something, anything. He had just begun digging for information, and already he was seeing things that led to new questions he would pursue. Who were they running from that made them wipe their history? Where did they get their money to live the life they lived? Why pay for everything with cash? Who was the guy staring at Hope and Mila? Maybe these questions would lead him nowhere, but they were questions no one before had bothered to ask.

"Tom?" said Annie.

Tom turned to her.

"Is everything OK?"

Tom nodded. "There's a lot here to go on."

"Like what?"

Tom smiled, but didn't respond.

"Are you going to tell me?"

"Once I sort everything out in my mind."

24.

Melanie gathered the documents on her desk and shoved them into her briefcase. She had to make a recommendation to Lance in the morning as to whether Ark Capital should invest in Peak River Mining. She had spent the day reading the information the new venture had sent her, but still needed to review other information she gathered through her various sources. She looked up when she heard Lance's voice.

"Hi," she said.

"You're here late."

"I was just packing up my things."

Lance smiled. "Good. I don't want you overworking yourself."

"You don't have to worry about that," said Melanie, smiling into his eyes.

"Listen, I had a dinner meeting this evening that got cancelled. I have reservations at Russell Ming's, which I'd hate to cancel. It's near impossible to get into that place. Do you have dinner plans?"

Melanie didn't know how to respond. She had left a message on Tom's phone that she'd swing by that evening to pick up the rest of her things. She had hoped that maybe he'd talk to her that night. A part of her knew it was over, but she wanted to understand what had happened to them. Her thoughts had been consumed with the breakup, and the idea of having dinner with another man had not even entered her mind. But, a part of her wanted to break away from Tom, and she wondered if having dinner with Lance was a distraction she needed. She stared at his gorgeous, gentle face, and smiled. "I don't have any plans," she said in a low voice.

Lance smiled. "Great. Let me just go get my coat and we can head out."

They walked into the dark room, surrounded by thick red drapes. A young shapely woman in a tight-fitting silk dress walked over with a tray with two flutes of champagne. Lance handed one to Melanie and he picked up the other. He tapped his glass against Melanie's glass. "To an enjoyable evening," he said as he watched her take a sip.

"Is this your first time here?" Melanie asked.

"Yes," he said, looking around.

Another woman led them to the dining room. The center of the room had a large column covered with cobblestones, with water cascading down over them from the ceiling. As they took their seat, a woman removed the white linen napkin in front of Melanie and handed her a black one, apparently concerned that the white linen would leave lint on her dark dress. She did the same for Lance. A tall man stepped up to the table.

"Would the lovely couple like something from the bar?" he asked.

Melanie could see Lance blushing a bit. He looked over at her. "Melanie?"

"I'd like a cosmopolitan," she said to the server.

"Vodka martini, up. Kettle One with olives," said Lance.

Lance watched the man walk off. "I'm sorry if that made you feel uncomfortable," he said.

"What do you mean?" asked Melanie.

"I know you're engaged, and I didn't know how you'd react to him calling us a couple."

Melanie smiled. "So, who was the investor that cancelled on you?" asked Melanie.

Lance smiled. "I guess you don't want to answer my question."

"Not until you answer mine," said Melanie.

The server returned with the drinks. "I'll leave you two for a moment and come back to tell you about our specials."

"Cheers," said Lance as he picked up his glass and took a sip. Melanie smiled and sipped her drink.

"There was no investor, was there?" asked Melanie.

Lance smiled. "I'm a bad liar."

"How'd you get the reservation here?"

"I had Jackie call a month ago."

Melanie stared at Lance with a surprised look.

Lance looked down. "Yes, I had this planned for over a month."

"What if I had said no?" asked Melanie.

Lance looked up and smiled. "Simple. I would've cancelled the reservation."

"And?"

"And everything would've gone back to the way they were."

"What happens now?" asked Melanie.

Lance stared into Melanie's eyes. "That is entirely up to you."

Melanie sipped her drink and looked down.

"Melanie, this has never happened before. I would never try to get involved with anyone who works for me. But, I can't control what I'm feeling. I wanted a chance to tell you this. What you do with it is obviously your choice. We can go back to work tomorrow as if none of this ever happened."

Melanie looked up. "But, it did happen."

Lance nodded. "Maybe it was naïve of me to think I could unload this on you and think there wouldn't be consequences, but I can take a rejection, and I can go into the office and forget that any of this happened."

"I don't think that's particularly realistic," said Melanie.

Lance nodded and put down his drink. "I'm sorry," he said.

"Why are you sorry?" asked Melanie.

Lance looked lost for words.

Melanie smiled. "I think we should look at the menu."

"Alright," said Lance as he stared at Melanie with a confused look.

25.

Tom listened to Melanie's voicemail message and shoved the phone in his pocket. He walked over to McLeary's Pub on the bottom floor of his apartment building and found a seat at the bar.

"Mr. Rose, haven't seen you in a while," said the familiar bartender who he only knew as Jenna. "What'll it be?" she asked.

Tom noticed her curvy figure and the tight tee shirt that left nothing to the imagination.

"Let's start with a beer. Pale Ale."

"You got it," she said as she stuck a frosted mug underneath the beer spout. "Where's Melanie?"

"We're not together anymore."

"So, you're a bachelor, huh?"

"Yea."

Jenna slid the mug of beer in front of Tom. She leaned toward him. "So, does this mean I can flirt with you?"

Tom chuckled. "No, but you can get me a burger and some fries."

"You're no fun," she said as she wrote down his order and placed it at the end of the bar. "So, what happened?"

"I'd rather not talk about it," said Tom as he picked up his beer.

"I guess she dumped you. Another man?"

Tom didn't answer. Jenna leaned in close to Tom. "You know, it's very dangerous for you to come in here and tell me you're a free man. I get off at two. Feel like buying me a drink when I get off?"

Tom put on a smile. "I can't stay up that late. I have work to do in the morning."

"Come on Tom. You've got to live a little. You can't spend the rest of your life just working."

"You have no idea," said Tom.

Jenna stared at him with a confused look. A server brought out a plate and set it down at the end of the bar. "I think my dinner's ready," said Tom, pointing with his chin.

Jenna rolled her eyes. She walked over to the end of the bar and returned with Tom's burger. "You know, one day I'm just going to stop giving you all this attention, and then you'll be sorry."

"I know I'll be sorry, Jenna," said Tom as he bit into his burger.

"You know, you don't look so broken up about Melanie leaving you."

Tom felt a shooting pain in his stomach. He dropped his burger and hunched over the bar.

"What's wrong? You OK?" asked Jenna.

Tom took in a deep breath. The pain wasn't subsiding. "I need to go," said Tom in a low voice.

"Go," said Jenna. "The burger's on me."

"That was wonderful," said Melanie as she stepped out of the restaurant. Lance followed close behind.

"Yes, it was. Thank you for joining me."

Melanie turned to face him. "I had a good time, and I'm glad you invited me. Even though it was under false pretenses."

Lance nodded. "Would you like for me to call you a car?"

Melanie shook her head. "I think I'll just walk. I need to clear my head."

"Clear it from what?"

Melanie looked down at the pavement. "From you."

She felt his hand beneath her chin. She looked up at him.

"I'm sorry if I made things awkward for you. That wasn't my intention."

Melanie stared into his gentle eyes, and the lines of his beautiful face. His soft touch warmed her, and the attention he gave her made her heart race. She hadn't experienced these feelings in years. Lance stepped close to her and kissed her. She didn't fight him. She put her arms around his neck and kissed him back. A part of her wanted to get lost in his arms. But, her mind started to wander. Thoughts of Tom filled her head. Is this betrayal? Lance pulled away, but his hands remained on her waist.

"Are you OK?" he asked in a gentle voice.

Melanie nodded. "I should go," she said.

Lance ran the back of his fingers down the side of her face. He gave her a small kiss on her lips and then smiled. "Will I see you tomorrow?"

"Yes."

"You're not going to quit on me, are you?"

"No," said Melanie. "I just have a lot to think about."

"I want to see you again," said Lance.

Melanie looked away. "I've got to go."

"OK," said Lance smiling at her.

"We'll speak tomorrow," said Melanie. She turned to start her walk to a place that she once called home; to see the man who no longer wanted her.

26.

Melanie opened the door to the apartment. She saw Tom sitting at the kitchen table with documents spread out all over. She saw a napkin on the table with what looked like blood.

"What is that?" she asked as she pointed to the napkin.

Tom looked down at the napkin. He picked it up and rolled it up into a ball. "Oh, I just had a bloody nose. It's nothing."

Melanie nodded. "Did you get my message?" she asked.

"Yes. Do you need any help with your things?"

"No. How was your day?"

"I'm busy with a new client," said Tom as he put down his pen. "Her name is Hope Kane."

Melanie stood frozen for a few seconds. She recalled reading about her in the papers. "The woman accused of killing her husband and daughter?"

"She didn't do it," snapped Tom.

"I didn't say she did," responded Melanie.

Tom stood. "You're right. I'm sorry."

Melanie shook her head. "Don't apologize for that. But I am entitled to an explanation about what happened to us."

Tom looked down. "It's better for you this way," he said in a low voice.

"That's not good enough for me," said Melanie as she felt the anger rising in her heart. "I deserve more than that."

Tom didn't respond. He turned and sat back down.

"Tom!" shouted Melanie. "Please talk to me!"

Tom picked up a pen and started writing on his notepad.

Melanie shook her head. "Is this the kind of human being you are? After all these years, you don't have the decency to be a man and tell me?"

Tom sat, without speaking.

"Is it someone else?" she asked, lowering her voice.

"It's nothing like that," said Tom.

"Just fucking tell me!" she shouted. "Why are you making me play this guessing game?"

Tom rubbed his face with his two hands and then looked up. "I can't tell you why. But I promise you, you will understand the reasons. Right now, what's best for you is to forget about me and move on with your life. I know it doesn't sound right or fair, but you have to trust me. It's best this way."

Melanie shook her head in disbelief. "I guess it really doesn't matter anymore. I'll get my things."

Tom's cell phone started to ring. He picked it up and answered.

"Hi Edward," said Tom into the phone.

She saw Tom hold the phone against his ear and close his eyes.

"Alright. I'll be right over," he said and ended the call. Tom turned to Melanie. "Edward's wife just filed for divorce. He said he was escorted out of the firm. He sounds like a mess. I need to go see him."

Melanie nodded as she watched Tom put on his coat and rush out of the apartment. She sat down on the sofa and buried her face in her hands.

Tom found a yellow cab on First Avenue. "72nd and Central Park West," he told the cab driver. The cab drove through Central Park and pulled up to The Dakota. Tom ran into the building. The doorman recognized Tom and sent him up. He knocked on the door and a few seconds later, Edward opened the door. He still had his tie on. He didn't say anything and walked toward the living room. Tom followed.

"You OK?"

Edward laughed, though there was nothing funny about Tom's question. "Am I OK?" said Edward almost to himself. He sat down on the couch and picked up a bottle of Scotch and poured it into a glass. "Want a glass?" he asked Tom.

Tom took off his coat and sat down across from him. "Sure."

Edward poured a glass for Tom, and then downed what was in his. He refilled it.

"Do you want to talk about it?" asked Tom.

Edward looked up at Tom. "There isn't much to talk about. This day was coming for a long time."

Tom sat, listening.

"Lisa found out about the call girls. I think it was that fuck, Tim Ryan. He accused me of sleeping with prostitutes, and then suddenly Lisa tells me we are through. That fucking scum!" Edward put down his glass. "And then, he had the nerve to have me escorted out of the office!"

"Why?" asked Tom.

"I threw something at the mirror in my office and shattered it. Dean Morris showed up with a couple of security guys and told me that I had to leave until I calmed down. It supposedly was a direct order from Timothy, that fucking asshole."

Tom closed his eyes and shook his head.

"You going to say anything?" asked Edward.

Tom downed the Scotch in his glass. "Edward, you knew Lisa would find out at some point, didn't you?"

Edward looked into Tom's eyes for a second, and then pulled away. He looked down at the floor. Tom could see the teardrops, dripping down his nose.

"I'm sorry you have to go through this, Edward."

Edward shook his head. "My life's falling apart, Tom. My wife's leaving me. I was escorted out of the firm that I helped to build. I have no kids. I have nothing."

Tom stared at the broken man, not knowing what to say.

"I'm a fucking failure," said Edward. "I can't even keep the promise I made you to make you a partner."

"You are not a failure, Edward," said Tom. He picked up the bottle and refilled his glass. "And, you didn't promise me anything."

Edward leaned back against the couch and closed his eyes. "Maybe I made the promise to myself," he said.

"Edward, you did all you could to help me. At the end of the day, it really doesn't matter. Becoming a partner at Stern is not what I want. Not anymore."

Edward lifted his head and looked at Tom. "What?"

Tom shook his head. "In a way we're both going through the same thing. I think we're both lost and we don't know where we're headed."

Edward stared at Tom without responding.

Tom put down his glass. "I never questioned you or the things you did. I watched it happen because I was in the same place as you. We both were on a path to somewhere, without thinking about where the road would take us. We stayed on because it was easy, and we dealt with the consequences the best we could."

Edward set down his glass and continued to stare at Tom.

"None of us knows when we'll die. If you and I were to die tomorrow, we both would have walked a path that was travelled by many before us. And so what? What would we have accomplished?"

Edward shook his head. "I fucking worked hard to get to where I am!" Edward shouted. He closed his eyes and then spoke in a whisper. "And I lost it all."

"What is it that you lost, Edward?"

"I'm a nobody." Edward opened his eyes. "I'm nothing."

"That's what I am."

"Bullshit! You have your entire future ahead of you. You'll do great things."

Tom shook his head. "You mean make another dollar? Fight like hell to be elected to the partnership?"

Edward didn't answer.

"And what will it all mean?" Tom put down his glass and looked into Edward's eyes. "I'm sorry Lisa left you, but she deserved more than what you offered her."

Edward looked up. "Is this your idea of trying to make me feel better?"

Tom stood. "No, but there's nothing I'm telling you that you didn't already know. You don't have to spend the rest of your life trying to hide from it, thinking that a bottle of liquor and the spread legs of a prostitute can solve your problems. Lisa had every right to leave you. You can do more with your life."

"How?"

"By making a difference."

"What is that supposed to mean?"

Tom stood and began putting on his coat. "You can do more with your life," Tom said again. "And I can too."

Tom walked to the door and stopped to look back at Edward. He sat with his face buried in his hands. Tom walked out onto Central Park West. He checked his watch, and it was nearing 11 pm. He looked back at the apartment building. Edward was living in a hell of his own creation. He now had to make a decision to lie dead or find a way out of that ugly place. Tom looked out into the darkness of the Park and then closed his eyes. The short time he had spent with Edward was as much for himself as it was for Edward. He made a promise to himself about Hope. Tomorrow he would find a way to keep that promise.

27.

Annie sat at her kitchen table and thought about Mila, the way she would come into the diner in her Sunday dress. She thought about Hope, and wondered if she really could be innocent. What if? She would be sitting in prison for the murder of the people she loved. Annie picked up the white business card. It said, "Thomas Hunter Rose, Attorney at Law." She thought about the evening with him. By the time they left Capri, he looked as if he had figured something out. What was it? Annie put the business card down and thought about the things he talked about. He said there was a large man at the gas station. Maybe the same man was at the diner? Strangers often stop by the diner for a quick bite. Lots of them are tall and big. The large man Vincent saw could've been any one of them. The bartender said the Kanes always paid with cash. Tom seemed fixated on that. Why? She closed her eyes and tried to think about Hope. She shook her head. It was so long ago, everything was fuzzy. Her mind drifted back to the Kanes paying only with cash. Annie opened her eyes. She remembered. Hope always paid with cash at the diner too. She hadn't told Tom that. Maybe that's something important that Tom should know about? Annie checked the clock on her wall that read 12:32 am. Was it too late to call? She flipped the business card over and saw his cell phone number. She dialed it. He answered on the first ring.

"Hello?"

"Tom, it's Annie. I'm sorry to be calling so late."

"I was up anyway," he said in a low voice.

"Is everything OK?" she asked.

"Yea, everything's fine."

"I'll be real quick. After you left, I thought about some of the things we talked about, and I remember you asking a lot of questions about Hope paying for things with cash. Well, I didn't think of it at the time, but I think the Kanes also paid with cash at the diner. I thought you should know."

"Thanks. That's helpful."

"Can I ask you why?"

"It's consistent with the fact that they have no history. Paying cash will not leave a trail as to where they may have been, unlike a credit card. I wonder if they were running from someone."

"If they were running from someone, then . . ."

Tom didn't let her finish. "Another thing that doesn't make sense is their lifestyle. They rented a nice, expensive home in Scarsdale, yet they had one used Toyota that they purchased for $8,000. They didn't have much money in the bank, although it seems money appeared in their account every month or so in $10,000 increments. But they had no problems dining at the most expensive restaurant in Scarsdale. We can't see anything that would suggest that either of them worked. There's nothing to explain how or where they got their money."

"And the man at the gas station? Do you think maybe he's the one who the Kanes were running from?"

"That would fit the theory," said Tom. "That the man chasing Hope is the one who killed her husband."

"How're you going to prove this?" Annie asked.

There was a long pause. "I don't know. I guess I'll continue to go and speak with people Hope may have interacted with before the murder. I was going to head up there tomorrow. The police found receipts from a place called the Petit Shoppe on Mamaroneck Avenue in White Plains."

"I know that store," said Annie. "My old roommate Heidi works there. I can go see her tomorrow. I have the day off."

"That's some coincidence," said Tom.

"Not really. A bunch of us grew up in New Rochelle, and a lot of my friends work in local stores and restaurants."

"I guess that makes sense," said Tom. "There's no need for you to talk to her. I was planning on being up there anyway."

"Well, OK. It's just that Heidi probably will tell me more than what she may tell you. After all, she doesn't know you."

"OK, then maybe you can talk to her first, and then we can meet her together."

Annie smiled. "OK," she said and hung up. She smiled at the thought of seeing Tom again. She liked him. He seemed honest, genuine. Then she thought about the large man at the gas station. What if Tom's theory was right? What if this man was following Hope, and ultimately killed her husband? What if he was at the diner? She tried to imagine a large man sitting at the counter, staring at the Kane family. There were many men who ate at the diner, and any one of them could've been him. Annie shook her head and walked to her room. She changed into a pair of shorts and a tee shirt, and climbed into her bed.

———————————

The cold gust of the wind made the tip of his cigarette glow brighter. He stood on the sidewalk, staring at the window. He watched her hand reach for the lamp by the window and shut off the light. Dom stood for a few minutes longer, looking up at the dark window. He turned and walked to his car. The file folder on the passenger seat was open. He picked up a picture and stared at the face of Annie Sharpe. He liked staring at it. She was pretty, even with a bad haircut. He liked her eyes. A smile spread across his face as he imagined meeting her and wondering what she would say to him. In time, he said in a low voice. In time.

28.

Tom watched the steam rise from his coffee. He thought about the incident at McLeary's. His heart started to race. Memories of his father coughing up blood came rushing back. The doctors had said the surgery didn't work, and the chemo treatments were just killing him. The cancer had come back with a vengeance. They had him hooked up to tubes to keep him alive. They made him a prisoner of his own body. Tom wiped the tears from his eyes. He took in a deep breath and started punching in the number for Dr. Klingman. Then he stopped. What's the point? What could he possibly do to change anything? The supposed best doctors in the world couldn't do anything to save his father. The memories of his father trapped on that bed made his mind freeze. Tom shoved his phone back in his pocket.

Tom walked up Third Avenue to his office building. He went by Edward's office, but the door was closed. His assistant said she hadn't heard from him yet. Tom walked to his office and booted up the computer, and then pulled out a memo pad. He wrote down everything he learned the day before in Scarsdale. He needed an investigator to help him. Mike Lynch, he thought to himself. Mike was the best investigator he knew with operations all over the country. Tom had worked with him a few years back in a case where a large corporate client believed someone was leaking confidential information to a competitor. Mike brought in a team of investigators and caught the mole in less than a week. Tom was just five years out of law school at the time, but Mike gave him a lot of deference, and often looked to Tom for strategy rather than running to Edward, who was in charge of the assignment. They had become friends and kept in touch when they could. Tom opened his Outlook Contacts and typed in "Lynch." He dialed the number.

"Lynch Investigations," said a woman.

"Could you put me through to Mike Lynch?"

"Mr. Lynch is with a client, but I can direct your call to another investigator."

"Please let him know Tom Rose is on the phone. He'll take my call."

"One moment."

Mike answered a few seconds later. "Mr. Rose, long time no talk. How've you been?"

"I've been good. How about you?"

"Busy. Very busy. Business is good."

"I hope you're not too busy to help me on a project."

"You kidding? For you, I'd drop everything. What's up?"

"I'm working on a pro bono project."

"Wait, wait. Pro bono?"

"Yea."

"I said I'd work with you, but I can't work for a non-paying client. Business is too good. Opportunity cost."

"Come on Mike. Hear me out before deciding she's not worth your time."

"Go on," said Mike. Tom could hear the keyboard clicking through the phone line.

"Alright, Mike. I can take a hint."

The typing stopped. "Sorry, I just had to get an email out. Tell me about the case. I'm listening."

"You hear about Hope Kane?"

"Who?"

"Hope Kane."

"Who the hell's that?"

Tom shook his head. "She was in the news about a year ago. She's suspected of murdering her husband. She was caught holding the murder weapon."

He could hear Mike chuckling. "Yea, I remember now. She was in the papers for a while. She's the one that doesn't speak, right? I never knew what the big deal was. Lots of nut jobs take out their husbands. Why are you getting involved with this?"

"It's more complicated than a routine murder. She has a three-year old daughter who's missing. And, you're right. She hasn't spoken a single word from the point when she was arrested."

"You haven't answered my question."

"It gets more interesting. She has no history."

"No history?"

"She lives in Scarsdale, New York. Moved there about four years ago. But, there's no information on her or her husband prior to them moving to Scarsdale. They have no records. No history whatsoever."

Tom waited for a response from Mike but heard nothing. "Neither she nor her husband worked. They had a bank account with about ten grand. They would draw down on that, and then they would refill it. No one knows where they got the money to replenish their account. They rented the house and paid the landlord with cash. They bought a used Toyota with cash. They used cash for everything. People in the neighborhood knew who they were, but no one knows anything meaningful about them."

"OK, so now you've convinced me you have a murderer who has some bizarre facts associated with her. You still haven't told me why you took this case on."

"I think she may be innocent."

"Didn't you just tell me they caught her with the murder weapon?"

"Yea, but there are things that don't make sense."

"Such as?"

"Such as the forensics report. Her husband was shot in his forehead. It looks like the shot was fired from a distance. They found a casing by the front door. Then there is a second shot. The second bullet hit him below the heart that went through the heart and got lodged in his shoulder blade."

Mike cut in. "Meaning he was shot when he was lying dead from the first shot. The second bullet was fired from near his feet."

"That's right."

"What does that prove? She popped him in his head because she was pissed, and when he fell dead, she shot him again to make sure the deed was done. Was there gun residue on her?"

Tom closed his eyes. "Yea. It was all over her."

"So, tell me again why you think she's innocent."

Tom paused for a while. "Because she's not the killing type."

"Excuse me?"

"It's her eyes. There was this innocence about her. I don't believe she could harm a fly."

"Look Tom, you know how much I like and respect you. But you've got to listen to yourself. Plenty of fine-looking women have been convicted of murder. Just because she has pretty eyes don't mean she didn't pop her husband."

Tom nodded but didn't respond.

"You still there?" asked Mike.

"Yea. Just thinking."

"I didn't mean to get you down, but I'm just trying to be real. In any case, what did you want me to do for you?"

"Nothing right now. I just wanted to pick your brain. Can you think of any reason why a couple would have no history like these people?"

"Yea. They could've been under a witness protection program. They could've been running from something and hired a guy to wipe their history. It could be anything. They both could've been married and decided to run from their spouses and start a new life. So they can live as different people."

"How hard is it to wipe your history? I mean create a new identity for yourself?"

"There are people out there who specialize in that sort of thing. I've used a guy once for a client. He's supposed to be the best in the business. Maybe you should put in a call to him. He'll be able to give you a lot of details about how this works."

"Can you give me his number?"

"Yea. Hold on. His name is Calvin Tines. He works out in LA."

Tom wrote down Calvin's phone number. "Thanks Mike."

"You bet. I'll put in a call to Calvin later today to give him a heads up that you'll be calling. He won't be in yet. Anything else I can do for you?"

"Yea. I recall you have friends at the FBI."

"I do."

"Is there a way to get them involved? This is also a missing person case. Hope's daughter's missing. Can you put in a call to them to see if they'll get involved?"

"I can put in a call to Washington, but they probably know about this case already. They probably made a conscious decision to not jump in."

"If that's the case, I'd still like to know why."

"Alright."

"There is one other thing."

"Go on."

"I saw a tattoo on Hope's left arm. It was in the shape of a heart with letters 'S' and 'D' in the middle."

"A lot of people have tattoos," said Mike.

"I know, but I wonder if the letters mean anything."

"Probably initials of someone in her life. You're really grasping at straws, my friend."

"I know, but I've got nothing here to go on. I'm just trying to find out who she was, where she came from. Something."

"Alright. I'll make some calls to contacts I have to see if anyone's seen a tattoo like the one you're describing. It'll take a while, though. This is like looking for a needle in a haystack."

"Thanks, Mike. I appreciate it."

"I'm happy to help but listen, Tom."

"Yea?"

"Don't get too crazy about this. You spending all this time to help her assumes she's innocent. From everything you've told me, she's guilty as hell. Don't kill yourself fighting a lost cause."

Tom hung up the phone and stared at his notepad. He thought through what Mike said. He tossed the notepad against the wall and buried his face in his hands.

"It's bad to throw things. I have first-hand experience in that department."

Tom looked up and saw Edward standing in his doorway.

"Edward, what are you doing here?"

"I'm a partner here, if you recall."

"They let you back in?"

"They have no choice, until the partnership votes me out. That may happen by the way, but it hasn't happened yet."

Edward walked in and picked up the notepad and began reading it. "Looks like you've got some good stuff here."

"It's not easy with an uncooperative client."

Edward nodded as he took a seat. "So, tell me about your theory."

"Theory of what?"

"Of this case."

"I don't have one yet, other than that I don't think she killed her husband."

"And what's the basis for that?"

Tom repeated his analysis about the bullet in Mark Kane's forehead, the location of the bullet casings, the angle of the second bullet.

"That doesn't tell me she's innocent," said Edward.

"I know, but there could be a plausible story that someone else shot Mark, and then made her shoot him when he was already dead."

"It's a plausible theory, but you have no evidence to support the theory."

"That's why I'm trying to figure out if she and Mark were running from someone; someone who may have wanted him dead."

"What else?"

"You already know that there are no records of these people before they moved to Scarsdale. The people who knew them thought they were a happy family but knew nothing about them. They were very private people. They paid for everything with cash. That bolsters the theory that they may have been running from someone. Their lifestyle also doesn't make much sense. Although they lived in a nice home in Scarsdale and regularly dined at an expensive restaurant, Hope doesn't seem to have any money. She can't even afford a lawyer. There is nothing to suggest that either she or her husband worked. And then there's the cash. They kept about ten grand in their bank account, which they would replenish with cash whenever it would run low. Of course, the cash deposits stopped once Mark died and Hope was arrested, which tells me they were depositing the cash themselves."

Edward stared at Tom. "Anything else?"

"There is a Mobile gas station in town, and the guy there said he remembered a man staring at Hope and her daughter. The gas station guy felt uneasy, so he wrote down the man's license plate number. But he didn't keep it, when he saw Hope the next day."

Edward leaned back in his chair, thinking.

"Oh, there is one other thing. Hope has a tattoo on her left arm. It's a shape of a heart with letters 'S' and 'D' inside of it."

"What's the significance of that?"

"I don't know. It just doesn't fit the image. A happy, young family who kept to themselves. Seemed to live a quiet lifestyle. The tattoo just doesn't fit in this picture."

"A lot of people have tattoos these days," said Edward.

Tom nodded. "Right now, this is all that I have. I'm heading back up to Scarsdale this afternoon to meet with a woman I met, who's helping me."

Edward looked up. "Who?"

"Her name is Annie. She's a waitress at a diner up there. She has a friend who works at a clothing store where Hope had shopped. Annie's going to see if she'll meet with me."

Edward nodded. "Sounds like we've got a long way to go before we can come up with a defense."

Tom furrowed his eyebrows. "What do you mean 'we'?"

Edward smiled. "My life is an utter mess. I have no family, and I'll likely lose my job. I have a big hole in my life that I have to fill. I may as well fill it helping you. And, if you're going to throw your career into the gutter, I'll help you do it in style. I have a lot of experience in that area."

29.

Annie stared into the window display. The red, orange and yellow sweaters and scarves that filled the window to the Petit Shoppe had already been replaced with what they call cruise wear, even though it was still January. She stared at the boy mannequin with white slacks, blue canvas belt with little white sailboats, a white polo shirt and a navy baseball cap on a faceless head. Next to it was a girl mannequin with a red dress with a white and blue collar. She imagined Mila in that little dress, walking into the diner with her beautiful parents. Annie opened the glass door and stepped into the store. She saw Heidi Meyer hovering over a large glass table, folding clothes and stacking them in neat piles.

"Hey kiddo," said Annie as she approached her.

Meyer looked up and smiled. "Annie, what's up? Haven't seen you in a while."

"Been busy with stuff. I had the day off so I thought I'd swing by to see you and to see if you could help me with something."

Meyer's smile vanished. "Is everything OK?"

"Yes, it's all just fine. I just need to ask you something."

Meyer looked up. "What about?"

"When do you take your break? I'll buy you a cup of coffee and we can talk."

Meyer put down the shirt she was folding. "I can take a fifteen-minute break now. No one's here. We can go in back," she said as she motioned for Annie to follow her behind the counter and into the storage area in the back of the store.

"Have a seat there," said Meyer, pointing to a folding table with four chairs around it. "I'll pour us some coffee."

Annie sat down, looking around the racks and racks of clothes covered in brown paper. Meyer placed a cup of coffee in front of Annie and sat down across from her. "You like it with cream and Splenda right?" Meyer asked.

Annie nodded. "Thank you. How's Ronnie?"

Meyer shook her head. "We broke up."

"Oh, I'm so sorry. What happened?"

"I caught him in bed with Pia."

"Pia? Your roommate?"

Meyer chuckled. "*Ex* roommate. Remember how she used to want to hang around Ronnie all the time? I don't know if you ever noticed before you moved out, but I always felt like she would just hang around, whenever Ronnie came over. Well, about two weeks ago, I wasn't feeling well, so I went home early. And there they were, going at it on my bed."

"Oh God, I'm so sorry. I can't believe it."

Meyer nodded. "Believe it. They're both assholes and deserve each other. This was all for the best. Now, what did you need my help on?"

Annie put down her coffee. "I met a guy, Tom Rose. He's a lawyer who's trying to help Hope Kane."

"Hope Kane?"

"Yes. He's representing her and thinks she might be innocent."

"Innocent? They caught her with the gun. How could she be innocent?"

Annie nodded. "I know, I know. It's hard to imagine, but he's trying to figure out what happened that night. Who knows? Maybe she really is innocent?"

"Well, alright, but how does that involve you?"

"He's trying to learn as much about Hope and her family as he can, and I know Hope used to shop here. I thought maybe there are some things you remember about her that might help him."

Meyer smiled. "You still haven't told me how you're involved in this. Is he that cute?"

Annie looked down. "It's really not like that. He just seems like he's trying to do some good, and he has no one to help him."

"Alright, I won't tease you. What did you want to know about Hope?"

"She used to shop here, right? He said that Hope had a receipt from this store."

Meyer nodded. "Yes, she used to shop here."

"She was here right after Christmas, right? The day of the incident?"

"Yes. She was here that morning. I remember as clear as day, because that was the day she killed her husband. I was in shock, because she seemed so happy that morning, and then to kill her husband that same day . . ." Meyer shook her head.

"She didn't show signs of anything being wrong?"

"No," said Meyer. "She was as sweet as ever. Her daughter Mila was with her, and she ran around the store like she always does. Hope bought a few things for Mila and then left. That was the last I saw of her."

"Did Hope pay with cash?" asked Annie.

"Yes, she always paid with cash."

"Is there anything else you can think of?"

Meyer thought for a moment. "You know, I really can't think of anything else."

"OK," said Annie. "Thank you for taking the time. Now that you got rid of Ronnie, maybe you have some free evenings? Maybe we should meet for dinner or something?"

Meyer smiled. "I'd like that. Just tell me when," she said as she stood.

Annie walked out of the storage room. Meyer followed her out. A man came into the store and walked up to Annie.

"Hi, I need to purchase a gift for my niece's birthday and need some help."

Annie turned and pointed to Meyer. "That's Heidi over there. She'll help you." Annie started to walk toward the door. She heard Meyer's footsteps behind her.

"Annie, wait."

Annie turned around.

"There's one other thing I just remembered. That morning when Hope was here, I remember a guy walking around the store. He never said anything to anyone, but seemed to be keeping an eye on Hope and Mila."

Annie's heart started beating quicker. "What made you remember that?"

Meyer nodded toward the man waiting for her by the register. "Him. Most guys who come in here don't have a clue. The first thing they do is run to me and ask for help picking something out. But the guy I saw didn't ask for any help. That's what made him stand out in my mind. He just bought something and left, right after Hope and Mila left."

"What did he look like?"

"I remember he was tall. Like over six feet. I don't remember what he looked like, other than that he was big."

"What color hair?"

Meyer shook her head. "I just don't remember. I think it was reddish and really short – like a crew cut." Meyer looked up at the ceiling. "But I could be confusing him with someone else. I don't know."

Annie thought for a second. "Did he pay with a credit card?"

"I think he did."

"Would you remember the name if you saw it?"

111

"I doubt it. A lot of people shop here."

"But if you look at all the receipts from that day, you might be able to separate out the people who aren't regulars, right?"

Meyer nodded. "I suppose, but there are a lot of customers who shop here. The chances of me locating the right credit card slip aren't very good."

"Could I ask you to take a look?" asked Annie.

"Well, I know we keep copies of the receipts, but I don't know if we keep them for over a year. I'll have to ask Mrs. Holmes."

"Okay. Would you mind meeting with Hope's lawyer after you check on the receipts."

"I don't know anything other than what I've told you. But, if you want me to, I'll talk to him."

"I just think he might be interested in hearing about the guy you remember seeing."

Meyer nodded. "OK. I'll take a look for the receipt."

Annie stepped out of the store and started for her car. She couldn't stop thinking about the guy Meyer remembered. Could it have been the same guy that Vincent saw? As she neared her car, she sensed someone was behind her. She turned and saw a figure turn into a side street. She took a step toward the street, but she stopped. Her heart was racing, and she couldn't breathe. She turned and got in her car and locked the doors. She turned again toward the street and saw an old couple walk out. She let out a deep breath. It had to have been them, she said to herself. It had to have been them.

30.

Tom waited for the clock to read 12:30. He nodded at Edward and dialed the number for Calvin Tines on the speaker phone. A man answered.

"Yea," he said in a gruff voice.

"I'm trying to reach Calvin Tines," said Tom, checking the number he wrote down.

"That's me," the man said. "Who's calling?"

"I'm Tom Rose and with me is Edward Miller. Did Mike Lynch contact you to tell you I'd be calling?"

"Yea, he did," said Tines in a slightly more upbeat voice. "What can I do for you?"

"We're lawyers for Hope Kane, who's being prosecuted for murder, and we were hoping to ask you some questions."

"Yes. Mike gave me the background about her. I'm happy to talk to you. What do you need to know?"

"We're trying to gather information on her. She has no history before she moved to New York. Mike thought maybe she may have worked with someone who does the kind of work you do to erase her history."

"Yea. She likely hired someone like me."

"How does it work? How do you erase someone's history?"

"Technically, you don't erase the history. You wipe the person's background by giving her a new identity, so she wouldn't have a history."

"Can you explain how you go about creating a new identity?"

"Giving someone new paperwork to match their new identity is the easy part. The more difficult part is making people change their behavior.

113

People have a tendency to fall into a routine. And it's that routine that makes it difficult for people to run away from their past. If people are willing to completely change their ways, then we have something to work with."

"How about moving to a different location and starting a new life?" asked Tom.

He heard Tines chuckle. "Yea. That's the first step. The second step is to change the way they live. Find new hobbies. If you used to like hanging out at museums, stop going to museums. Start going to ball games. Stuff like that."

"Are there a lot of people who are in your line of work?" Tom asked.

"There's a handful, but there are only three other guys who really know what they're doing. If you're trying to figure out who did the work for your client, it's probably one of these guys."

"How do you know?"

"The fact that you're calling me tells me that they did a good job on her."

"How well do you know these guys?"

"I know them."

"Do you think they'll be willing to speak to me?"

Tines chuckled. "Doubt it. I agreed to talk to you as a favor to Mike. I owe him big. But people in my business don't like to talk about the work they do. Our entire business is built on confidentiality. The minute any one of us starts to talk about our past clients, we lose all credibility. No person who wants to ditch her past will hire you if she knows you'll tell the world who she really is."

"I get that, but what possible harm could come from revealing Hope's history now? Her husband's dead and she's in prison?"

"Think about what you just said."

Tom fell silent.

"You wouldn't be calling me to find out about her background if she wanted you to know about her past. If she doesn't want you to find out who she is, she sure as hell ain't gonna want the guy who helped her wipe her history to start blabbing on about her past."

"What do you suggest I do?" asked Tom.

"Let me talk to them. Maybe I can get something from them that can help you. But I wouldn't get your hopes up."

"Thank you."

"One thing," said Tines. "This is between us. No one can find out I helped you. As I said, I'm doing this as a favor to Mike. But even that can go only so far."

"Understood."

Tom looked over at Edward as he ended the call. "I guess we can call that progress."

"Progress?" asked Edward. "How do you call that progress?"

"He said he'll talk to the guys he knows."

Edward shook his head.

31.

Tom sat in the passenger seat of Edward's Mercedes S550 as they sped up the Henry Hudson Parkway. He stared out of the window, thinking about Hope; the way she looked up at him with the lone tear drop on her cheek. There was an honesty about her that he didn't anticipate. He knew he had nothing to prove her innocence, but for reasons he didn't understand, his gut told him she was. Hope Kane was not a killer. The ringing of his cell phone brought him back to the moment.

He saw Annie's name pop up on the caller ID. "Hi," he said.

"Where are you?" she asked.

"We're on our way up to see Hope."

"I met with my friend Heidi at the Petit Shoppe."

"Go on."

"She remembered seeing a tall man at the store on the morning of the murder. She thinks he had red hair with a crew cut. She said he was staring at Hope and Mila who were at the store that morning."

"What does she remember about him?"

"Not much, other than what I told you. He bought something with a credit card, so Heidi's checking the store's records to see if she can locate the receipt."

"Where can we meet you?"

"We?"

"Another lawyer from my firm, Edward Miller. He's working with me."

"Oh. Why don't we meet at Mel's. When will you get there?"

"By 1:30."

Tom put down his phone and looked over at Edward. "That was Annie. Her friend remembers seeing a tall man with red hair staring at Hope and Mila the morning of the murder."

Edward nodded. "Yea, I gathered. How'd you meet her?"

"I met her at a diner when I first came up here."

"You fucking her? Is that the reason you broke things off with Melanie?"

"No, Edward."

"Why's she helping you?"

"I don't know. She didn't tell me. Maybe because she agrees with me – that Hope may be innocent."

"That couldn't possibly be the reason."

"Why do you say that?"

"Because, other than you, and a very small part of me, nobody thinks Hope's innocent."

"Then why are you helping me?"

"Representing a client has nothing to do with whether or not she's guilty. She's entitled to have counsel represent her interests. Have you forgotten what you learned in law school?"

Tom turned toward the window. "I'm not interested in due process and the technical gamesmanship that may get a guilty killer off. I'm only interested in proving her innocence because I believe she's innocent."

"That's not our job as lawyers," said Edward.

"None of that much matters to me."

"What about Melanie?"

"What about her?"

"What happened?"

"I don't want to discuss it."

Edward shook his head. "Listen Tom, we've known each other a long time."

"Just drop it," said Tom, not letting him finish. "I have my reasons."

32.

Annie returned with a pot of coffee and refilled the three cups sitting on the table. She slid back into the booth and sat down next to Tom. Meyer wasn't ready to meet with them. She had trouble locating the receipts and needed more time. Annie repeated the story about the man Meyer saw on the morning of the murder.

"Heidi thinks the receipts may have gone to storage. She'll need to wait until after she closes shop to go look for them; it'll be after five. I don't think my boss will appreciate us sitting here until then," she said.

"We don't have to stay. I think we should take a ride to Hope's house," said Tom.

"Why?" Annie asked.

"They're doing construction across the street from her house. There are guys working there. I haven't had a chance to speak with any of them to see if they saw anything."

Edward turned to Tom. "What did you say? Did you say construction?"

Tom nodded. "Yea."

"What kind of construction?"

"It looked like a brand new house, although the chimney looked old."

"Sounds like a partial tear-down. It's common for people to tear down an old house, keep some portions of the house and build around them. There are tax benefits to doing it that way. The question is, when did they start the project? We may get lucky."

Tom furrowed his eyebrows. "I'm not following you."

"Whenever you have a major construction, it's common for the builders to install a twenty-four hour camera that records all activity around the house. They usually do it as a security measure to deal with vandalism. If they had a camera and it was aimed out toward the street, it may have caught something that could be helpful to your theory that someone else killed Mark Kane. The problem is, these constructions usually take less than a year. My guess is they started the project less than a year ago, meaning if any cameras were installed, it would've been after the murder."

Tom stood. "Let's go. We have to start getting lucky at some point."

"Wait," said Edward. He looked at Annie. "Annie, would you like to work for Stern and Hobbs?"

"Excuse me?" asked Annie, with a surprised expression.

"You're taking a lot of time to help us, and I want to make sure we pay you for your time."

Annie shook her head. "Oh Edward, thank you, but there's no need. I made one visit to a friend. I don't need to be paid for that."

"There's something else," said Edward. "Right now, because you don't work for our law firm, our conversations are not privileged, meaning the prosecution can get you to tell them everything we've talked about. If you come to work for us, we can preserve the privilege."

"But I'm not a lawyer."

"We can hire you as a paralegal."

"I don't have any experience . . ."

"It doesn't matter. You're helping with the investigation and you have all the experience you need. What do you think?"

Annie turned toward Tom. "I, I don't know. I didn't start this to get a new job."

Tom nodded. "Just think about it. You don't have to decide anything right now. We just have to be a little careful about what we discuss."

"Are you concerned about money?" asked Edward.

"No, it's not that at all. I make plenty here, and I like my life. I just don't know if I can change everything on a moment's notice. I got involved with this because I wanted to help."

Edward nodded. "OK, Annie. Let's do it this way. We'll hire you on a part time basis. This way, you can keep your job here, and you can work with us just on this project during your spare time. We just need this arrangement to protect our conversations."

Annie nodded. "I guess that could work."

"Good," said Edward. "I'll have my assistant put together a letter agreement."

They walked to the silver Mercedes waiting in the parking lot. Annie climbed into the back and leaned against the soft leather seat. They pulled out of the lot as Tom directed Edward to Hope's house.

She saw workers on the roof, laying shingles down, and hammering away. They got out of the car and headed toward the house. Tom waved at the men on the roof. One of the men came down the ladder.

"Can I help you?" he asked Tom.

"I'm Tom Rose. We're lawyers for Hope Kane," said Tom, pointing toward Hope's house across the street.

The man nodded. "I'm Frank Bowers. What can I do for you?"

"How long was this house under construction?" asked Tom.

"A year and a half," said Bowers.

"Why so long?" asked Edward.

"The homeowner ran into financial problems. He lost his job, so we had to stop all work. He wound up selling the house to a new family, and they hired us to complete the project."

"Then this house was under construction in December, two Christmases ago?" asked Tom.

"Well, we started in the later part of the summer and then the home-owner lost his job in November. So, there was no activity here from I'd say November through May of last year, which is when the house was sold."

"Do you have cameras in place to keep an eye on the house?" asked Edward.

Bowers pointed toward the roof of the house. "Yes sir. See? We have two cameras going twenty-four seven. That one there is aimed at the street so we can see who's coming onto the property." He pointed at the tree next to the curb. "That second one there is pointed at the house, so we can see if anyone comes near the house."

"Were the cameras running between November and May when the project was suspended?" asked Tom.

"Definitely," said Bowers. "Since we weren't coming here regularly, we had more of a reason to keep the cameras going to check against vandals. It doesn't cost us anything to run the cameras. Just some electricity. That's about it."

"Do you keep the recordings?" asked Edward.

"I don't know, but I assume so. It's all digital stuff and it gets saved on the builder's hard drive. I'm pretty sure he loads everything onto CDs and files them away."

"Where can we find the CDs?" asked Tom.

"Back in the GC's office in White Plains."

"Could we see the recording?" asked Tom.

"I don't see why not, but you gotta talk to the GC."

"What's his name? How do we get a hold of him?"

"His name is Nick Glorioso. You have a pen? I'll give you his number and address."

Tom pulled out a pen and his memo pad and wrote down the information Bowers gave him.

"Give him a call," said Bowers. "He's a nice guy. He'll be happy to help you."

Dom parked the car a block away beneath a tree. The bright sun and the shade of the tree shielded him from being detected. He sat in his car staring at Tom Rose. Blood shot up to his head and he gripped the steering wheel tighter. He sat frozen as he watched Tom pull out his cell phone.

They walked back to Edward's car. Tom dialed Glorioso's number. A woman answered.

"NEG Construction, this is Tina. May I help you?"

"This is Tom Rose speaking. May I speak with Nick Glorioso?"

"One moment." A few seconds later, a man got on.

"Hello, Nick speaking."

"Mr. Glorioso, My name is Tom Rose."

"Yes sir, what can I do for you?'

"I'm a lawyer for Hope Kane. She lives across the street from where you guys are constructing a house on Mulberry Street."

"Yea, I've read about her. How can I help you?"

"So, you know about the murder of her husband?"

"Yea. Such a horrible story."

"Yes, it is. We're trying to get any information we can about what happened in Ms. Kane's home on the night of the murder. We spoke with Frank Bowers."

"Yea, he works for me."

"He tells us that you may have recordings of the area near the house. Is that right?"

"That's right, but we don't record the house twenty-four seven. The video camera is connected to a motion sensor. It only goes on if it detects movement. Every once in a while, we load the recordings onto CDs, which we keep in our office."

"Did you see the recordings?" asked Tom.

"Nah. It would take too much time. We would only go in to look if something were missing or if the house was damaged. We haven't had any problems there, so there was no reason to look. It's a nice neighborhood."

"Will you let us see whatever was recorded?"

"I don't see why not. I have everything in my office. Swing by whenever you want and I'll let you see it."

"Would you mind if we came this afternoon?"

"I leave around six, so if you can get here before then, you can take a look."

"We'll head over right now."

Tom put away his phone. "He'll help us. Let's go. Maybe things are starting to break the right way for us," said Tom.

Edward smiled. "See Tom, I'm already paying dividends for you."

They drove onto Mamaroneck Avenue and headed toward White Plains. Edward found a parking spot in front of the building. They took the elevator up to the third floor and walked over to suite 364. Tom opened the door and stepped in. Edward and Annie followed. He didn't see anyone sitting at the receptionist's desk by the door.

"Hello," said Tom, but heard nothing. He walked past the table and down the hallway. "Hello," he said again, and heard no response. He walked to the end of the hallway and saw an open office door on the left. He walked toward it and knocked on the door and peaked in. That's when he saw the two dead bodies.

33.

Annie shook violently in the back of the police car as Tom pulled her close to him trying to calm her. She said she'd never before seen a murdered victim; then again, neither had he. He saw Edward walk toward the car and tap on the window. Tom stepped out of the car.

"The woman's name is Tina Martin. She was Nick's receptionist."

"Did they find the CDs?" Tom asked.

Edward shook his head. "No. There were no CDs."

"Then whoever did this took them," said Tom.

"Don't jump to conclusions. There's also cash missing. It looks like an ordinary robbery."

Tom shook his head. "Come on, Ed. Why would a robber take CD recordings of a construction project?"

"I don't know," said Edward. "They don't have anyone in terms of a suspect right now. There's a surveillance camera at the building, but there are a ton of people who walked in and out of the building. They don't know who to focus on."

"We have to tell them about the CDs," said Tom.

Edward shook his head. "I did. But the police is focused on the victims and they have their hands full right now. They're not much interested in hearing about our conspiracy theory about some CDs that are supposedly missing. How's Annie?"

"She's in shock. Understandably."

"Is she still up for going to meet her friend?"

"I doubt it."

Tom heard the car door open and he turned to see Annie walking toward them.

"Hey, you OK?" Tom asked.

Annie had a blank expression. "I may have seen him."

"Saw who?" asked Edward.

"The man who Heidi and Vincent saw. It happened earlier today. I was walking to my car and I could've swore that someone was following me. When I turned back, I saw someone walk into an alley."

"What did he look like? Did he have a crew cut?" Edward asked.

Annie shook her head. "I just saw his back. I didn't see his face or his hair, but if it's the same guy, he's following us."

Edward put his hand on Annie's shoulder. "Annie, if you didn't see this man, how can we assume he's the same guy, or the person who killed these people?"

Annie didn't answer.

"The police said they have surveillance cameras in the building," said Tom. "Let's see if there's a guy who fits the description of the redhead."

"Wait," said Edward. "Give me your cell phone."

Tom looked at Edward. "Why?"

"If your crazy theories are right, whoever this guy is, he's listening to your conversations. You called Glorioso to tell him we were heading over to see the recording. He had to have heard that conversation. That's the only way he could've known."

Annie sat in front of the monitor as Officer Fitzsimmons cued the recording to the right time-period. Tom and Edward stood behind her staring at the monitor. They asked Fitzsimmons to play the recording over and over again.

"Nothing?" asked Fitzsimmons.

"No," said Tom. "It could be any one of these guys, but they're wearing hats or hoods. We can't see their hair."

Fitzsimmons shook his head. "I'm sorry, but I really don't see how you can connect some random guy that some people remember seeing over a year ago with these murders. We have no idea who this guy is, and you don't see him on the recording. We have nothing to connect whoever this guys is to what happened here."

"But he could be any one of these guys," said Annie, pointing at the monitor. She pointed at a guy with a ski hat. "This guy. This guy could be it."

"And he also might not be. This video clip shows nothing that'll be useful," said Fitzsimmons.

Another officer entered the conference room. "We're done analyzing Mr. Rose's phone," she said. "It was hacked. Looks like it was hacked through an email he opened with his iPhone. We cleaned it so you can use it now," she said as she handed the phone to Tom. "Don't open any suspicious emails with this phone if you want to avoid another bug."

"Is there any way to trace who did it?" asked Tom.

She shook her head. "No."

"Oh my God," said Annie. "So it is true. He's been following us and tracking our calls."

Fitzsimmons stared at Annie. "What are you saying?"

Tom stepped to him. "Look, as I told you. We're investigating the murder of Mark Kane. We think whoever hacked my phone is the guy who murdered these two people, because he must've heard me tell Glorioso that I was going to his office to see the recording of Hope Kane's house on the day of the murder. That's why the CDs are missing."

Fitzsimmons shook his head. "Listen, I don't know who hacked into your phone, and I don't know if these people kept any CDs at their office." He pointed at Annie. "Maybe her friend saw a man who was staring at

Hope Kane over a year ago, but even if that's true, that's just not enough for us to assume that the same guy killed these people. None of this adds up to anything. We have nothing to connect these events to these murders or Hope Kane. Glorioso and his assistant were victims of a robbery. Their wallets were emptied out. It looks like they had a cash box for subcontractors, which was also cleaned out. Unfortunately, these things happen."

"You're not seriously suggesting there's no connection here, are you?" asked Tom.

"I just don't have enough to tie these two murders to what you're doing for Hope Kane," said Fitzsimmons as he walked out of the room.

"But my friend saw a man on the day of the murder!" shouted Annie at the closed door. She brought her hand to her mouth. She turned to Tom. "I told you about Heidi when I called you, didn't I?"

"Shit! You did," Tom said as he ran after Fitzsimmons.

34.

Annie dialed Meyer's cell phone from Edward's car. She answered right away.

"Hi Annie," she said.

"Oh thank God. Are you OK?"

"Yea. Why wouldn't I be?"

"You might be in danger. Are you at the store? We're on our way there right now."

"What, what do you mean I'm in danger?"

"Go in the back of the store and hide. We'll be there in a minute."

"Annie, what's going on? You're scaring me!"

"Just do as I say!"

"I'm already in back. Mrs. Holmes is in front."

"I think you should just leave the store. Go out the back," said Annie.

"OK," said Meyer. Annie heard her gasp. "Oh God, the door lock is broken."

"What?"

"The back door. The lock is broken. Someone must've broken it."

"Is there anyone there?"

"No."

"We're almost there."

Edward parked his car behind the police car, and Annie ran after the police officers into the store. She saw Meyer standing by the register. Annie ran to her and hugged her. "Thank God you're OK."

Two officers spoke to Mrs. Holmes and ran to the back of the store. Meyer pulled away. "Someone tell me what the hell's going on."

Tom walked up to her. "I'm Tom Rose. I'm Hope Kane's lawyer and Annie's been helping me. We think there's someone out there who's trying to prevent us from gathering evidence to defend Hope, and may even harm those who get in his way. I know you were trying to locate a credit card receipt from the day of the murder of Hope's husband, and we were concerned this guy might try and stop you."

Meyer stared at Tom in shock

The police officers returned from the storage area. Fitzsimmons walked over to Meyer. "I'm Officer Fitzsimmons. When did you first notice the lock in the rear door was broken?"

"I just noticed it a few minutes ago."

"Mrs. Holmes said she hadn't been setting the alarm for a while. When was the last time you checked that latch?"

"We get our deliveries through that door once a week, so we would've noticed it if it were broken. The delivery guy was here three days ago, so it had to have happened in the past two or three days."

Mrs. Holmes walked in from the back of the store. "Someone picked the old safe. The door's wide open," she said.

Fitzsimmons took a step toward her. "Anything missing?"

She shook her head. "It's an old safe. We used to keep cash in there, but we stopped keeping cash in the store. We close out the register every night and I make a deposit on my way home. That safe hadn't been used for years. Whoever broke in here probably didn't know that so thought he might've found some cash in it."

Fitzsimmons looked over at Tom. "Look, I know you're trying to tie all of these things to Hope Kane, but this was a burglary."

"But you're dismissing the things that tie everything together. My phone was hacked. I called Glorioso, and when we got there, he was found dead. I spoke with Annie on that same phone, and she told me about Heidi and the receipt. And now, we see that the store had been broken into. You're just refusing to see these things for what they are. There's someone out there who's trying to impede my investigation."

"I'm not overlooking anything. Under different circumstances, I might be persuaded to think that there's more to this, but not now."

"What do you mean 'under different circumstances'?"

Fitzsimmons lowered his voice. "Where the person you're trying to protect is not a murderer."

"She hasn't been convicted."

"That doesn't mean she didn't commit the murders. You're trying to piece together a story that says your client's innocent, and the real murderer is trying to stop you from gathering the evidence to prove her innocence. I get the strategy. I've seen plenty of lawyers try it. But the problem is, there's no way you'll ever convince me that someone else committed that murder. She was caught with the murder weapon in her hand, standing over her dead husband. There's no way you're going to convince anyone that she's innocent. And, there's no way you're going to get any officer's attention to start a new investigation to connect these separate, innocuous events to help you weave a story of Hope Kane's innocence."

Tom didn't respond. Fitzsimmons tapped Tom's shoulder. "Listen, I know you're trying to help your client, but open your eyes. Before we can even start to think about piecing these different events together, we would have to be convinced that someone's trying to frame Hope Kane. That's where we hit a brick wall. We just are not gonna get there."

Tom didn't move as he stared at Fitzsimmons walk back into the storage room. Annie put her arm around him. "Forget about him," she said.

Tom shook his head. "Maybe he's right."

35.

Tom returned to Edward's car after he walked Annie to her apartment. Tom turned toward Edward as he started the engine. There was a time when he looked to Edward to fix all that went wrong in a case. Tonight, everything was different. Edward was just a man, just like him. He had no answers.

"How is she?" Edward asked.

"She's still in shock."

"Not surprising. It's not every day you see murdered people."

Tom nodded. Edward put the car in drive and pulled out of the parking lot. "I have to hand it to you, Tom. I'm not saying I buy into your theory or strategy yet, but everything that happened today does leave you wondering if there's more to this story," said Edward.

Tom didn't answer.

"I thought you were chasing a rainbow. There was no doubt in my mind she was guilty. But, after today, I have my doubts. The task now is finding out what really happened and then telling that story to the jury."

Tom shook his head. "And how are we going to do that? We have nothing. We know there are people out there who are trying to get in our way, but we don't know why and we don't know who. We have no leads." Tom turned to the passenger window and looked out into the darkness. "Maybe Fitzsimmons was right," said Tom. "Maybe this is just one big coincidence that proves nothing about Hope's innocence."

"You sound like you're giving up," said Edward.

Tom turned to Edward and stared at him. He didn't know what to say.

"I didn't want you to take this case to begin with, so it'll sound odd for me to say this," said Edward. "In a matter of days, you managed to at least raise some questions about Hope's innocence. Why would you give up now?"

Tom looked away again. "Yea, and I also may be responsible for the deaths of those two people."

"No Tom. That's not true. There's a murderer out there. You're not responsible for the actions of a madman."

Tom closed his eyes. In that moment, the sight of the two dead people flashed in front of him. He couldn't breathe. He wanted to scream.

"You OK?" Edward asked.

Tom looked up and nodded as he fought to take in a breath.

"I'm sure there's a lot going through your head, but remember this. You just scratched the surface on Hope Kane. Sleep tonight. You can always decide what you want to do in the morning. I'm behind you either way."

36.

Tom sat down at the kitchen table and poured the Scotch into his glass. He stared at the brown liquid for a few seconds and then downed it. The burning liquid in his throat did nothing to calm his nerves. He closed his eyes and took in a deep breath. Tom refilled his glass. His mind drifted to thoughts of Melanie. All his life, he knew exactly what he wanted. And he made Melanie believe she was a part of the world he was going to create for them. He never anticipated that he'd wake up one morning and realize he had to leave her. There was no choice. He had to leave. It wasn't fair to selfishly keep her trapped with him. She had to be free of him. He knew he made her a promise of a life together, but he knew he was no longer able to keep that promise. These thoughts froze his mind and chained his ability to offer an explanation to Melanie. All he could do was to just say goodbye.

The meeting with Doctor Klingman opened his eyes to the ignorance with which he had led his life. He didn't know who he was and what his life meant. None of it ever really mattered before. When death isn't staring you in the face, it's easy to think you are immortal. Immortality meant you had the luxury to allow days to go to waste. But the news of his illness forced him to look at everything differently; to reflect on the life he had lived and to decide how he was going to live the precious time he had left. Then, Hope Kane entered his life. It was the way she looked at him and the way she cried. After that first meeting, he was certain that finding a way to help her was what he wanted; what he needed. Hope was going to be the guiding light to give him purpose. But now, he was pouring Scotch into an empty glass at 2 o'clock in the morning, knowing he had a hand in the deaths of two innocent people. Tom buried his face in his two hands, wishing he could go back and change the decisions he had made. But there would be no going back. He was stuck on the path he had chosen, even though he had no clue what price he and others might have to pay.

Tom pushed aside the half empty bottle. He had to move on. He had to think about tomorrow and the decisions he would have to make. Tom was certain everything was connected – his hacked cell phone, the phone call with Annie about Meyer and the missing receipt, the call to Nick Glorioso about the recording and his death. The police dismissed everything as a mere coincidence. Tom shook his head. He understood that it's easy to dismiss facts right in front of you, if the same facts couldn't coexist with the story they had chosen to accept. Hope's guilt was a tale that already had been told, and one that had been engraved into the minds of anyone who had heard the story. Today, he didn't have enough to get people to understand that they had gotten it all wrong. Tom stood and walked to the window to stare out at the 59th Street Bridge. The carefully placed lighting along the edges of the bridge brought out its beautiful shape, its grand structure. Tom looked below the lights and the portions of the bridge that light couldn't reach. The dark night had disguised the grime and the rust that covered the decades old beams that held up the bridge. He swallowed hard and sat down on the windowsill. People died because of the things he had set in motion. He knew he was responsible, and the only way he could try and make sense of the price they had to pay was for him to finish the job he started. Tom walked toward the bedroom, leaving behind the view of the bridge, and the world of illusions that showed men and women only what they wanted to see.

––––––––––

Melanie stood in the enormous foyer, staring at the bright lights flickering outside of the floor to ceiling windows. She had never before been inside of a penthouse apartment that took up the entire floor of a high rise. The smell of the wood burning fireplace and the deep glow of the candles warmed the room. She felt his hands as he gently helped her out of her coat. He poured wine into two crystal glasses and handed one to her. She willingly took it and smiled into his eyes. Lance stepped to her and kissed her. She put her arms around his shoulders and kissed him back. He slowly unbuttoned the front of her dress and she felt his hands against her breasts. He kissed her again and pulled her hand toward his bedroom. Her mind began to drift toward Tom, but the alcohol and his gentle touch distracted her just enough to lose herself in the moment. They fell onto his bed as they undressed. The passion flowed with every touch, every kiss. Then, the thoughts of Tom came rushing back. She pulled away and sat up.

"What's wrong?" he asked.

Melanie turned from him and covered her face with her two hands.

"I'm sorry," he said in a gentle voice.

"No," said Melanie. "Don't tell me you're sorry. Just hold me."

Lance put his arms around her and brought her into an embrace. "Just hold me," she whispered again, hoping that sleep will come fast and help her run from her thoughts of Tom Rose.

37.

Edward stared at the blank wall that once held up the eight-foot mirror that he had shattered. He thought through the Hope Kane investigation and then shook his head. Yesterday, for a short while he thought Tom had stumbled onto something. This morning, he wondered if he had just gotten caught up in the moment. He had done it many times before in his career – get caught up in your own bullshit, only to realize in a saner moment that the story just didn't work. Tom was going for a home run with Hope Kane. He wasn't trying to get her off. He was trying to prove her innocence. Edward knew he had to talk to him. Tom had become near obsessed with Hope Kane. He couldn't just sit by and let Tom go down this path. Edward walked down the hall and knocked on Tom's door. He didn't hear a response. Edward opened the door and saw Tom sitting on his chair in the dark, staring out of his window.

"How're you doing?" asked Edward as he sat down on the chair in front of the desk.

Tom turned to Edward. "Just thinking."

"About?"

"Next steps."

"And?"

"Still working it out."

"You really think you can prove her innocence?"

"Yes, because I believe she is."

"Based on what?"

Tom turned back to the window. "It was something I sensed from the very beginning."

"The law doesn't operate on people's senses. It operates on evidence."

Tom nodded. "I know."

"So how are we going to gather the evidence to support your theory?"

"I don't know. But I believe we'll find a way."

Tom leaned back against his chair, still looking out of the window. Edward sensed he didn't want to speak any more about the case.

"So what happened with Melanie?" Edward asked.

Tom turned back toward Edward. "She can do better than me."

Edward chuckled. "What in the world are you saying? You two are perfect for each other."

"No," said Tom.

"Look Tom, I've known you a long time. I know how much you love her. I don't know what you're going through right now, but you will get over it. I promise you. You will get past whatever it is you're dealing with. Don't make life's decisions at a time when you may not be thinking straight."

"Thanks, Edward," Tom said in a low voice.

"That's it? That's all you're going to say?"

Tom didn't respond. Edward got up. "We're going to continue this conversation, Tom. I'm not going to let you make this mistake."

Tom nodded and turned back toward the window. Edward stood and stared at Tom's back. After a short while, he stepped out of Tom's office, knowing that the conversation had ended a long while ago.

38.

The two dozen red roses sat on the center of her desk. Melanie read the card.

I feel as if I've been waiting for you all my life. Last night will forever be a part of me that will never leave me. I want to experience life with you by my side.

With all my heart, Lance

Melanie put down the card and walked to the window. Her heartbeat quickened as she thought about Tom. She tried to fight back the tears, but it was no use. Though he wanted to part ways, a part of her believed it wasn't over. She had hoped in time things would go back to the way they were. But last night, she didn't have the patience to wait. She needed him and he wasn't there for her. So she ran from her hopes and into the comforts of Lance's embrace. None of it was planned. It just happened. She got lost in the moment, and her needs overwhelmed her. Now what? She shook her head and buried her face in her hands. After last night, she knew she was lost. It was no longer about Tom and what he may be feeling. It was now about her own thoughts and questions – whether she could ever go back . . . whether she wanted to go back, even if he wanted her.

Tom sat at the conference room table, laying out the story in his mind. He knew he had no evidence, but the events of the past two days fit into the story he pieced together. "She's innocent," he said as he looked up at Edward on the other side of the table.

Edward leaned back. "Let's hear it."

"You know the story, Edward. It fits perfectly. You were there and saw for yourself. Hope's husband was murdered by the same man who murdered Glorioso and Martin. His goal is to keep Hope in prison, which is the reason he stole the CDs. And the same reason he broke into the Petite Shoppe and took the receipt."

Edward nodded. "I agree that all of those things could be true. But the part that I can't work through in my mind is why would the murderer go through the trouble of trying to keep Hope in prison when he could've just as easily killed her that night? What would motivate a person to kill the woman's husband, keep her alive, and then somehow take away her ability to speak? It's a difficult story to explain. That's the reason we can't convince the police of this story. And guess what? We're going to have the same problem with the jury."

Tom looked at Edward with a blank stare. Edward continued. "This is important, Tom, because whatever story we tell the jury, it has to be credible. This one question has no answer, and that's what could kill our story."

Tom looked up at the ceiling, knowing Edward was right. "That piece will have to wait," Tom said. "Right now, everything else falls together. We had two separate leads that they cut off, and we now know they did it by listening in on my phone conversations."

"The other problem we face is time," said Edward. "Whatever story we ultimately decide to tell, we need time to gather the evidence. Right now, all we have is a series of random events that seem to fall into a story that we're trying to tell, but we have no evidence. We have nothing to connect the true murderer to Hope Kane. With a trial coming up in just over a week, we have zero chance of completing our investigation to gather what we need to tell our story."

Tom stared blankly at Edward. The excitement of convincing himself of Hope's innocence had clouded his ability to see the difficulties he faced. Edward brought him back to the cold reality. He had won nothing yet. "What do you suggest we do?" asked Tom.

"We have to ask the judge to adjourn the trial, but it'll be a challenge. Judge Gonzalez is all business and likes to clear his docket quickly. This case has received a lot of media coverage, yet it's just been sitting and gathering dust. The judge will want to move it. The evidence is stacked up against Hope. He's not going to see the point of adjourning the trial again. The prosecution's chomping at the bits to get this done and over with. So, we're going to have to push real hard at the pretrial conference to kick this thing back."

"I don't want an adjournment," said Tom.

"What? Have you lost your mind?"

"I don't want Hope sitting in prison any longer than she has to."

"I understand that, but she'll be sitting in prison for a hell of a lot longer if we don't get the time we need to build our case."

"I'll push for a short adjournment. Maybe a week, but nothing more."

Edward shook his head. "OK. I'll let you make that call. But I want to raise something else with you. We have to constantly stop and adjust our thinking. I know you think she's innocent, but we have to stop focusing on her innocence and start focusing on a story that'll either raise a reasonable doubt of her guilt, or provide justification for what she did."

"And what story is that?" asked Tom.

"I don't know, but we haven't explored any of it. Maybe she killed her husband in a jealous rage? Crime of passion. Maybe she found out he was having an affair?"

"We have no evidence of that," said Tom.

"Have we looked?"

Tom shook his head no.

"This is precisely the problem with latching onto one theory. We ignore everything else. And, we have no evidence that she didn't kill Mark, and no actual evidence that someone's trying to frame her. The point is we have to keep our options open. If we buy into your theory, we lose another defense that may be more plausible."

"Edward, the theory of her innocence didn't come from thin air. We've been on this case for just a few days and in that time, the theory came to us from the questions we asked. As you say, we don't have time. And that means we don't have time to do a dance to figure out which theory to pursue. I believe we have to pursue her innocence, because I believe she is."

Edward let out a deep breath. "Alright Tom, I understand. But there's one more thing we need to think about. If your theory's right, then there's a murderer out there who's willing to kill people to keep Hope in prison. Where does that put us?"

Tom stared into Edward's eyes. "I've thought of that."

"And?"

"If the murderer's goal is to frame Mark's murder on Hope, he couldn't come after us. Killing or attacking her lawyers would be an all out admission that she's being framed."

Edward leaned back and nodded. "Are you willing to risk our own lives based on that logic?"

Tom didn't respond. He sat and stared at Edward. The ringing of the phone broke the silence. Tom pressed the speaker button on the phone.

"Tom, it's Helena. Mike Lynch's on the phone. Do you want to take it?"

"Yea," said Tom. He heard Helena connect the call. "Mr. Rose's on the line," she said before hanging up.

"Hello? Tom?"

"Hey Mike."

"Calvin Tines is with me."

"Hi Calvin. I have Edward Miller here."

"Edward, how's it going," said Mike. "Been a while."

"Yes. Too long," said Edward.

"Alright. Calvin, tell them what happened," said Mike.

"I got a visit earlier today from two guys. One held a gun against my head while the second one went through my computer. They made me give up the names of my three friends who I told you I was going to call. After they got what they wanted, they told me I better not help any lawyers, and if they find out I did, they'd come back and take care of me and my son. They told me they'd do the same if I called the police. They then knocked me out. When I woke up, they were gone."

"Not help lawyers?" asked Tom.

"There's more. I called my three friends to warn them, but it was too late. Some guys visited them too, and pretty much told them the same thing. I tried to find out if one of them had done work for Hope Kane, and they wouldn't talk. They said it wasn't worth dying for."

"Do you know the guys who attacked you?" asked Edward.

"No. Never saw them before. But the thing is, whoever these guys are, there's a bunch of them. The guys who visited my friends were different from the ones who worked me over."

"How do you know?" asked Tom.

"I'm in LA. One of these guys is in Denver, the other's in Phoenix and the third is in Vegas. All three of us got a visit within a couple of hours of each other."

"I take it no one ran to the police about this?" asked Tom.

"No. I believed their threat and my friends did too. Police weren't going to do shit anyway, especially when no one knows who these guys are. We're better off getting protection from Mike, which is the reason I got my son and flew here to Chicago."

"What about your friends?" asked Edward.

"They're packing it in for a while. An extended vacation until this thing blows over," said Tines. "I flew here because I didn't want to take a chance that these guys are listening in on my phone conversations. How else could they have found out about my friends?"

"They found out because my cell phone was hacked," said Tom.

"What? Where's your phone now?" asked Mike.

"It's with me, but the police cleaned it," said Tom.

"When did you get the police involved?" asked Mike.

"We were following up on a lead. We talked to a guy who was building a house across the street from Hope's house. He said he had a recording of her house on the night of the murder because he has cameras installed on the house he's building. We went to see him, and we found him and his assistant dead in their office. The police checked out my phone and confirmed that it had been hacked."

"Shit. This is getting serious," said Mike. "Is the police helping you with your investigation?"

"No. They think the murders were random acts, and refused to draw a connection to my phone getting hacked or to Hope."

"No real surprise there," said Mike. "Look, I suggest you get your techs to check out your office phone to make sure no one's tapping it. Until that's done, I don't want to discuss this anymore by phone. You guys need to get over here right away."

"It'll have to wait until tomorrow," said Tom. "Edward and I have to be in court in the morning for a pretrial conference."

"Alright. Just get over here as soon as you get done."

"We'll need security," said Edward.

"I got it covered," said Mike. "I'll have guys from my New York office travel with you."

"You know we can't pay you," said Tom. "Why are you helping us?"

"I don't like people fucking with my friends," said Mike. "I gotta run. We have work to do."

39.

Tom sat next to Edward and Hope at counsel table. He looked over to his left and saw Linda Starr in her finely pressed blue suit. And in the gallery, he saw a large crowd of people, mostly reporters with notepads and laptop computers. The bailiff told everyone to rise. "The Honorable Daniel Gonzalez presiding," he said. "The people of the state of New York versus Hope Kane." Linda walked to the podium.

"Good morning your honor. My name is Linda Starr with the Westchester County District Attorney's Office."

Tom leaned toward the microphone sitting at counsel table. "My name is Thomas Rose and with me is Edward Miller, here for Hope Kane."

Judge Gonzalez nodded toward the lawyers. "Welcome. Mr. Rose, Mr. Miller, I understand you've taken on this case pro bono."

"Yes, your honor," said Tom.

"I would like to commend you and your firm for doing so. We need more involvement by large private firms like yours in cases like these. I wanted to acknowledge you for that." He looked over toward the prosecution's table. "Ms. Starr, let's proceed."

Linda nodded. "Yes your honor. We're here to report that we're ready to proceed to trial. Discovery's been completed, and now that Ms. Kane has counsel, the prosecution is prepared to proceed with jury selection and then trial on February 8 as previously scheduled by your honor. While I know Mr. Rose's going to ask for more time, there's no reason to delay this case any longer. The evidence is what it is, and we don't believe adjourning the trial will make any difference."

"Mr. Rose?" said the judge as he turned to Tom.

Tom stood. "Your honor, my firm took on this case less than a week ago, and we do request a brief adjournment of the trial." I've reviewed the record in this case, and what is clear to me is that no one, neither the police, the DA's office nor Ms. Hope's prior counsel, engaged in any real analysis to determine whether Ms. Kane committed the murder of her husband."

The judge gave Tom an expressionless stare. "Mr. Rose, you are aware that this case has been on my docket for over a year. Now, I'm not pre-judging this case, but from what I recall, the defendant was caught with the murder weapon in her hand, standing over the victim. What possible benefit will more time bring?"

"No one saw Ms. Kane pull the trigger," said Tom.

"Mr. Rose, you'll have to do better than that," said the judge.

"Your honor, until we were retained, Ms. Kane did not have lawyers looking out for her interests. The people who were tasked with represent-ing her interests did nothing to understand what might have really hap-pened that night when Ms. Kane's husband was murdered. The interview notes show that no one bothered to ask the right questions; questions that may actually shed some light on whether there may be an explanation for what happened that night. Let me spend five minutes describing what we were able to uncover during our short investigation. Yesterday, we learned that the house that sits across the street from Ms. Kane's home is under construction, and has video recording cameras installed around the house. That meant the video cameras may have caught people going in and out of Ms. Kane's home on the night of the murder. Neither the police, the prosecution nor the attorneys who represented Ms. Kane even bothered to ask about the recording. When we went to the contractor's office to obtain access to that recording, the two people who were holding the recording were found murdered, and the CDs holding the recordings had been taken."

"Objection, your honor!" shouted Linda as she stood.

"Objection to what?" asked the judge.

147

"Mr. Rose is making representations to the court that we have not heard before, and the prosecution has had no opportunity to determine whether they are accurate."

"Ms. Starr, there's no jury here. Mr. Rose is not presenting evidence. He's trying to convince me to give him more time to investigate this case so that he can come up with his defense. Do you have a problem with that?"

"Yes we do, your honor. Any lawyer can stand up here and make representations to the court to buy more time, and I don't believe it's appropriate for Mr. Rose to be seeking an extension based on representations that simply may not be true."

Judge Gonzalez leaned back. "Ms. Starr, if as you suggest, Mr. Rose is making statements to the court in order to get an extension, and if I subsequently learn that those statements were false, there will be a price to pay."

The judge turned to Tom. "Mr. Rose, am I making myself clear?"

"Yes, your honor. To be clear, everything I've represented to the court is documented in the police report that was filled out yesterday in White Plains. I have a copy of it right here, which I would like to hand up."

"Objection, your honor," said Linda. "The prosecution has not seen the police report."

The judge rolled his eyes. "Mr. Rose, do you have an extra copy?"

"I do your honor," said Tom as he handed a copy to Linda. Judge Gonzalez read the report and then put it down. "Mr. Rose, all this report says is that two people were found dead in their office. It doesn't say anything about the defendant here."

"Your honor, I understand that that report does not tie the murders to Ms. Kane, but it does say her lawyers discovered the victims when they visited their offices. And I'm representing to the court that we were there to get access to the recording of Ms. Kane's home. Ms. Kane has a constitutional right to be able to present her defense. Under these circumstances when it seems everyone, including her own lawyers, appeared to have accepted her guilt before a jury was even selected, it is obvious that she was not given such an opportunity."

The judge looked down at the report again and then looked up at Tom. "Mr. Rose, let's just say you are right, and there's some mad man running around and killing people. Explain to me again how this ties in to Ms. Kane."

"We believe Mark Kane was murdered by someone else. When we started to pursue leads that may shed light on what really may have happened that night, the true murderer threw roadblocks in our way. And they did it by listening in on my phone conversations. The police report sitting in front of your honor shows that someone is trying to impede our investigation."

"Other than this report, what else do you have to suggest that someone else may have murdered Mr. Kane?" asked the judge.

"We don't have anything concrete, but we have other things. We have a witness who saw a man staring at Ms. Kane on the morning of the murder. We have . . ."

"Wait," interrupted the judge. "Did you say someone was staring at Ms. Kane?"

The crowd in the courtroom burst out in laughter. The judge chuckled as he waited for the courtroom to quiet down. "Mr. Rose, with all due respect, the fact that a man stared at the defendant on the day of the murder may be remarkable in your mind, but it hardly passes as evidence that someone else murdered her husband."

The laughter in the courtroom continued.

"Your honor, there's more than just a man staring at the defendant," said Tom.

"You say more, but what? If you have something more to add, then now's the time," said the judge.

"That's just it, your honor. We're just starting to tie different pieces together, and that's the reason we need more time. With just a little more time, we'll be able to complete our investigation. What is clear is that no other lawyer has bothered to even begin an investigation. I believe Ms. Kane is entitled to more than that. She has a right to representation, and she's had none. On this record, I don't believe a conviction will hold up on appeal. New counsel was just retained, and we've had no time to adequately represent Ms. Kane."

The judge stopped laughing and stared at Tom with a serious look. He apparently was taken aback at Tom's refusal to back down.

"How much time do you need, counsel?" the judge finally asked.

"We are asking for a one-week adjournment," your honor.

The judge leaned back. "Now, why didn't you just say up front that you need only one week? That I can accommodate. Ms. Starr?"

Linda stood. "Your honor, the prosecution objects to even a one-week adjournment. I've reviewed the police report, and this report provides zero support for any delay whatsoever. All it says is that Nicholas Glorioso and Tina Martin were murdered in their office and some money and other things had been taken. I don't believe this comes close to demonstrating that more time will yield anything new for the defense."

Judge Gonzalez nodded. "I'll give you one week, Mr. Rose. Complete your investigation, and I want everyone back here on February 15 for a conference and to select a jury. Anything else?"

"Nothing further, your honor," said Linda.

Tom looked at her and then turned to the judge. "We have nothing else."

The judge stood and left the courtroom. Tom watched two guards help Hope up and escort her out of the courtroom. She suddenly turned and stared out toward the gallery with a frightened look. Tom followed her eyes, but all he saw were open doors to the courtroom with the crowd piling out. He turned back to Hope and saw her frightened eyes fixated on the doors as they took her away.

40.

The iron gates opened slowly as the Maybach pulled up. He drove along the long driveway, lined with boxwoods on both sides. The large fountain in front of the house was framed by a three-foot wall made of granite, flown in from Italy. Ian Ramsey stepped out of the car and stared at the water shooting out into the sky from different spouts hidden behind the granite wall. The red and yellow lights underneath flashed on and off with rhythmic bursts of the water. He turned back to the car and saw the passenger door open. She stood and stared at him. With the dim lights falling from the trees, he could see the curves of her body, hidden underneath the thin white dress. She looked nervous and unsure, but he knew she would relax. In time.

The double oak doors opened and he saw Tony Remo standing off to the side. "Let's go," he said to her. She took small steps and caught up to him. He pulled her close and kissed her. She didn't fight him. He knew she wouldn't. He ran his hand down her back and felt the curve of her hips. The excitement of the intimate moments to come made his heart race. He leaned back and smiled into her green eyes. She looked down. He put his arm around her thin waste and pulled her into the house. Remo stepped to the side without saying a word. He saw her looking around the marble foyer and the giant chandelier providing a soft glow to the room. She willingly followed him up the circular staircase. They stepped into a large sitting area, with freshly cut flowers in vases all around the room. He uncorked the champagne sitting in a silver ice bucket and filled the two flutes resting on a tray. He handed one to her and watched her bring the glass to her luscious lips. "Don't move," he said to her as he took off his jacket and sat down on the couch. She stood, frozen. He stared at her perfect figure, barely visible underneath the dress. "Unbutton your dress," he said. She put down her flute and began undoing the buttons. "Slowly," he said, and she slowed down. When she got to her navel, he told her to stop.

"Come over here."

She walked to him and stood in front of him. He brought his two hands up her dress and around her hips and slowly pulled her down to straddle him. He pulled her dress down to her waste. Her quiet moaning excited him, even though he knew she was faking it. She put her arms around his neck as he picked her up and brought her to the bed. After he had finished, her eyes remained closed and her chest moved up and down with each breath. He stared at her for a while, hoping to regain the excitement she gave him just a few moments earlier. There was no use. It was gone.

He rolled off of her and zipped up his pants. "Go," he said to her. She opened her eyes and began buttoning her dress. She stood and walked quickly to the door and left. He reached for the intercom box on the nightstand.

"Yes, Mr. Ramsey," he heard Remo say.

"Have Sean take her back to the club."

"Anything else?"

"The girl."

"The same. Still crying for her mother."

Ian leaned back against the bedpost and closed his eyes. He slammed his fist down on the mattress. "Fucking bitch," he said under his breath. He opened his eyes and reached for the Las Vegas Centennial and read the headline. "Celebrity Mobster Ramsey to Donate $5 million to Build New Playground." He stared at the picture of himself standing next to the Director of Parks and Recreation. It was a good picture of him.

Ian leaned back again. He tried to think about the girl he just fucked, but he couldn't. She wasn't special; not different enough. Ian sat up and pressed the red button on the remote. The monitor flickered on. He stared at the girl sitting on the floor with a pile of untouched toys surrounding her. He smiled and thought about her mother. She would sit in prison in New York for the rest of her life, knowing that he put her there. But that wasn't enough. She would have to die in that prison, deprived of her ability to utter a word of her innocence. Only then would he achieve his revenge for what she did to him.

41.

Annie saw Meyer behind the register, speaking with Mrs. Holmes. She walked over to them.

"Hello, Annie," said Mrs. Holmes. "How're you doing?"

Annie put on a smile. "I'm doing OK. Crazy huh?"

"Unfortunately, crime happens everywhere honey," said Mrs. Holmes as she started to walk toward the back. "You two girls talk."

Annie looked over at Meyer. "You doing OK?"

She nodded. "Yea. It was unsettling, knowing someone broke in here. Things happen, I guess. They fixed the lock yesterday."

"Did you find the missing receipt?"

Meyer shook her head. "No. And now I'm thinking about it, I have no reason to believe the man I remembered seeing was after Hope Kane. I'm just remembering something that probably never happened."

Annie stared at Meyer with a puzzled look. "But you were so certain before. You remembered the man here, the day of the murder."

Meyer smiled. "Our minds can do funny things sometimes. I guess I was just looking for a way to help you. Yesterday, like you, I was convinced that Mr. Kane's murderer was the one who broke in here. But the police said that whoever got in here was after money. He broke into the safe in back. It looks like it was an ordinary burglary attempt."

Annie nodded. She wondered how Meyer was so certain just a day before that the man was staring at Hope, only to say just a day later that it didn't really happen. "Well, if you remember anything else, will you call me?"

Meyer nodded. "I will, but nothing's going to change. Frankly, there was a time when everything seemed to fit in to what your friend's trying to prove for Hope Kane. But once you take a look at what really happened that night, there's no way he can show she's innocent. They caught her with the murder weapon, for Christ's sake."

"I understand," said Annie as she turned to leave. Meyer called out after her.

"Annie, I know you want to help your friend, but you have to open your eyes. Don't get caught up in his crazy ideas."

Annie stared at Meyer without speaking.

Meyer continued. "I'm just saying, don't drive yourself crazy over this. It's a lost cause."

Annie walked out of the store and headed to her car. She looked in her purse for her keys when she sensed someone behind her. She tried to turn when a hand with a handkerchief covered her nose and mouth. She couldn't breathe and things started to become blurry. A second later, everything turned black.

42.

He leaned back in his chair in his library and closed his eyes. He tried to imagine her sitting on the concrete floor of a prison cell. He tried to picture her with matted down, tangled hair covering her face. This is all your fault, he thought. You brought this on yourself. You fucking bitch, he said in a low voice.

"Mr. Ramsey."

Ian opened his eyes and saw Sean Boles standing a few feet from him.

"We received the shipment. It's good stuff."

Ian looked up at Boles and stared at him, grinning ear to ear, hoping for praise for a job well done. The last shipment had crap in it that made some users lose their shit. Police in Vegas were crawling all over the place looking for the dealers. Luckily, they didn't get close to him, which at the end of the day was all that really mattered. But it was still bad for business. This time, they apparently didn't fuck up. A bullet in the knee of the delivery boy sent the right message. They wouldn't fuck up again because the next bullet was aimed at their chief.

Boles' grin slowly vanished, as Ian continued to stare at him without expression. Boles cleared his throat.

"Oh, and I got a report from Dom."

Ian leaned back. "Go on."

"Looks like Rose's been stirring shit up."

"What the fuck's that supposed to mean?"

"He's got Lynch Investigations working with him," said Boles.

"Big shit," said Ian. "He can get the National Guard to help him, but there's nothing anyone can do that would matter."

"Uh, one other thing," said Boles, looking uneasy.

"What's that?" asked Ian.

"Uh, there apparently were video cameras near her home that were running that night."

Ian turned to Boles. "What? What the fuck are you talking about?"

"The house across the street," said Boles with a shaky voice. "It, uh, it's under construction, and it had cameras recording the area twenty-four seven. Rose was about to get the CDs to see what was in them."

"How the fuck did he figure that out, and we didn't?"

"I, uh, I don't know, but Dom took care of everything. He got to the people who were holding the CDs before Rose could get there."

"So, what happened?" asked Ian.

"He had to pop them," said Boles.

"What?"

Boles took a step back. "Um, he had to take them out before Rose got there."

"Fuck!" shouted Ian. "We fucking left a trail?"

Boles shook his head. "Uh no, we didn't. No one knows who killed these people."

"If this lawyer Rose has half a brain, he'll connect these hits to Hope Kane. How the fuck could we allow this to happen?"

"I, uh, I don't know, Mr. Ramsey."

Ian closed his eyes and took in a deep breath. Rose can try and figure shit out, but the evidence against Hope Kane was damning. These two deaths did nothing to help her defense.

"What's she been up to?" Ian asked, lowering his voice. "We know if she's talking?"

"She's not talking as far as we know."

"As far as we know?"

"We'll find out for sure."

"Make sure we send a message."

"Yes sir."

"How good is Rose?"

"I, uh, I don't know. We have Dom keeping an eye on him."

"Find out exactly what Rose's up to."

"OK, but Dom can't listen in on his conversations anymore."

"Why not?"

"He figured out his phone was bugged."

Ian closed his eyes. "You fucking tell Dom he better stop fucking this thing up! Understand?"

"Yes. Yes sir."

"How's the girl?"

"The same. Same crying."

Ian shook his head.

"Anything you want us to do with her?"

Ian didn't respond. He turned his head away from him and closed his eyes. He heard Boles' footsteps against the marble floor, walking away from him. He thought about her again. A surge of blood shot into his head. "Fuck you, you fucking bitch!" he screamed. His voice echoed through the marble room, bouncing off of the arched ceiling. He heard footsteps.

"Everything OK, Mr. Ramsey?" asked Remo with Boles standing behind him.

Ian walked passed them toward his room. There was no need to respond. They both had heard the scream before.

43.

Edward closed his briefcase when he saw Timothy Ryan. "I saw the news coverage of today's hearing," Ryan said.

"We had a good day," said Edward.

"Yes, you did. This is good, Edward. I think we're definitely scoring some points in the media. I heard through the grapevine that the Law Journal is planning a story on the importance of pro bono work and wanted to interview us. I think you getting involved with Tom was a smart move. The MC's easing up a little about what you did to that mirror."

Edward nodded. "Thanks, Timothy. I've got to catch a plane. We'll catch up later."

"Plane? Where are you going?"

"Chicago. We're meeting with investigators. Lynch Investigations."

"Lynch? How're you affording Lynch?"

"They're doing it pro bono."

Ryan smiled. "Good man. I can't believe you got Lynch to help you."

"It wasn't me. Tom got them involved."

Ryan took a step toward Edward and spoke in a low voice. "Edward, this is going well, but don't drag it out beyond the extra week the judge gave you. The best way to score with the media is to do a quick in and out. We got the PR for taking on the case. It's better if we get to a quick trial and she gets convicted. We keep everyone's interest. We wouldn't want people to get bored with the story, which is what'll happen if this thing plays out too long. You get what I'm saying?"

Edward took a step toward the door. He stopped and then turned back to Ryan. "I'm glad that you and the MC approve of the job we're doing, but let me make one thing clear. You may think we're doing this as a PR stunt, and that's fine. But for me and Tom, we're lawyers and we're representing a client."

Ryan stood frozen without responding. Edward stepped closer to him. "I will tell you something I've been meaning to tell you for a long time. You remember when you bought me that mirror the day we elected you to the partnership? The one that I broke?"

Ryan nodded. "Yea. I wanted to thank you for making the big push for me."

"I remember when you had it hung in my office. I used to stare at the reflection of people coming in and out of my office. And I remember watching you come in and sit in my office, hoping that I'd put you on one of my high profile cases. You remember that?"

Ryan stayed quiet, staring at Edward.

"Well, I didn't mind that sight very much, because at least you were honest. You had just become a partner and wanted to keep busy. You wanted to have your name in the press. I get all that. But then, as you started to make a name for yourself largely from leveraging off of other talented lawyers, you began to think you were something special. You forgot who you really are."

Ryan took a step back and crossed his arms. "And who do you think I really am?" he asked with a grin on his face.

"You're more interested in making another buck than acting like a lawyer. What I see is a sniveling lawyer who became a politician and conned everyone into believing he's more than what he is. Someone who forgot where he came from. What I see is a pathetic man who thinks he can solve the world's problems with trickery. That's who you are. But the very mirror you bought me never forgot who you really are. You are the same sniveling con artist who didn't earn an ounce of what you think you earned."

Ryan glared into Edward's eyes. Edward smiled. "Timothy, any asshole can buy gifts and tell lies. But all of that shit will catch up to you. I didn't need the mirror anymore to remind me of what a pathetic human being you are. That's why I wasn't afraid to get it out of my life. I know exactly who you are, and I no longer need a mirror to remind me."

44.

Melanie stared at her phone, debating whether to call him. They had been together for so long. If it had to end, she didn't want it to end this way. But then, how did she want it to end? He had pushed her away. It wasn't her fault. What would be the point of calling him? What would she say? That she found his replacement? With Lance, her boss? Why would he even care? He's the one who left her? Why should she feel guilty? Melanie shook her head. Everything about Lance was so wonderful. Then why was she clinging onto Tom? Why? The knock on her door brought her back to the moment. She turned away from the door and wiped her eyes with a tissue.

"You OK?" asked Lance.

Melanie tried to force a smile. "Yes."

"Do you want to talk about it?"

Melanie didn't respond. His voice, his concern warmed her.

"The sun's shining," said Lance. "We can get a couple of cups of coffee and take a walk through the Park. And we can talk about what's upsetting you, or we can just say nothing. Whatever you want."

Melanie nodded. Lance walked into her office and took her coat off of the hanger. He held it up for her. Melanie stood and allowed him to help her into the coat. She pulled her silk scarf around her neck and followed Lance out of the office.

They walked to the coffee shop on the bottom floor of the building. Lance handed her the cappuccino and picked up his cup. They headed across Fifth Avenue and into Central Park. The bright sun warmed her. Even though it was 30 degrees out, with no wind and the bright sun shining, the February chill didn't seem so daunting. They walked and walked, but Lance didn't say a word. She finally touched his arm and stopped.

"You haven't said a word to me," she said.

Lance smiled. "I know. This was supposed to be about you. If you want to talk, then you should. Otherwise, it's just a walk."

Melanie looked down. "I don't know. I don't know what to think. What to say."

"You shouldn't have to know any of those things. You should go with what you might be feeling. Life isn't that complicated. We make it so."

"But I've been with Tom for so long. We were going to be married."

"And how do you feel about that now?"

"It doesn't matter," said Melanie, looking away. "He left me."

"He left you because he probably wasn't the right man for you," said Lance.

Melanie looked up and into his eyes. She saw the genuineness in them.

"Look, I want to be with you, and I think you want to be with me. You never would've given me a chance if he was right for you," said Lance. "We both know that."

Melanie allowed those words to sink in. He made it so real, so simple.

"I care about you, Melanie. Holding you last night was important to me. And I believe it meant something to you too. Just promise me."

"Promise you what?"

"That you'll give us a chance," said Lance as he took her hand.

Melanie stared into his deep blue eyes and smiled. Lance put his arm around her. "You warm enough to walk to the fountain?"

Melanie nodded. "Sure."

As she put her arm around Lance's waste, her cell phone rang. She pulled it out of her purse and saw it was Tom. She stared at his name for a few seconds. She pressed ignore and leaned her head against Lance's shoulder.

45.

Tom and Edward followed Lynch's guys out of O'Hare International. A black Suburban pulled up. The larger guy, Peterson, opened the rear door and motioned for Tom and Edward to get in. Peterson got in the passenger seat and told the driver to go. They sped down Interstate 90 to Chicago and pulled up to a large building on North Michigan Avenue.

"Follow me," said Peterson as he stepped out of the car. He waited in front of the glass door until a buzzer sounded and the door unlocked. He walked in and waited for Tom and Edward to follow. Two armed men waited by the door. Peterson led them down a long hallway and opened the door to a large conference room. Tom saw Mike Lynch and another man. Mike had been out of the military for more than twenty years, but he maintained the same look – shaved head, muscles on muscles on his five-foot ten-inch frame. Tom didn't recognize the man behind him. He had a full graying beard that didn't quite match his long dark hair. They both stood as Tom and Edward stepped in.

"Tom, Edward, good to see you," said Mike as he shook their hands. "This is Calvin Tines. You spoke to him on the phone." Tines walked over and shook their hands. Mike motioned for Tom and Edward to take a seat. "We have a lot to discuss."

"Any progress on figuring out who helped Hope with her identity?" asked Tom.

Mike shook his head. "Not yet, but that may not be so important anymore."

Tom leaned back and waited for Mike to continue.

"A lot's happened since when we spoke yesterday. Remember when you asked me a few days ago about a tattoo?"

Tom nodded. "Yea. S and D in the middle of a red heart."

"I sent out a note to the guys in all my offices to keep an eye out for this tattoo. I got a call yesterday. One of the guys in my Vegas office frequents strip clubs, and he said he knew of the tattoo that's on Hope's arm. There's a place on the strip called Shangri La Dream, and apparently there's a VIP room and the women who service those customers all have a tattoo of a red heart and the letters S and D in the middle. If your client's tattoo is the same tattoo, then she may have been a dancer at that club."

"What do we know about the club?" asked Edward.

"Not a whole lot in terms of actual facts, but there's a bunch of rumors bouncing around. And if the rumors are right, we may have stepped into a shit storm. The club's privately owned by some company called SD Entertainment. The corporate documents we were able to get our hands on don't say much, but what we hear through the grapevine is the club's indirectly owned by Ian Ramsey."

"Ian Ramsey? The celebrity mobster?" asked Tom.

"Yea, that Ian Ramsey. The one that's getting a lot of press for his donation to the parks and recreation charity to build a playground."

Ian Ramsey was a well-known mobster who managed to evade the authorities for years, and somehow became a quasi-celebrity by pretending to do good deeds for the public. Tom shook his head.

Mike continued. "The authorities have been keeping an eye on Ramsey for years, hoping to find something illegal to pin on him, but they've gotten nothing. After repeated dead ends, the cops have thrown up their hands. The guy's a genius at covering up his bad deeds. He's never been caught. The word on the street is everyone who works for him is scared shitless of him, and that's how he makes sure no one blows the whistle on him. And, he's brilliant in playing to the media by acting like a philanthropist. And our fucked-up society is fascinated by an accused mobster who plays the limelight and does good deeds. He's an enigma and the rags can't get enough of him."

"Do we know why the dancers have this tattoo?" asked Tom.

"My guy has a favorite dancer at the club who he's gotten to know. She told him about the women in the VIP room and their tattoos. She thinks it's a way to let the other clubs know these women belong to SD, and they shouldn't try and steal them."

"Sounds like branding your property," said Tom.

"Yea. The other thing we know is only a select group of people who frequent the club are given access to the VIP room with these dancers. My guy was never invited, but according to his dancer friend, the VIP room caters to extremely wealthy men who like illegal drugs and high-class whores. She made my guy promise her he wouldn't repeat any of this because she was afraid Ramsey would come after her."

Tom closed his eyes, trying to piece everything together. Mike continued. "Bottom line, if Hope Kane was a dancer at that club and decided to run, that'll explain why she wanted to change her identity. It may also mean we're fighting against Ian Ramsey."

"Are you willing to take him on?" Tom asked.

The room fell silent. "I guess you don't beat around the bush," said Mike. "I don't run from a fight, but there's only so much I can do to protect everyone. Even though he's never gotten caught, I don't have a doubt he's a ruthless murderer who knows how to go after people. If we're going to fight him, we better make sure we win."

"We'll find a way to beat him," said Tom.

Mike nodded. "And what's your strategy?"

"I need more time, but I'll come up with something."

Mike nodded. "Well, make sure whatever you come up with, that it'll work. I don't even want to think about the consequences if we fail."

"We are not going to fail," said Tom.

Mike stood. "Look, as I said, I'm behind you. But before we go down this road, everyone should consider the fact that we don't have to continue this fight. We can drop the case now and hope that Ramsey leaves us alone."

Tom shook his head. "If Ramsey's behind all this, he's not going to leave us alone. We have to face him."

Mike nodded. "Alright, but if we're going to do this, we need all the help we can get. I'm going to call my buddies at the FBI and see if they'll help us."

"What do you expect they'll do?" asked Edward. "You think they'll go after Ramsey based on a tattoo?"

"Until my friend Tom thinks of a better idea, I'm not too proud to ask for help from anyone who's willing to listen to me."

46.

She walked down the concrete hallway. Up ahead was a row of human cages that held the criminals. It was a walk she took every night at the same time. This was the worst part of her job, but it was part of her job description, and the video recording devices made it impossible for her to skip the walk. She would have preferred to sit back at the office with the other corrections officers and play cards, but until they hired someone else, this was her task. As she approached the first cell, she tried to guess what the prisoner would be doing. This was a little game she created to make the walk more bearable. She would try and guess the position of the inmate, and if she got it right, she'd award herself a point. If she got it wrong, she'd lose a point. On her back sleeping, she said to herself as she stepped in front of the first cell. She shook her head as she saw Cecilia Mack lying on her side. Minus one, she said. On her belly, she said as she approached the second cell. There she was, lying on her stomach. She smiled as she approached Hope Kane's cell. This was an easy one. She knew Hope would be sitting in the corner of the cell. She was there every single night, without exception. She used to ask Hope what she was thinking about, but she never answered. She would just sit, stare into the wall and say nothing. As she walked past Hope's cell, she noticed something was different. She turned to face the cell. Hope was not in her usual spot where she always sat. She pulled out her flashlight and aimed it into the corner of the cell, and there was no one there. The flashlight caught something on the floor. Then she saw her. Hope was lying on the cement floor in a pool of blood. She pressed the alarm and opened the cell. Hope was still breathing, but barely. Her left wrist had been shredded. Her right hand held a piece of plastic; what looked like a handle of a plastic fork.

47.

Annie opened her eyes, but it was too dark to see. She tried to stand, but she was tied to whatever she was sitting on. She blinked her eyes a few times trying to see in the darkness. "Hello?" she said. A few moments later, she was blinded by a bright light as someone opened the door to the room and walked in. The room returned to complete darkness when the door closed. She could feel someone standing in front of her.

"Who are you?" Annie asked.

"You have been working with Tom Rose," the man said in a low voice.

"Who are you?" she asked again. He slapped her face hard that sent her flying to the floor, along with the chair she was sitting on. He laughed out loud and then picked her up. Her ear was ringing and the entire side of her face felt numb. She felt blood on her lips. Tears came flowing out and her throat tightened. She tried to breathe.

"Answer me," he said in the same low voice.

"Yes, I was helping him," she said.

"What does he know about Hope Kane?"

"He doesn't know anything. All he knows is that some people were supposed to give him a recording of a house near her house, and those people were killed."

"I don't give a shit about that."

"That's all I know."

"What does Mike Lynch know?"

"Who?"

"Mike Lynch. What do you know about him? What's he doing for Rose?"

"I, I don't know. I've never heard the name before."

The man turned on a light. He was in a black ski mask. He reached behind him and pulled out a gun and aimed it at Annie's forehead.

"No," she said through her tears. "Please, please. Don't kill me," she pleaded.

He kept the gun aimed at her. "You want to live, don't you?"

Annie nodded as the tears dripped down her face. She tried to speak, but the only sounds she heard were her sobs.

"You are going to do exactly as I say from now and until Hope's been tried and convicted. If you defect from anything I tell you to do, I will hunt you down and point this gun at your head again. But before I pull the trigger, I will tear you apart, piece by piece until you beg me to kill you. I promise you, you will suffer. I also know your grandmother lives in New Rochelle. We will find her and torture her right to her death. We have a long list of people you care about, and we will go after each and every one of them until they have all suffered the worst possible death imaginable. And just think. All of that pain and death would be because of you."

His words sent a shock through Annie's body. The tears stopped flowing. The thought of the pain and death he was threatening against the people she loved froze her mind and body alike.

"The only way you're going to avoid this fate is if you do exactly as I tell you. Do you understand?"

Annie nodded, staring into his black eyes.

He pulled out a knife to cut the rope holding her against the chair. He then reached back and punched her face. Annie went flying to the floor as she lost consciousness.

48.

Tom stared at the blank notepad. He hadn't written a word in the thirty minutes he sat in the small conference room. Mike got through to his friends at the FBI. As predicted, they weren't moved by the tattoo or the beating Tines took. Mike did get them to talk to the agents who had investigated Mila Kane's disappearance. They said the file was closed three months after she went missing because they presumed she had been murdered by Hope Kane. Tom knew he had a story that may explain what happened that night and exonerate Hope, but he had no proof. Tom knew he didn't have enough to win Hope's innocence. He needed more.

His mind started to drift to thoughts about Melanie. He called her before he left for Chicago. He knew it would confuse her, but he wanted to hear her voice; to know she was well. He knew it was selfish. Now, he was grateful that she didn't answer. He pulled out his iPhone, and realized he never turned it on when the plane touched down at O'Hare. He turned it on and waited for it to boot up. He saw he had seven missed calls and had a voicemail message. He punched in his pin and listened.

"Mr. Rose. This is officer Johnson from the Bedford Hills Women's Prison. Please call me back as soon as possible. It's an urgent matter regarding your client, Hope Kane."

Tom dialed the number Johnson had left.

"This is Tom Rose. I'm returning your call."

"Hope Kane's in intensive care at the Northern Westchester Hospital."

"What? What happened?"

"She tried to take her life. She slit her wrist with a plastic fork. A corrections officer doing a routine check found her. She's lost a lot of blood."

"My God."

"I was directed to call you and let you know what happened."

"What's her condition now?" Tom asked.

"I don't know. You can try calling the hospital."

Tom ended the call and walked into the conference room. Edward looked up. "She tried to take her life," said Tom.

Edward closed his eyes and shook his head. "How is she?"

"They don't know. She's in intensive care. I need to go see her," Tom said.

"We have work to do here," said Edward. "There's nothing we can do for her right now. Let the doctors do their job."

Tom shook his head.

"Maybe you can send your friend Annie to check in on Hope," Edward said.

Tom nodded. He dialed her number. She answered in a weak voice.

"Hello."

"Annie, it's Tom."

"Hi. Where are you?"

"I'm in Chicago. You don't sound right. Are you OK?"

"Yes. What're you doing in Chicago?" she asked.

"I'll tell you later. We just learned that Hope tried to commit suicide."

"Oh my God," she said.

"Could you go see her to see how she is?"

"OK."

"She's at the Northern Westchester Hospital."

"I'll go see her."

"Are you sure you're OK?"

"Yes. Please call me later about Chicago."

"I will. Why are you so curious about Chicago?"

"I'm just curious. Are you in Chicago for Hope?"

"I'll call you later. Please check on Hope and call me."

49.

"We got a lot more info," said Mike as he walked into the conference room.

Tom turned to him.

"One of Calvin's friends called him from a secure line. He realized he was in danger, and thought he'd be better off working with us. He's the guy who helped Hope change her identity. He gave us information in exchange for security."

"Go on," said Tom.

"Hope lived and worked in Vegas. Her real name is Hannah Silver, and her husband, Mark Kane's real name is Steve Wolfe. Wolfe was an accountant and kept the books for Ramsey. They developed a secret relationship. At some point, they decided to run away together. That's when they hooked up with Calvin's friend to change their identity. He thinks Hope was pregnant at the time they came to him."

Tom nodded. "That confirms the tattoo. She worked for Ramsey and decided to run. Will he work with us? Will he testify to all of this?"

Mike shook his head. "No. The deal is he doesn't testify. He gave us this information to get protection from us; not to stick his neck out into a firestorm. If we put him on the stand or run to the authorities, he'll deny ever talking to us."

"Then what good is this information?" asked Edward.

Mike didn't respond.

"We can use it," said Tom.

Edward turned to him.

"We may not have evidence, but now we know what happened. She and Wolfe were running from Ramsey. They changed their identity and moved to New York. Ramsey caught up with them and killed Mark Kane."

Edward shook his head. "But why not kill Hope? That's the part that we can't explain."

Tom suddenly stood. "Annie," he said aloud.

"What about Annie?" asked Edward.

"When I spoke with her, she didn't sound right. She was trying to get information from me about what I was doing in Chicago. She expressed no concern about Hope."

"You think they got to her too?" asked Mike.

Tom didn't answer. Mike stepped up to Tom. "Give me her address. We need to get her."

50.

Annie leaned back on her chair and ran her fingers gently down the side of her face. She could feel the swelling over her cheekbone. Her hands trembled as she dialed the number he gave her. He answered, but didn't say anything. A tear flowed down her cheeks.

"He's in Chicago," she said into the phone.

"Why?"

"He wouldn't tell me."

"Find out."

"OK."

Annie ended the call and closed her eyes. Why? she asked. Why is he doing this to me? Annie thought about her grandmother. She buried her face in her hands and wept. How could she have put her own grandmother in danger? Who are these people?

The knock on her door made her jump. Annie sat up and looked around. She heard another knock. She went to the door and looked through the peephole. Two men stood in front of her door. Her heart pounded. She didn't know what to do. She ran back to the sofa and picked up her cell phone. She began dialing 911, then stopped. He said he'd kill her grandmother if she called the police. She had no way out. Annie walked to her door and opened it and stared into the eyes of the two men standing in her doorway.

"Are you Annie Sharpe?" one of the men asked.

"Yes."

"I'm Jimmy Kulter and this is Bobby Cano. We're with Lynch Investigations."

"What can I do for you?" Annie asked.

"Can we come in?" Kulter asked.

Annie nodded and took a step back into her apartment. They followed her in and closed the door. She pointed them to the sitting area.

"Our boss Mike Lynch has been working with Tom Rose in connection with Hope Kane," said Kulter. "We have reasons to believe you were contacted by some very bad people."

Annie didn't know how to respond. He had said he'd kill her and her grandmother if she told anyone about him or what had happened to her.

Cano leaned toward her. "We're here to help you. They probably threatened your life as well as anyone else who may be important to you. We're going to protect you and your friends."

Annie couldn't control the fear and emotion that ran through her body. She closed her eyes and began to sob. "How do I know you are not with them?"

"Look at me," said Kulter. Annie looked up. He smiled into her eyes. "If we were the bad guys, why would we be having this conversation? We came here to protect you. Whoever these guys are, they don't scare us. Bobby and I are former police officers. Our boss, Mike Lynch, was with the special forces when he was in the military. Most of our investigators come from the police force or the military. We can protect you."

Annie wanted to trust them. She nodded. "OK."

"Tell us from the beginning. What happened?" said Kulter.

"I don't remember everything. I remember looking for my car keys and then I blacked out. I woke up in a room tied to a chair. A man was there."

"Describe the man," said Cano.

"I can't. He was wearing a mask. He was tall. Over six feet. All muscle. He had frightening black eyes."

"He did that to you?" Cano asked pointing at Annie's cheek.

Annie nodded. "Yes, and he said he'd torture and kill my grandmother and anyone else who was dear to me, unless I did exactly as he said."

"Where is your grandmother now?" Kulter asked.

"She lives in New Rochelle. I spoke to her this morning, and she seemed fine."

"Annie, we need to take your grandmother to a safe location where they can't get to her," said Kulter. "Do you think she'll mind going to Florida for a little while? We have a place where she can stay until this thing blows over. Is there anyone else you think might be in danger?"

Annie shook her head. "I don't know. My parents passed away a long time ago, and my grandmother raised me. She's the only family I have."

Kulter nodded. "OK. We'll need to take a ride together to go and see your grandmother."

Annie nodded. "And then what?"

"You are going to come with us to Chicago, and we'll get direction from Mike and Tom Rose."

51.

"She tried to do what?" Ian asked Remo and Boles.

"She slit her wrist. That's what Jacob told Dom. We don't have any more details," said Remo.

Ian started laughing out loud as Remo and Boles stared at him with a confused look. Ian thought about what Hope was going through. The torture was working. She couldn't take it, so she tried to end it. But, she failed, so he still had her. Ian nodded and stood.

"Is she going to be able to go through with the trial?" he asked.

"We don't know yet. All we know is she's alive. Dom's been working with Jacob to find out."

"Tell Dom to let me know as soon as he knows. What about Rose? What's he up to?"

"Dom had his meeting with the waitress," said Remo. "She's starting to feed him information about Rose's movements," said Remo.

"I don't give a shit who's feeding him information. I want to know what Rose's been up to."

"We're trying to get that information," said Boles. "We did hear that Rose's in Chicago."

"What the fuck's he doing in Chicago? He's got a trial that's gonna start soon."

"We're trying to get to the bottom of it," said Remo.

"What about Tines?" Ian asked.

"We don't know where he went. He disappeared after our guys paid him a visit."

"Alright, but make sure he doesn't cause a problem," said Ian. "I don't want that fucker running to the police."

"He couldn't be that stupid," said Remo. "And even if he is, he has no idea who paid him a visit. No one will ever be able to connect what happened to them with us. Don't worry."

"I don't worry about the dumb fucks that fill this world," said Ian. "But the one guy that worries me a little is Tom Rose."

"Why's that?" asked Boles.

"Because that fucker hasn't gone away yet. And the fact that he wants to represent her when no other lawyer does makes me wonder what makes him tick."

"He's just a kid probably just following his boss's orders," said Boles.

Ian nodded. Boles was right, but something about Rose made him feel a little uneasy. "Don't lose sight of him," said Ian as he walked off.

52.

Dr. Cavanaugh stared at Hope Kane as she tried to sit up. The straps held her down. Her wrists were chained to steel bars on each side of the bed. She slowly opened her eyes. "I'm Doctor Cavanaugh," he said, hovering over her. "How're you feeling?" he asked. Hope didn't answer. She just stared at him. He wasn't surprised. He had examined her before and was fully aware that she refused to speak. Seeing Hope lying in front of him chained to a bed gave him a strange feeling of satisfaction. That she tried to take her own life angered him. After what she had done to her family, he wanted to see her pay the price, to watch her suffer, and there was no way he was going to let her run from the consequences of her evil acts by taking her own life. He was the one who treated her and stitched her up. And now, she was alive and aware. She would be able to sit through her trial and receive the public punishment she deserves for what she had done. By keeping her alive, he felt he did his part for society in making sure Hope Kane got what she deserved. He smiled into her eyes.

"Ms. Kane, you tried to do something very bad to yourself. Now, we can't permit that to happen. We fixed you up the best we can, but I don't want to see you here again. Do you understand?" he asked in a gentle voice.

Hope continued to stare at him. The doctor turned to the nurse. "We should keep her overnight to make sure she's OK."

"Yes, doctor."

"And if her vitals are good, we can send her back tomorrow or the next day."

The nurse furrowed her eyebrows. "I thought we were going to send her for a psychiatric evaluation."

"What for? She doesn't speak."

"Isn't that what we normally do for suicide . . ."

"Stupid," said the doctor, not letting her finish. He turned to Hope. "I think those evaluations are useless. You just made a mistake. You did something silly, but you're OK now. I want to make sure you don't miss the important trial coming up."

Hope continued to stare at him. The doctor turned to the nurse. "Let's get her out of the straps. She couldn't harm herself again with her wrists chained to the bed."

He turned back to Hope. "You take care now," he said. "And good luck with your trial."

53.

Annie walked into the conference room. Tom saw the bruise on her face. He rushed over to hug her. "I'm sorry I dragged you into this," he whispered.

She buried her face into Tom's chest and cried. Tom helped her to a chair and sat down next to her.

"Annie, we crossed paths with some very bad people," he said. He pointed to Mike. "This is Mike Lynch. He runs this investigation firm."

Mike motioned for others to sit around the table. He looked over at Annie. "You're safe now. He can't get to you, and your grandmother is well protected in Florida. There's no way they'll find her." He turned to Tom and Edward. "Gentlemen, we have chosen to go to war with Ian Ramsey. I can provide security, but that's where our expertise ends. You know that. You have to come up with a plan. Without a plan, we are dead in the water. If you're going to take a shot at the king, we'd better make sure we kill him. If we miss, we'll have a real problem."

"Ian Ramsey?" said Annie, looking up at Mike.

"Yes, Ian Ramsey," said Tom.

Edward turned to Annie. "You up to telling us what happened to you?"

Annie nodded and recounted everything, going back to when she blacked out near her car. "He told me to get information about what Tom was up to and to feed him information. He said if I didn't cooperate, he'd kill me, my grandmother and anyone else I cared about."

"Did you see what this man looked like?" asked Tom.

"No. He was wearing a mask. He was very tall, very big. He had black eyes."

186

"Anything else?" asked Mike.

Annie shook her head. "No. He gave me a number to call whenever I had any information." She pulled out a piece of paper from her pocket and handed it to Mike. "This is the number."

"I'm sure it belongs to nobody," said Mike. "It's probably a burner phone that's not attached to any individual." He turned to Tom. "So, what's our plan?"

Edward leaned forward before Tom responded. "Do we have enough to go back to the police or the FBI?"

"No," said Tom. Everyone turned to him.

"We can't go to the police," Tom said. "This explains why Hope doesn't speak."

"What?" asked Edward.

"Look at what they did to Calvin and his friends. Look at what they did to Annie. And then ask yourself why isn't Hope speaking. Her daughter's missing. Everyone assumed she's dead, even though no one's seen her body. They have her. That's how they're making Hope cooperate. Just like the way they tried to make Calvin, Annie and everyone else cooperate with them. They're threatening to kill Mila to keep Hope quiet from telling the world what really happened that night. Threaten the life of her daughter to get her to do what they want. If we go to the police, they will kill Mila, which is the only reason Hope's been sitting in prison in silence."

Everyone nodded in agreement. Tom stood and walked to the window. "We know he's a whore for the limelight," he said. "We need to know everything about Ian Ramsey. What do we know?"

Mike cleared his throat. "Not much more than what I've told you before. My friends at the FBI told me there's an entire team of guys at the Bureau who devoted years trying to get information on Ramsey to take him down. After hitting enough brick walls, they pretty much threw up their hands. But they did gather some basic information on him."

"Let's hear it," said Tom.

"His primary game is drugs and prostitution. The belief is he sells drugs and prostitution through his strip club. He's got a lot of people working for him, but they are tightlipped and won't ever snitch on him. He's a master manipulator, and he's managed to convince his guys that they are better off going to prison than to turn on him. He feeds on the fact that he's not been caught, and he rubs the feds' faces in it by staying in the limelight.

"Something else we know about him from the papers is he thinks he's a celebrity. You see more pictures of him in the gossip rags than the Kardashians. Even though he's a low-life criminal, he acts like he's legit by going around rubbing elbows with the rich and famous and by throwing a lot of money at charities. And, to a certain extent, it's working. The media has turned him into a second tier celebrity, and he loves it. He can't get enough of the limelight."

Tom nodded. "Helpful," he said.

Edward shook his head. "I don't know what you're planning Tom, but I'm a simple-minded lawyer. All of this is very interesting and may even be something worth discussing at a cocktail party, but I'm still at a loss as to how we're going to gather evidence to put on a case for Hope."

Tom came back to the table and smiled. "I have a plan," he said and looked over at Mike. "What contacts do you have with the press?"

54.

The icy rain slapped against his face, but he didn't feel any discomfort from it. Dom's mind was too fixated on Hope Kane's condition to worry about getting wet or the chill that would follow from a drenched wool coat. The trial couldn't get delayed any more. He was sick of waiting for that day to come. Living in Westchester wasn't so bad, but knowing he was trapped there until her conviction made each waking moment unbearable. And, for what? For some fucking game that Ian Ramsey wanted to play? Dom sucked hard on the cigarette and tossed what was left in the gutter. He saw Dr. Cavanaugh walk out of the hospital. The long gray hair and the boney face he saw on the internet matched the smallish man walking toward the parking lot. Dom intercepted him before he got to the lot.

"Doctor," he said, sticking his hand out. The doctor looked at him with a puzzled look. "Do I know you?" he asked.

Dom smiled. "No, you don't know me. You're Doctor Cavanaugh, right?"

The doctor nodded. "Yes. What can I do for you?"

"I'm Mick Hennessy. I write for an internet blog and I've been following the Hope Kane story."

The doctor nodded. "I don't give interviews regarding my patients," he said and walked into the parking lot. Dom walked alongside of him.

"Doctor, I wasn't planning on interviewing you. I won't be doing any reporting until her trial starts. I just wanted to know what her condition was. Will she be in shape to proceed with her trial?"

The doctor stopped and turned to Dom. "Yes, I believe she'll recover in time for the trial."

Dom nodded. "Thank you doctor. After what she'd done, I think the public's anxious to see her tried and convicted and put away for a very long time. More delay is not what the public needs."

The doctor tapped Dom's arm. "I agree with you. Now, I'm late for a dinner, so good evening," he said.

"Wait, can I assume she's out of intensive care?" Dom asked.

"Yes, she's in the recovery area."

"That's up on the third floor, right?"

The doctor nodded. "Yes. I really do need to run."

"OK doctor, thank you."

The doctor took a few steps and then stopped. He turned back to Dom. "What paper did you say you're with? Maybe I will give you an interview once all's said and done with the trial."

Dom smiled. "It's not a paper. It's a startup internet blog that reports on high profile crimes. You wouldn't have heard of it. I just might take you up on your offer to be interviewed, but that won't be for a while. Thank you doctor."

Dr. Cavanaugh nodded. "OK. Well, good evening to you."

Dom watched the doctor walk into a white S Class Mercedes. He stared at the car as it drove off. Dom checked his watch and walked to the rear of the hospital. He put on his hat and leaned against the building by the metal door. A moment later, it swung open and two men walked out. He slipped into the building before the door closed. The service elevator was to the left. He took it to the third floor. A nurse sat behind a counter, but otherwise, the recovery area was empty. Dom walked up to her. The nurse looked up. "May I help you?"

"What room is Hope Kane in?" he asked.

"One moment," she said as she pulled out a clip board. He could see 318 written next to Hope Kane's name.

The nurse shook her head. "I'm sorry sir, Ms. Kane's not permitted to have visitors."

Dom nodded. "Oh, OK. Thank you," he said and walked out toward the elevators. He leaned against the wall just enough to be out of the nurse's line of vision. After a few moments, he saw her get up and disappear into one of the rooms. Dom walked back into the recovery area and toward room 318. The door was locked. Dom pulled out two wires and stuck them into the keyhole. He had picked locks like these many times before. The lock unlatched and he slowly opened the door. He turned on the light and he saw her lying on the bed hooked up to an intravenous line. She turned toward him and froze. Her eyes were large. Dom smiled at her.

"I'm watching you. Don't forget our deal."

He could see the tears flowing down Hope's face. "Remember. We know everything you're doing. Taking your life is a violation of our deal. Don't try it again. You know the consequences."

Dom smiled at her and shut the lights off. He walked out of the room and made sure the door was locked. Just a little longer, he said to himself as he made his way back to the service elevator.

55.

Ian sat in the back of the Maybach as Remo drove down the long driveway. "Mr. Ramsey, look," said Remo as he pointed toward the iron gates. Ian sat up and looked and saw the mob of people standing on the other side of the gates.

"What the fuck is that?" Ian asked.

"I'll find out," said Remo as he stepped out of the car. Ian stared out at Remo as he spoke with people holding tape recorders and cameras. He was too antsy to sit and wait for Remo. Ian got out of the car and walked up to the gate. "Mr. Ramsey, do you have a comment on the allegations?" asked a woman holding a microphone. Ian looked behind the crowd and saw news vans lined up on the street.

"What allegations?" Ian asked her.

"The allegations in the complaint that was filed against you and your companies," said a different reporter.

Remo turned to look at Ian. Ian turned around and started to walk back to the car when he heard the question that made him stop in his tracks.

"Mr. Ramsey, is it true that you murdered Mark Kane and are holding his daughter hostage?"

"The complaint was filed this morning," said Stuart McBride, Ian's long-time lawyer. "It's completely insane what they allege."

"Who's the plaintiff?" asked Ian.

"Hope Kane and Annie Sharpe. The defendants are Shangri La Dream, SD Entertainment, and you individually. Let me tell you, Ian. In the thirty-five years I've been practicing law, I've never seen anything like this. I think this is Rule 11 territory. We can get them sanctioned for making these horrific and baseless allegations."

Ian sipped his Scotch and looked away into the distance. He spoke in a calm voice. "Tell me about the allegations."

McBride began flipping through the complaint. "It says that you own SD Entertainment, which in turn owns Shangri La Dream. You treat all the people who work at the club as your property, and you never allow them to leave. They are your prisoners. You brand all of your prisoners with a tattoo to make sure the world knows the women belong to you. Hope Kane tried to escape from your prison, but you caught up with her. You killed her husband and kidnapped her daughter to keep her from telling the authorities what you tried to do to her."

Ian took another sip of his drink. "What about the other plaintiff? What does it say about Annie Sharpe?"

"It says Annie Sharpe was working with Tom Rose to investigate your involvement in the murder of Kane, and you tried to silence her by having one of your men assault her and threaten to kill her and her grandmother. These are pretty crazy allegations."

Ian turned to McBride. "Leave the complaint with me and leave."

McBride nodded. "OK, but I want to start preparing a Rule 11 motion. I need to send it to Tom Rose to review so he has an opportunity to voluntarily withdraw the complaint. I don't want to lose any time."

"I said leave me the complaint and leave," said Ian in an even tone.

"Uh, OK. I'll wait until I hear from you," said McBride as he stood.

Ian watched Remo escort McBride to the door. "Get Sean," Ian said to Remo. "And get Dom on the phone."

His heart was pounding and he started to feel perspiration forming on his forehead. Ian heard footsteps and saw Boles step in. He stepped next to Remo as Ian heard Dom's voice on the speaker phone.

"Yea, Dom here."

"What the fuck did you do?" shouted Ian from his chair.

"What do you mean?" asked Dom.

"What did you do to Annie Sharpe?" asked Remo.

"I did what I had to do to get her to cooperate," said Dom. "Why do you care all of a sudden?"

"Because we just got sued by her and Hope Kane for what you did to them," said Remo.

"I'll take care of it," said Dom.

"No!" shouted Ian. "We can't touch them. It would just be admitting to what they're alleging in the complaint."

"Then what do you want me to do?"

"Nothing, you fucking moron!" shouted Ian. "I told you to keep an eye on Rose. It was a simple task, but you had to take it too far and fuck everything up!"

"I don't understand why you're going crazy," said Dom. "She's going to trial soon, and then she'll sit in jail for the rest of her life. This is what you wanted, Mr. Ramsey, and you're going to get what you wanted. What difference does it make that they sued you? They can't prove shit anyway."

Ian stood. "I told you this had to be perfect. For an entire year, everything was going perfectly. That bitch was in jail for killing her husband, and no one had a clue as to what happened. Now we have two dead people, and a fucking complaint accusing us of everything we did down to the last fucking detail. This is far from perfect! This is turning into a complete clusterfuck!"

"Like I said, just tell me what you want me to do and I'll take care of it. I really don't see a problem here. Any asshole can file a complaint. It doesn't mean shit unless they have proof, and they have no proof here."

"We have to do something," said Ian. "But I don't know what."

"Let me have a word with Tom Rose," said Dom.

"Didn't you hear me? We can't touch any of them without giving credence to what they're saying in the complaint." said Ian.

"He won't know who I am. We wouldn't be giving him any more proof than what he already has. I'll speak with him. Get him scared, and maybe he backs off. If he doesn't, they're no further ahead than where they are right now."

Ian slammed his fist down on his desk. "You put us in this mess. Go ahead and talk to him, but don't leave a mark on him. But, once this is all over, I want his fucking head. And if this goes sideways, I'm going to want your head."

Ian could hear Dom laughing. "I'll deliver his head on a platter," he said as he hung up.

56.

Linda Starr stared at the headline on the front page of the New York Times – "Ian Ramsey accused of framing Hope Kane." She shook her head and picked up the complaint styled, Hope Kane and Annie Sharpe v. Ian Ramsey, et al. Anger started to fill her head as she tried to think through Tom Rose's strategy. She looked up when she heard a knock on her door.

"What do you think?" she heard Heather Palmer ask.

"I call it a desperation move. She has the nerve to sue Ian Ramsey? These people will stop at nothing to manufacture a defense."

"I was asking about Hope's condition," said Palmer.

"I think she's alive, but don't know much beyond that," said Linda.

"You don't seem particularly worried about her."

Linda smiled. "I don't have a lot of sympathy for murderers."

"But she has to be physically able to stand trial."

Linda nodded. "I believe she'll be fine. We heard from her doctor, and he thinks she'll be discharged in a couple of days."

"What do you think about the complaint against Ian Ramsey?" Palmer asked, pointing at the complaint sitting on Linda's desk.

"He knows he has nothing and can't get her off, so he launches a media campaign with a preposterous complaint. He's trying to taint the jury pool. Scum bag."

"Maybe, but we're not dealing with amateurs here," said Palmer. "Do we have anything to refute what they're alleging?"

Linda shook her head. "No, but why's it relevant? He doesn't have any proof in my case. He can say what he wants over in the federal district court, but it has no impact on his ability to defend Hope. She's guilty as hell. His self-serving complaint won't get her off."

"Linda, I don't want to second-guess you, but maybe it would be prudent to depose this Annie Sharpe. I suspect Tom Rose will call her as a witness at Hope's trial."

"Let him," said Linda. "I've had witnesses try and lie before. The jury will see right through them."

"Linda, you're my star prosecutor. You know how I feel about you. You've found your place here pretty quickly, and part of the reason I think you've risen so quickly is because you're aggressive and have good instincts. So I'll go along with you, but sometimes it's good to take a step back and reassess. There's something about this case that doesn't sit right with me."

"Thank you Heather, but I know what I'm doing. I'm going to put Hope in prison for a very long time."

Palmer nodded. "OK. Come talk to me if you want to brainstorm. My only advice is don't take Rose too lightly."

Linda stared at the door for a few seconds after Palmer left. She tried to anticipate what Tom was going to do next. She shook her head. This was an open and shut case. There wasn't a damned thing Tom could do about it. All this trickery may get some people's interest, but it won't be enough to buy Hope's freedom. Linda smiled and stood. She felt like getting a latte from Starbucks.

57.

Tom sat in the conference room and stared at the steam rising from the coffee. The reaction of the media was exactly what he anticipated. The complaint got their attention, and they in turn got Ian Ramsey's attention. The small success, however, did nothing to ease his nerves. He had to get past many more hurdles to achieve his goal. The next hurdle was to get discovery from Ian and his companies. Tom knew he'd get nothing in terms of documents. People who ran criminal organizations generally don't keep incriminating evidence lying around. If he was going to get anything useful out of this lawsuit, it had to come through testimony. Tom began to outline the questions he would ask – questions for which Ian Ramsey would have no easy answer.

Edward walked into the room, noticeably upset about something.

"What's wrong?" Tom asked.

"Those fucking morons," he muttered.

"What?"

"I've spent the last half hour having a screaming match with Mobley and Ryan. They're pissed that we filed the complaint without clearing it through them first."

"Why do they care?"

"They're concerned about the firm's reputation. Ryan thinks the allegations in the complaint are so far-fetched that we are risking Rule 11 sanctions. He doesn't want Stern's name associated with a complaint like this."

Tom smiled. "I guess it's a good thing we didn't clear it with them before filing it."

Edward sat down across the table from Tom. "He said we are done at the firm unless we withdraw the complaint. He's going to put out a press release saying that we're rogue attorneys who'll no longer be associated with Stern and Hobbs."

Tom sat quietly staring at Edward.

"I couldn't get Ryan to change his stance. We need to make a decision on this complaint," said Edward.

"I'm not withdrawing it," said Tom.

Edward leaned toward Tom. "Think this through before you make up your mind. You're potentially flushing your entire career down the toilet."

"I understand the ramifications. I've made up my mind. I'm not withdrawing the complaint. They can fire me if they want."

"How can you take this so calmly?" Edward asked.

"It's not that difficult of a choice. I can let Hope Kane rot in prison for a crime she didn't commit and keep my job that I don't give a shit about, or try and save Hope. It's not much of a decision."

Edward leaned back in his chair and laughed.

"What's so funny?" asked Tom.

"You have a way of seeing things so clearly," said Edward. "Didn't notice it before. You're right. Our choice is pretty clear if you put it the way you just did. Fuck these assholes."

Tom smiled.

"Looks like it's me and you kid," said Edward. "We'll see if they have the balls to follow through with their threat."

58.

Timothy Ryan waited impatiently as he watched the six other managing partners walk into the conference room. Their assistants said they were too busy to meet on a moment's notice, but they all found a way to get to the meeting once they heard what the meeting was about. He watched Bob Mobley step in and pour a cup of coffee. They made their way to the large marble table and sat down.

"Thank you for making the time to meet on short notice," said Ryan. "You all have heard about the complaint Edward and Tom filed against Ian Ramsey. The allegations in the complaint go beyond the realm. It's been all over the news. We don't need publicity like this."

"Timothy and Bob, didn't *we* ask Tom to represent Hope Kane?" asked Shari Morton, who ran the Mergers and Acquisitions Department.

Ryan nodded. "Yes, but the deal was to get in and see if he can get information on the whereabouts of her missing daughter. It was supposed to be a quick in and out while getting some good PR. We didn't authorize him to bring this lawsuit with these outrageous allegations and fuck up the entire strategy."

"That's not the point," said Morton. "We asked Tom to represent her. Maybe he found something? Maybe what he alleges really is true?"

"Come on Shari," said Mark Thompson, the chairman of the Banking and Finance Department. "The complaint reads like a fucking novel. There's no way he's going to prove all that shit."

"Since when did you become a litigator?" asked Morton, shaking her head.

"Look," said Ryan, raising his voice. "Any normal person reading this complaint will reach the same conclusion. This was written to appeal to the press and the masses. That's the reason the media went crazy over it. I don't like this firm's reputation getting tarnished with this sort of horse shit. We don't make up stories to stick into a complaint. Bob's already received calls from the GCs of major clients of this firm, demanding to know how we allowed this to happen. This is sanctionable."

"Which clients?" asked Morton.

"They run the gamut," said Mobley. "Financial institutions, airline clients, automotive, private equity funds, you name it." He looked over at Morton. "Even your clients have called, Shari. Everyone under the sun read the stories about Hope Kane. She was headline news a year ago because she was this freak who decided to kill her husband and daughter and then become a mute. Everyone knows she's guilty. So our star associate and one of our partners file a complaint that everyone knows is pure fiction, and everyone assumes they did it to get Hope off. They don't like the fact that their top shelf law firm is playing these types of games to get a known criminal off."

Morton nodded. "Alright. I get it. What do we want to do about it?"

"Bob and I spoke with Edward and demanded that he withdraw the complaint," said Ryan.

"And?" asked Thompson.

"He said no. I told him that he and Tom may not have a job tomorrow."

"What did he say to that?" Thompson asked.

"He told me he had to think about it. He later called me back to tell me to go fuck myself."

Morton chuckled. "That Edward. He hasn't changed a bit."

"I want to call a partners' meeting and vote on removing Edward from the partnership. We can fire Tom any time," said Mobley.

"What will that accomplish?" asked Morton.

"We'll distance ourselves from these cowboys. It'll be a nice public statement that Stern and Hobbs won't tolerate this type of behavior," said Mobley.

"Wait," said Ryan. "Now that I think this through, she's right. Firing Edward and Tom won't do any good. It won't address the harm they did to our reputation. There's no denying that two of our lawyers filed this lawsuit while working for Stern. Firing them will just look like we're trying to do damage control, without solving the problem."

"What are you suggesting?" asked Mobley.

"We need to make the case go away quietly and quickly," said Ryan. "That means we cut a deal with the prosecution, and make Edward and Tom drop the civil action. This way, we still get the good PR, and clean up the mess they created at the same time."

Morton nodded. "That works for me. How're you going to convince Edward to cut a deal?"

"I can be very persuasive," said Ryan. "And if that doesn't work, I know Heather Palmer. I helped her run her campaign for District Attorney. She owes me. I'll do it myself."

59.

Tom saw Annie looking out of the large window at the runway. His heart ached, thinking about the hell she had to go through – all because of him. She turned, seemingly sensing that he was staring at her. Tom walked to her.

"How're you feeling?"

She smiled. "I'm fine."

"I wanted to tell you that I'm sorry," Tom said, looking into her eyes.

"Sorry for what?"

"For dragging you into this."

Annie looked down. "Don't be sorry. No one knew it would come to this. I jumped in to help you because . . . well because I did. Whatever happens, I'm not going to second guess my decisions." Annie looked up at Tom. "Are you sorry you took on this case?" she asked.

Tom looked away from her, thinking through Annie's question. "You know, I've asked that question many times, ever since Nick Glorioso and Tina Martin were murdered. If I could've seen the future and saw what was to come, I don't know what I would've done. But, I don't get to go back and change the past. And, knowing what I know, I can't imagine just walking away."

Annie smiled but didn't say anything.

"Why are you smiling?" Tom asked.

"Because it's good to see that there are still good people in the world."

Tom shook his head. "I took this case on as much for me as for Hope Kane."

"What do you mean?"

Tom chuckled. "I don't really know, but what I do know is that I stopped spending my waking hours wondering what I should be doing with the rest of my life."

Annie stared at him with a puzzled look.

Tom put his arm around her. "Don't try and make sense of what I'm saying. I'm not sure I fully understand."

"We're boarding," said Edward as he walked by them and toward the gate.

Annie picked up her bag to follow Edward. Tom took her hand. "Can I tell you something?"

She nodded.

"I promise you that this will all turn out OK. We're going to get through this and you are going to get your life back. I don't know why I believe that or how I'm going to pull it off. But I believe I can make that happen."

Annie smiled as she looked into his eyes. "I believe you," she said.

60.

"What the fuck is this?" Ian asked, tossing the document on the table.

"It's a deposition notice. They want to examine you," said McBride.

"Can they do this? They just sued us. We haven't even answered their complaint."

McBride shook his head. "No. Normally you talk to the other side and you come up with a discovery schedule and get it approved by the court. These guys just aren't following the rules. I'll prepare an objection, and then they'll have to file a motion to compel you to appear for the deposition. Don't worry about it."

Remo stepped into the study holding a newspaper. "Mr. Ramsey, did you see this?" he asked, handing the newspaper to Ian.

Ian read the headline. "Kane's Lawyers Demand Ramsey Testify." He read the article.

> Tome Rose with the prestigious New York City law firm, Stern & Hobbs, served a deposition notice on Ian Ramsey. In the complaint Mr. Rose filed in the United States District Court for the Southern District of New York, the plaintiffs allege that Mr. Ramsey orchestrated the murder of Mark Kane, Hope Kane's husband, and has kidnapped their daughter, Mila, to prevent Ms. Kane from blowing the whistle. It further alleges that Mr. Ramsey began a campaign to threaten and torture anyone who sought to assist Mr. Rose in his investigation of Mr. Kane's murder, including the imprisonment and torture of Annie Sharpe who is assisting Mr. Rose in his representation of Hope Kane. The complaint seeks money damages in the amount of $100 million for pain and suffering, loss of consortium, false imprisonment and other torts. Importantly, Mr. Rose stated, "Mr. Ramsey knows what he did. That's why he will find a way to not show up for his deposition to testify. We all know, if he really is innocent of these allegations, he would insist

on going on the record to tell the world that he is innocent.
Mr. Ramsey won't do that, because he knows he is guilty of
everything that's been alleged in the complaint."

"That fuck!" shouted Ian. "He's playing with me. He's fucking playing with me." Ian looked over at McBride. "What the fuck are we going to do about this?"

"Like I said, we'll file an objection. They have no right . . ."

"No, you idiot!" Ian cut him off. "We can't object. We would be playing right into his hands. He'll just do another fucking interview with the media and claim that he predicted this. He's turning this into a circus, and my reputation is getting clobbered."

"Mr. Ramsey, you have every right to object to this. Don't let his games force you to give up legal rights you have," said McBride.

Ian threw the newspaper at McBride. "We are not going to object. We're going to do something different. Tony, show Stuart out."

"I, uh, I don't understand," said McBride.

"I'm going to deal with this my way," said Ian.

Peterson drove the black van out of LaGuardia Airport and onto Grand Central Parkway. Tom sat in the back with Annie and Edward. Edward had a concerned expression.

"What's wrong?" Tom asked.

"The people we're dealing with. They don't play nice."

Tom nodded. "We didn't start the fight."

"I understand, but we need to think about our own safety."

"They would be out of their minds to harm us in light of what we alleged in the complaint."

Edward nodded. "I know. You've said that before, but I'm a little uncomfortable making life or death decisions entirely on your logical reasoning."

Tom looked out of the window. "What choice do we have? They know who we are. If they want to come after us, they will. We just have to keep on giving them reasons that'll persuade them to stay away from us."

Edward nodded. Tom turned back to Edward. "I'm sorry I put us here, but we are at a point of no return."

The van dropped off Annie at her apartment in Westchester, and then drove to the Dakota to drop off Edward. They pulled up to Tom's building.

"You look tired," said Peterson as Tom stepped out of the van. "Get some sleep."

"I will," said Tom.

"More importantly, be careful."

Tom nodded. Peterson pulled away. He saw the doorman and waved at him as he walked into the elevator. Exhaustion started to set in as he stuck his key in his door. He had been running nonstop for 48 hours. The apartment was dark. He reached for the light switch when someone grabbed him. A gloved hand covered his mouth and he felt a blade against his throat. Tom elbowed the man's stomach and spun around. He took a swing at the man, but he blocked it. The man grabbed Tom's throat and picked him up and tossed him to the floor like a ragdoll. He jumped on Tom and put the blade against his throat. Tom felt the blade cut him and he thought this was the end, but the blade stopped. He felt the warm blood dripping down the side of his neck. Tom tried to look at the man's face, but he couldn't make it out. It was too dark.

The man kept the blade against his throat and spoke in a whisper. "You are bleeding. It's a small cut. If I press the blade just a millimeter deeper, I will hit your artery, and you will bleed to death in less than a minute. Maybe that's what you really want – to die a quick death. If so, just nod and I will make it quick for you. Otherwise, listen very carefully to what I'm going to tell you. You have decided to fuck with the wrong people. We don't let people fuck with us. No one threatens us. No one plays with us. But you've chosen to take us on. We admire you for your courage or stupidity, whatever it is that might be causing you to do what you're doing. I'm going to leave you with a decision to make. You and your friends can walk away and you get your life back, just the way it was. You can go back to work, go and get married to Melanie. Annie Sharpe can go back to waiting tables. We are giving you that choice. You have 24 hours. Next time I see you, the blade goes in all the way and then your friends come next."

The man pulled the blade away and allowed Tom to get to his knees. As he tried to stand he felt a hard blow to the back of his head and every-thing went black.

Tom opened his eyes, lying on the floor of his apartment. He slowly sat up. His head was pounding. He ran his hand against the lump on the back of his head. Faint light started to stream in through his window. Tom checked his watch. It was just after seven in the morning. Everything started to come back to him – the man waiting for him in his apartment, the blade against his throat and the decision he had to make. "Melanie," he said as he dialed her number. She answered right away.

"Tom?"

"Yea, it's me."

"Why are you calling?" she asked in a low voice.

"I, I just wanted to make sure you were OK."

Melanie didn't answer.

"Melanie?"

"Yes, I'm fine."

"OK. I just wanted to make sure. Just be careful."

"Why are you saying this?"

"I've picked a fight with Ian Ramsey."

"Yes, I saw it on the news."

"He's a dangerous man. I just wanted to make sure he didn't do anything crazy."

"I'll be fine."

Tom held onto the phone as Melanie hung up. He listened to the silence and closed his eyes. He walked to his bedroom and stared at the unmade bed and the open closet. Melanie had taken all of her clothes. He opened the drawers in her dresser and saw they were empty. At that moment, it all sank in. She was gone from his life. It was something that had to happen, but the reality of it made his heart ache. The envelope on his nightstand caught his eye. He opened it.

> *Tom, I had hoped to speak with you. I waited and waited for you to call. I know you've been consumed with your new case. As much as it hurt to lose you, a part of me was happy to see you doing what you seem to love. I don't know what happened to us, but I guess it's no longer important. You needed more than what you had in your life, including me. I'm sorry I couldn't give you what you needed.*

> *I held off in gathering my things, but I finally realized that I needed to move on with my life. I'm sorry I had to say goodbye like this, but I didn't know how else to do it.*

> *Love always, Melanie*

Tom sat down on the bed and looked down at the floor. A surge of emotion overtook him. His heart tightened as the tears came pouring out. It was as if he had awoken from a trance. He wanted to hold her and tell her it wasn't her fault. But telling her that would defeat the very reason he had to end the relationship. She deserved more than what he could give her. He didn't want her to be sad. He wanted her to be able to go on with her life when it was all over. "I'm sorry Melanie," he said in a low voice.

Tom walked to the bathroom and turned on the light. He stared into his swollen eyes, the small cut on his neck, and dried blood on his shirt collar. "You want me to run?" Tom shouted into the mirror. "Fuck you, Ian Ramsey! Fuck you!" Tom peeled off his shirt. "I'm coming after you!" he shouted. "I'm fucking coming after you!"

61.

Tom opened the door to his office and saw the message light flashing on his phone. He set down his briefcase and pressed the message button.

"Tom, it's Timothy. I would like to have a meeting with you and Edward about the Hope Kane matter. Please be at my office at 10 this morning."

Tom looked up and saw Edward standing by his door. "Ryan wants to see us," said Edward.

Tom nodded. "Yea. I just listened to his message."

Edward stepped in and closed the door. Tom sensed something was wrong. "What's wrong?" Tom asked.

"I want to talk about our strategy," said Edward, taking a seat.

Tom nodded.

"I like the aggressive strategy in going after Ramsey, but I'm concerned we're getting too close to the line."

Tom furrowed his eyebrows. "I don't see that, Edward. We have a factual basis for everything we allege in the complaint."

"Do we?" asked Edward.

"Why are we having this conversation again?" Tom asked. "We discussed this repeatedly before we agreed to go this route."

Edward shook his head. "Tom, the story we want to tell is all plausible, but the entire story is based on conjecture. Is it plausible? Yes. But could it be wrong? Absolutely."

"We are not wrong."

"How about the allegation that Ramsey's framing Hope? Where's the factual support for that?"

"He's sending people to stop us from gathering evidence to show her innocence. My phone getting hacked. The visits to Tines and his friends. Glorioso and Martin. Annie. What more do you need?"

Edward nodded. "All of those things show that someone's trying to get in our way, but they provide no evidence that Ramsey put them up to it, much less show that Ramsey killed Mark Kane."

"It's circumstantial evidence," said Tom.

Edward nodded. "OK. Let's take your circumstantial evidence and say the jury buys it. Tell me about Mila. What factual basis do you have to allege that Ramsey kidnapped Mila?"

Tom didn't respond.

"Good. We're now making some progress. We have nothing to support that. And even worse, we don't even say that the allegation is upon information and belief."

"We had to make the allegation credible. We had to make the world believe it's based on facts. That's the foundation of this strategy," said Tom.

"I get the strategy, Tom. But we are making shit up. There's something called ethical rules and Rule 11 sanctions. At some point in time, we have to operate with facts, not conjecture and guesswork."

"I signed the complaint, Edward. I'm on the hook for whatever problems we face."

"That's not the point! I'm trying to look out for you. You violated all of the discovery rules by serving a deposition notice on Ramsey a day after we filed the complaint. You think the judge's going to look kindly to that?"

"Don't worry about looking out for me," said Tom. "You want to play by the book? We may as well pack it up and go home. We are not going to get anywhere if we follow the rules. You know as well as I do that Ramsey's behind all of this. We know the story, but we don't have the evidence. The only way we are going to piece together the evidence is by sticking to our script and luring him in to take the bait. That's all we've got."

Tom heard his intercom. It was Helena. "Tom, Stuart McBride's on the phone. He said he represents Ian Ramsey and the SD companies."

Tom looked up at Edward. "Put him through," said Tom.

Tom heard the call connect. "Tom Rose speaking," he said into the speaker phone.

"Mr. Rose, Stuart McBride here."

"What can I do for you?"

"I wanted to discuss your deposition notice for my client, Ian Ramsey. I don't believe your notice is in compliance with the rules and wanted to suggest that we reschedule it for a date after we've had a conference with the judge. We haven't even answered the complaint yet."

"I'm sorry, but we can't agree to that," said Tom.

"Excuse me? You are aware that it's improper to serve a deposition notice at this stage of the litigation, are you not?" asked Stuart, raising his voice. "It directly violates the judge's rules."

"The only thing I'm aware of is the fact that I served your client with a deposition notice that requires him to appear for his deposition, tomorrow at 10 am. It's up to him if he wants to object, but I have no intention of adjourning the deposition."

Stuart cleared his throat. "We reserve our rights to seek relief from the court," he said in a firm voice.

"Reserve whatever the hell you want, but you tell Ramsey that I intend on examining him tomorrow, and that he had better appear."

"Mr. Rose, I don't think you're hearing me . . ."

Tom cut him off. "No, you are not hearing me! Have your client at the address we listed on the notice or be prepared to explain to the world why your client is ducking me! That's all I have to say to you."

Tom didn't hear a response. "If there's nothing else, I will see you tomorrow," said Tom as he ended the call.

Edward shook his head. "And what's your plan if he doesn't show?"

"We go back to the press."

"And why are you so convinced that he gives a shit about what the press has to say?"

"No one's had the nerve to go public with any accusations against him. Even the FBI and state police have never followed through on anything against him because they never could gather sufficient evidence. Even though everyone under the sun knows he's behind all kinds of bad shit, he's been successful in keeping them at bay. You heard Mike. He likes the limelight. He likes the idea of being a big shot who's legit. And to a large extent, he's succeeded by avoiding prosecution. The recent reports in the press have changed all of that. And if my hunch is right, he's going to show up tomorrow, because he doesn't need me telling the world that he's a criminal who is too afraid to testify. That's why I'm convinced he'll show."

"I'm not going to change your mind, am I?" said Edward as he stood.

Tom didn't respond.

"We've got a meeting with Timothy. Let's go," said Edward.

Tom stood and followed Edward to the elevator. Edward didn't speak. Tom knew he didn't like the strategy. It was too risky and on the edge of what was permitted. Edward was an aggressive lawyer, but he always played within the rules. It was no surprise that he had reservations with what Tom was trying to do. They got out of the elevator and walked to Ryan's corner office. The door was closed. "You can knock and go in," said his assistant. "He's waiting for you."

They stepped into the sun lit room. Ryan stood from his desk and walked over to shake Edward's hand and then Tom's.

"Gentlemen, thank you for coming by," he said, gesturing to sit at the sitting area on the other side of his office. A few seconds later, a tray was brought in with coffee and pastries. "Help yourselves," said Ryan as he poured a cup of coffee.

"We're a little busy," said Edward. "What did you want to meet about?"

Ryan smiled. "Okay, I see you want to get right to the point. It looks as if you've been using the media to create an uproar in the Hope Kane matter."

Tom and Edward didn't respond.

"The reality is, I think we've gotten all the PR we want out of Kane. The management committee is grateful that you took on this case. Now I think it's reached the end of its useful life. We think you should agree to a plea deal with the prosecution and be done with this case."

"We can't ask Hope if she'll negotiate a plea deal because she doesn't speak or respond to us," said Edward.

"Bullshit," said Ryan. "You know you can get around that. Give her a written proposal. Ask her to scribble something on it, which will be treated as her written consent. You know you can make that happen."

Edward shook his head. "I think I need the client's permission before I can negotiate a deal with the prosecution."

Ryan smirked. "Sometimes we have to adjust our actions based on the circumstances."

"That's not gonna happen," said Tom.

Ryan turned to Tom. His smirk was gone. Tom wasn't surprised at his reaction. He obviously was looking to Edward to make the decision. Edward is the partner on the case. Why should a lowly associate have an opinion that anyone would care about?

"What exactly do you mean by that?" asked Ryan.

"Just what I said. We are not going to negotiate a plea deal without her consent, and we certainly are not going to fake her signature on a deal she never asked us to negotiate."

Ryan laughed nervously. "No one said anything about faking her signature."

Tom stood. "It really doesn't matter Timothy. We're not going to send her off to prison because you decided she's no longer useful for your purposes."

Ryan turned to Edward. "Are you going to tolerate this behavior from your associate?"

Edward smiled. "It's his case," he said as he stood. "We're meeting with the guys from Lynch Investigations, so we've got to run. As for making a plea deal, Tom makes the final decisions. It was your idea to put him in charge of this case, remember?"

Ryan stood and started to laugh.

"What's so funny?" asked Edward.

Ryan pulled out an envelope. "Here," he said. "This is a written plea offer from the Westchester DA, Heather Palmer. They'll agree to a plea deal for twenty-five years, and they'll drop all charges for the murder of Mila Kane. It's a good deal. Tell your client to take it."

Tom lunged at Ryan and grabbed him by his collar. Edward pulled him away and restrained him.

"You fucking asshole! You went behind my back! She's not your client!" shouted Tom.

"Wrong," said Ryan. She's a client of Stern and Hobbs, and you don't have a say in this. You are a fucking associate who's lucky to have a job, and now, you're going to have to deal with a criminal charge of assault." He turned to Edward. "You know your ethical duties, Edward. You are duty-bound to present this offer to Kane. She gets to decide what she wants to do. Not him."

Edward released Tom. He snatched the envelope from Ryan's hands, then took a step closer to Ryan. "I will take this to Hope Kane but remember. If you try and go after Tom for assault, deal's off, and as the only witness here, I wouldn't tolerate you lying to the authorities about an assault that never took place. Think about that before you embarrass all of us by running to the police."

62.

Tom and Edward sat in the back of the black Suburban with Mike as Peterson sped up I-684. As much as Edward wanted to rip up the envelope, he felt they had no choice but to present the offer to Hope. He was willing to cross the ethical bounds in dealing with Ian, but he was not willing to deprive Hope of her right to make this decision. They pulled into the visitor's parking lot at the Northern Westchester Hospital. The receptionist directed them to Hope's recovery room. Mike and Peterson waited by the door as Tom and Edward entered the room. Tom saw Hope lying on a bed, with her wrists chained to the sides of the bed. Hope looked up and stared at Tom.

"We heard what happened," said Tom.

Hope turned away from Tom and stared off into the distance.

"We need to talk about your case," said Edward. "We received a plea deal from the prosecution."

Hope turned to Edward and stared at him.

"I know you don't speak," said Edward as he pulled out the letter from the white envelope. "But if this is something you want, all you have to do is take this pen and sign at the bottom of the page. If you sign this, you'll go to prison for 25 years for the murder of Mark Kane, but the prosecution will drop all charges for the murder of Mila. If you want this deal, you just need to sign it."

Hope looked down at the paper. She looked up at Edward and held out her hand. Edward pulled out a pen from his breast pocket and handed it to her.

"You don't have to sign it," said Tom. She turned to him. "We are doing this because we have to, but this doesn't mean our view of this case has changed. I believe you are innocent. Now more than ever."

Hope stared at Tom for a few seconds, then brought the pen to the bottom of the plea deal sitting on her lap.

"Hope, I know Ian Ramsey's behind all this." Tom turned his head and showed the cut in his neck. "See this? Ramsey's people did this to me."

Hope looked up and stared at the small cut on Tom's neck.

"What?" said Edward as he took a step toward Tom.

"They're doing this because they know we got them figured out. Hope, they're desperate. We have them where we want them. I believe Mila's alive and the only reason you've played this game with them is because you're trying to save Mila. But if Mila is alive, what kind of life will she have, living with that monster? That's no life at all. We have a chance to give her the life she deserves. And we have a chance to give you your life back."

Hope looked down at the page again.

Tom continued. "If you sign that piece of paper, it's over. Mila grows up in the same prison Ramsey has created that you tried to escape. Do you think he'll give her a life that she deserves? He'll raise her in captivity. Maybe even turn her into a dancer, just like you."

Hope looked up at Tom again and stared into his eyes.

"Hope, Mila shouldn't have to grow up with that monster. She's entitled to grow up with her mother. Give me a chance. If I can't deliver on my promise, you can sign it then. But please. You have a chance to fix all of this. Don't take away my chance to help you."

Hope didn't take her eyes off of Tom. Tom could see her hand shaking. Her eyes started to well up. Hope looked down and dropped the pen and buried her face in her hands and cried.

"We're going to find a way to bring Mila back to you and we're going to make Ramsey pay for what he's done to you and your family," said Tom.

Tom reached down and picked up the plea deal and started for the door. He turned back and watched Hope, lying on the bed as the tears streamed down the sides of her face. "I will bring Mila back to you," he said in a soft voice. "That is a promise."

63.

Ian sat back in his chair, as Boles led McBride into the library.

"You have good news for me?" Ian asked.

McBride fidgeted. "Uh, no, Mr. Ramsey."

"What did he say?"

"He's moving forward with your deposition tomorrow. He said object if we want to, but then you'll have to explain to the world why you are ducking the deposition."

Ian threw down the newspaper he was holding. "Fuck! I knew he wouldn't back down. I fucking told you that!"

"As, as, uh, as I said, we can object to this . . ."

"No!" said Ian as he stood. "I'm not going to let that fuck play me to the media. I have no choice. I have to let him depose me."

McBride took in a deep breath. "I would advise against doing that," he said.

"I don't give a shit what you advise. Where do I have to go for the deposition?"

"They rented conference space at a local firm here in Vegas."

"Give Sean the address and I'll meet you there," said Ian as he turned away from McBride.

"We should spend some time to prepare," said McBride.

Ian turned back to him. "I don't need to prepare. I know exactly what that asshole's going to try, and I'll put him in his place. I'll run circles around him. He doesn't know who he's fucking with. Now, get out."

McBride lowered his head and headed toward the door. Ian turned to Boles. "Get Dom on the phone."

Boles dialed Dom's number.

"Yea," said Dom.

"I thought you said you gave him the message," said Ian.

"I did."

"It didn't get through. That fuck's going forward with my deposition tomorrow."

Dom didn't respond.

"What did you tell him?" Ian asked.

"I told him I'd kill him if he doesn't back off."

"It wasn't enough."

"I should have pushed it further when I had the chance. I might not be able to get him alone again."

"Why?"

"He's got guys following him everywhere. I think they're Lynch's guys. The waitress has guys hanging out in front of her apartment. It'll be hard to get to either of them without having to deal with Lynch's guys."

Ian sat down in his chair. "We may have underestimated him. What about Hope? Will she be able to start trial on time?"

"Yes. I also made sure she lives by our deal."

Ian chuckled. "Good."

"What do you want me to do about Rose?" asked Dom.

"Nothing. I can handle him. What's the prosecution doing about all this shit?"

"I'll find out."

"I want more than a status report. I need to know how they're planning on dealing with Rose's bullshit."

"I'm on it."

64.

The plane pulled up to the gate at Las Vegas International. Edward hadn't said a word the entire flight. Tom was fine with that. He knew Edward was upset that he kept the attack against him a secret, and he was just as glad not to have to explain himself. Peterson ran out to get the car while Mike waited back. A few moments later, Tom saw the black Suburban pull up. "Let's go," said Mike.

"We'll be there in a second," said Edward as he grabbed Tom's arm. Mike nodded and walked to the car.

"So, what happened?" Edward asked.

Tom shook his head. "It's not important."

"Yes, it is!" said Edward in a firm voice.

"What difference does it make? It happened. I'm alive."

"Tell me what happened," said Edward.

"A man was waiting for me in my apartment. I don't know how he got in. He put a knife in my neck and said if I don't back off, he'll kill me. It doesn't matter, because I know they're not stupid enough to make good on that threat."

"What matters is you kept it from me. You kept it from all of us. When they start attacking us, everyone on this team has a right to know."

"Why?" asked Tom.

"Why? Because each one of us has a right to walk away. This isn't some game. This isn't some litigation where the winner takes the money. This is our lives we are talking about. You have no fucking right to decide for everyone else whether or not they should risk their lives for the sake of Hope Kane."

Tom looked down. He spoke in a low voice. "I'm not backing out of this, Edward. I made a promise to Hope."

"Those are decisions you made," said Edward. "And that's something you have to live with."

Tom looked up as he heard Mike calling to them. "Let's go guys," Mike said.

Edward turned to him. "I'm not going."

"What? Why?" asked Mike as he stepped closer.

"Tom was attacked last night by one of Ramsey's guys. His theory about Ramsey not coming after us is obviously flawed."

Mike turned to Tom. "Is this true?"

Tom nodded. "Yes. I was attacked. But it was just a scare tactic. They could've killed me right then and there, but they stopped. They stopped because they knew they couldn't kill me without jeopardizing their goal of framing Hope."

"Why didn't you tell us?" asked Mike.

"I didn't think it was relevant."

Mike grabbed Tom's arm. "Bullshit!" he said with gritted teeth. "I have bent over fucking backwards to help you, and you thank me by lying to me?"

"I'm through," said Edward as he picked up his luggage. "I didn't jump into this to have Ramsey take out a contract on my life. My years are numbered. I plan on holding onto them as long as I can." He turned and headed back toward the gates.

Tom turned to Mike. "You can walk too. They told me to walk away if I want to live. I assume you are all safe if you walk away."

Mike stared at Tom without speaking.

Tom looked away. "Look, Edward's right. You're right. I should've told you. Maybe I was afraid you'd all run. I'm not running because I can't. If I stop now, Hope will take the plea deal and spend the rest of her life in prison, while Mila grows up to be Ramsey's slave. I can't allow that to happen."

Mike nodded. "Alright. I'll get you through the deposition. After that, we are going to have a conversation. Got it?"

Tom nodded.

Tom sat as Ian and two other men stepped into the conference room. He didn't bother standing. A tall skinny man with glasses walked over to Tom. "I'm Stuart McBride, Mr. Ramsey's attorney."

Tom nodded but didn't bother shaking his hand. "I'm Tom Rose. Are we ready to get started?" he asked, staring at the court reporter. The woman nodded. "Yes."

McBride stepped to the other side of the conference table and sat down next to Ian.

"Please swear in the witness," said Tom.

"Wait," said McBride. "Can we at least get some introductions of others in the room first?"

Tom nodded. "This is Mike Lynch, but he's leaving."

Tom looked into Ian's eyes. "I assume you are Ian Ramsey. Who's the other guy?"

"That's Sean Boles. He works for Mr. Ramsey," said McBride.

Tom turned to the court reporter again. "Please swear in the witness."

She looked over at Ian. "Please raise your right hand. Do you swear that the testimony you are about to give will be true and correct to the best of your knowledge, so help me God?"

225

Ian stared at her for a second. "God? I don't believe in God," said Ian with a grin.

Tom smiled. "You will."

Ian stopped smiling. "Excuse me?"

"You will believe in God once I get through with you," said Tom in an even voice.

"Objection," said McBride.

Tom ignored him. "Are you or are you not going to give truthful testimony?" asked Tom. He could see Ian's face turning red. Anger was building.

"I'll give truthful testimony," he said, glaring at Tom.

"Please state your full name and your home address," said the court reporter.

Ian looked over at McBride. He cleared his throat. "Mr. Ramsey will give you his business address. His home address is private."

The court reporter turned to Tom. Tom nodded. "I already know where he lives. In fact, every reporter in Las Vegas knows where Mr. Ramsey lives." Tom looked over at Ian and smiled. He could see Ian tensing his jaws. Tom turned back to the court reporter. "I'm fine with his business address."

The court reporter turned back to Ian. He cleared his throat. "Ian Ramsey. 2589 Prospect Avenue, Las Vegas, Nevada."

Tom sat up and leaned over the table. "Mr. Ramsey, the address you just gave, what business do you conduct there?"

"Objection," said McBride. "What relevance does that have to this action?"

Tom ignored McBride's question. "Please answer, Mr. Ramsey."

Ian looked over at McBride, looking for guidance.

"Uh, Mr. Rose, I have stated an objection to your question."

Tom didn't take his eyes off of Ian. "Relevance objections are not appropriate in a deposition. You know that, and if you don't, Mr. Ramsey should get himself a better lawyer."

"I've said my objection, and I direct my client to not answer," said McBride. "Since you've chosen to not play by the rules, I'll do the same."

Tom turned to McBride. He knew McBride's objection would not hold up if he were to take the dispute to the judge, but he couldn't get into a debate about what is and is not permitted under the discovery rules. After all, he himself had violated every one of them to get Ian into the room. But the entire strategy would be doomed if Ian refuses to answer a single question. Tom had to remind him of the consequences of Ian refusing to respond.

"Mr. Ramsey, you can choose to not respond to my questions. I'm fine with that, and in that event, we may as well just terminate the deposition now. I've already told your lawyer what I was going to do if you had chosen not to appear for today's deposition. If you are going to refuse to answer my questions, then let's just call it a day and I'll proceed as if you never showed up for today's examination. It's entirely up to you."

Tom could see the anger building in Ian's eyes. "How would you like to proceed?" Tom asked.

Ian gritted his teeth. "Ask your questions."

Tom nodded. "Mr. Ramsey, are you aware that my clients brought a lawsuit against the Shangri La Dream and SD Entertainment?"

Ian laughed. "If you want to call that piece of garbage a lawsuit, then yes, I'm aware," said Ian.

"Do you know if Shangri La Dream is a corporation?"

"I don't know."

"Mr. Ramsey, do you own Shangri La Dream?"

"No, I do not."

"How about SD Entertainment? Is that set up as a corporation?"

"I believe that is set up as a corporation."

"Does SD Entertainment own Shangri La Dream?"

Ian fidgeted in his seat and then looked over at McBride. He nodded, signaling that Ian should answer the question.

"I'm not sure, but I think it does."

"Who owns the shares in SD Entertainment?"

"I don't recall exactly who," said Ian.

"Do you own any shares in the company?"

"I believe I have a small interest."

"Are you testifying that you don't know if you own some shares in the company?"

McBride cut in. "Asked and answered. He's already answered the question."

"Are you objecting?" asked Tom.

"Yes, asked and answered. Objection."

Tom turned back to Ian. "Please answer my question."

Ian cleared his throat. "I believe I have a small ownership interest in SD Entertainment. The majority of the shares are owned by Peter Russo. That's my best recollection."

"Who's Peter Russo?"

"He's a business associate of mine."

"What business?"

Ian looked over at McBride. He sat up. "Objection."

"What are you objecting to?" asked Tom.

"Uh, I, uh, Mr. Ramsey's business is not relevant to this action."

Tom shook his head. "It's a baseless objection and you know it. But let me get at this slightly differently to address your relevance objection.

Mr. Ramsey, are you in any way involved in the businesses of Shangri La Dream and SD Entertainment?"

"I am not."

"You did say you are a minority owner of SD Entertainment, isn't that right?"

"Yes."

"But you are not involved in the business operations of SD Entertainment or Shangri La Dream?"

"Correct."

"Mr. Ramsey, do you spend any time at Shangri La Dream?"

"Yes, I do."

"Isn't it correct that there is a special room for important people at the Shangri La Dream?"

Ian looked over at McBride and then turned back to Tom. "Yes."

"Have you been invited to this special room?"

"Yes."

"How does one get invited?"

"I don't know."

"How did you know that you were invited?"

"The host came to me and told me that I was invited to go to the VIP room."

"Is that what it's called? The VIP room?"

Ian nodded.

"Please respond verbally," said Tom. "The court reporter can't transcribe you nodding your head."

"Yes," said Ian.

"Now, in the VIP room, isn't it correct that the women who entertain the guests all have a tattoo with a red heart and the letters 'S' and 'D' inside of the heart?"

Ian fidgeted in his seat. He looked over at McBride. "Objection," said McBride.

"What's the basis for your objection?" asked Tom. "We specifically allege that Hope Kane has a tattoo, the same tattoo that is on every woman in that room. There's no relevance objection here."

"We need to take a five-minute break," said McBride.

Tom smiled. "You can take your five-minute break after Mr. Ramsey answers my question."

McBride looked at Ian and nodded. Ian stared at McBride for a few seconds and then turned to Tom. "I've seen some women with that tattoo, but I can't say whether they all have it."

"We'll take our break now," said McBride.

Ian grabbed McBride's collar the moment they stepped out of the conference room. "You are my fucking lawyer. Do something!"

"I, uh, I am, but there's not much I can do. He's entitled to ask these questions."

Ian released him. He turned to Boles. "I don't like where this is going."

Boles cleared his throat. "What choice do we have? He's going to make it look like you're running if we don't finish this."

Tom heard the door open. McBride and Ian walked in with Boles trailing them.

"Are we ready?" Tom asked.

"Whenever you are," said McBride.

"Mr. Ramsey, do you know who Hope Kane is?"

"No. The lies in the complaint were the first time I've heard of her."

"You've never met her before?"

"No."

"How about Mark Kane?"

"I don't know who he is."

"Mila Kane. Do you know who she is?"

"No."

"Do you know who Hannah Silver is?"

Ian leaned back as his face turned red.

"Mr. Ramsey, please answer my question."

"I, uh, I don't know her."

"How about Steve Wolfe?"

"Never heard of him."

Tom leaned in over the table and looked Ian in the eyes. "I am going to ask you two questions, Mr. Ramsey, and I want you to think long and hard about my questions before you respond. Whether you choose to answer or not, it's up to you, but if you were my client, I would advise you to not answer the questions."

Ian stared back at Tom. Tom could see Ian gritting his teeth. He was angry and nervous – just the way Tom wanted him.

"Did you have Mark Kane killed on the evening of December 26?"

"Objection!" shouted McBride.

"Do you want to plead the Fifth Amendment?" asked Tom.

"Objection," said McBride again.

Tom didn't take his eyes off of Ian. "Think about that last question, Mr. Ramsey, and decide whether or not you want to answer. Now, I'll ask my second question. Did you kidnap Mila Kane?"

McBride began banging the table with his hand. "Stop! Objection!"

"That's a baseless objection, and you know it Mr. McBride." Tom turned to Ian. "Mr. Ramsey, if your lawyer were doing his job, he'd instruct you to plead the Fifth Amendment, and not incriminate yourself. Since he's not giving you that direction, I feel I should help you here. You can either answer me with a lie and commit perjury, or you can plead the Fifth. It's up to you."

Ian turned to McBride and then turned back to Tom. "You think you're so fucking smart. You don't have a clue who you are fucking with."

"Stop!" shouted McBride. He pointed at the court reporter. "We are going off the record. Stop typing!"

"No!" shouted Tom. "Stay on the record. Mr. Ramsey, are you done with your response?"

"I object," said McBride. "Mr. Ramsey hasn't responded, and you are mischaracterizing his testimony."

Tom smiled. "I think he did answer my question."

Ian stood. "Let's go," he said and walked out of the door.

Tom stood and followed Ian out the door. "Hey Ramsey!" he shouted. Ian stopped and turned back.

"Your boy sent me a message. And I got it loud and clear."

Ian stood still.

"I have some good news for you."

"What's that?" asked Ian.

"My co-counsel Edward Miller is out. Annie Sharpe is out and so is Lynch Investigations. They took your boy's advice and have decided to walk. You should be happy about that."

A slight grin went across Ian's face.

Tom smiled. "But I also have some bad news. I'm not out. I'm in this thing until the very end. And you are going down."

"Fuck you!" shouted Ian. He opened the glass door to the street and followed Boles and McBride through the crowd of reporters and flashing cameras. Tom followed them out and the reporters rushed him. "I have a statement to make," Tom said loudly enough for Ian to hear. He saw Ian turn around as Boles held open the door to their car.

"I just completed my examination of Mr. Ian Ramsey. I will make them public in the court filings I will be making shortly. But let me give you a hint. Mr. Ramsey just admitted to me that he kidnapped Mila Kane and had Mark Kane killed."

Pandemonium set in as the reporters tried to get to Ian. Tom saw Ian jump into the black car and drive away. Tom went back into the building and closed the latch to keep the reporters out. He walked out of the rear entrance where Mike was waiting. They jumped into his car and drove off.

"What was it that you were trying to accomplish with that stunt?" asked Mike.

"To tell him how it's going to be."

"And what's that?"

"A man who is not afraid to die can be very dangerous."

65.

Jacob Milstein heard his cell phone ringing. The caller ID was blocked. He answered.

"Jacob? It's me, Mick," said the familiar voice.

"Yes. Hi Mick. What can I do for you?"

"You've seen the papers about Rose?"

"Yea. Nutty, huh?"

"What're you guys going to do about it?"

"I don't know."

"Find out."

Milstein chuckled. "Listen Mick, like I told you before, I can get you status reports on the case, but it's not easy for me to get details on what Linda's planning. It's her case."

"How much have I paid you?"

"What?"

"I've paid you over fifty grand. You think I paid you all that money for you to just tell me when the next hearing is? This is when you're going to start earning your money."

"The deal was I keep you in the loop on the progress of the case. I never agreed to share confidential strategy with you. That would be improper."

"You think it's proper to take money for supplying the information you've been giving me?"

Milstein shook his head. "I haven't given you any confidential information. There's nothing wrong with you paying me for that."

"You want to play it that way? I'll call Heather Palmer directly and see what she has to say about it."

"Wait," said Milstein, wiping the sweat off his brow. "You do that and you won't get any more information from me."

"I figured that much out. But it won't be because you've decided to not give me information. It'd be because you'd be out of a job and may even get in some hot water. Tell me how it's going to be."

"Alright, alright. I'll try and get what you need, but I can't guarantee anything."

"Just get me the information, or I'll be calling your boss."

Milstein heard him hang up. His hand trembled. The deal was to keep him informed of the progress of the case. There was nothing improper about sharing the information he previously shared. He said he worked for an internet blog and wanted up to date information. Milstein never thought it would hurt anyone to keep him updated on upcoming hearings and the outcome of those hearings. Now, he wanted more. If Palmer were to find out about this arrangement, he'd be fired for sure. And the press would twist the facts to make him look like a mole for a blog. His career would be ruined. He had no choice. He'd talk to Linda and get as much as he could. Hopefully, that'll be the end of this.

66.

Calvin Tines stared at Ian's car as Peterson drove the van, staying about two blocks behind.

The Maybach pulled up to a driveway with large iron gates. They opened slowly and the car drove in. Tines and Peterson crept slowly toward the gates.

"We need to get as much detail as we can about this place," said Tines.

"We're already on it," said Peterson. "We already got shots of the property, and we're tracking down the architect who designed the house."

Tines nodded. "Alright. Tom wanted us to be seen by them. Go and park in front of the gates."

67.

Tom followed Mike into the building. They took the elevator up to the 18th floor and walked to the glass doors with the steel sign, "Lynch Investigations."

Tom saw Edward and Annie sitting with Tines and Peterson in the conference room.

"I thought you left," Tom said to Edward as he walked in.

Edward shook his head. "I've had the misfortune of seeing you in the news while waiting for my flight back to New York. I came back to try and knock some sense into you. You're playing with fire. If you give a shit about your life, you need to drop this. Hope's a lost cause, and you're risking your own life to scale a mountain that no one can climb."

Tom turned to Annie and stared at her bruised face and then back to Edward.

Tom lowered his head. "I'm sorry," he said in a low voice. "I'm sorry I dragged all of you into this fight. I had no right to keep things from you. I told Ramsey that you are all out, that you got his message. This is now between me and him. I believe he understands that. You can go back home. He no longer has any reason to come after you."

"What about you?" asked Annie. "How can you take him on without my testimony about what he did to me?"

Tom shook his head. "Edward was right all along. Your testimony wouldn't have changed anything. You can't testify as to who attacked you or how he's connected to Ramsey. Putting you on the stand is nothing more than an open invitation to Ramsey to come after you again."

Tom turned to Mike. "Thank you for everything you've done for me."

Mike stood. "Tom, this is crazy. We had a shit case to begin with, and now you don't even have Annie's testimony. What's the point? Why fight a fight that you know you are going to lose?"

"I made her a promise."

"Promises have to be broken sometimes," said Edward.

Tom looked up at everyone. "I wish I could tell you that all of this is about Hope. But it's not. This has always been about me."

Everyone stared at Tom in silence.

"I watched my father die not so long ago. All of us go through our lives, not thinking about how fleeting life can be. We waste so much of it, thinking it lasts forever. Then, when the end becomes a reality, we start to think about what we could have done. It can all end tomorrow, yet we waste days doing nothing with it. I've spent most of my life, going through the motions to chase after something that meant nothing to me or anyone else. I need to start doing something with my life. Doing something that matters."

Tom wiped the tears from his eyes. "I need Hope Kane as much as she needs me. I need to know that I did something that mattered. I need to know that I made a difference."

Tom looked up at everyone. "I believe Hope's innocent. And so do all of you. I can't walk away knowing what I know. She has given me a chance to do more than just go through the motions in this one life I was given. She's given me a chance to fix something. To save a life. I need this more than anything else right now. That's why I can't walk away. I refuse to die with regrets."

The room fell silent. Tom walked to the window and looked out at the flat desert outside. "In the end, what else is there? The only question that's going to matter is how did you live your life?"

68.

Ian stared at the black van on the screen.

"They've been just sitting out there," said Remo. "They're not even trying to be discreet. They're sticking their camera out of the window and taking pictures of the house."

Ian heard footsteps. He turned and saw McBride and Boles walking into the study.

"What now?" asked Ian.

McBride handed Ian a document. "What's this?" Ian asked.

"It's a trial subpoena."

Ian looked at the document. "He wants me to testify at her trial?"

"Yes, but you don't have to. You're outside of the jurisdictional boundary. They can't force you to appear in New York."

Ian threw the subpoena at McBride. "Then why are you bothering me with this horseshit?"

McBride's voice shook. "Well, Rose can use your deposition testimony at the trial."

"Fine. I didn't say shit anyway," said Ian.

McBride shook his head. "Well, technically you are right, and I agree with the decision to not appear for the trial. But Rose claims he has enough from your deposition to blame you for Mark Kane's murder and the kidnapping of his daughter."

"Bullshit! He doesn't have shit!" said Ian.

"Well, you didn't deny it when he asked you about Mark and Mila. He's going use that to tell whatever story he's going to tell. That doesn't mean you should go to New York, but you should know what he's going to do."

Ian threw his glass against the wall. The crystal exploded into a thousand small pieces and fell to the oak floor.

"Stuart, you are a fucking idiot! You are useless!"

McBride stood frozen.

Ian turned to Remo. "Make travel arrangements so that I'm in New York for the trial," said Ian.

"I, uh, I don't understand. You're going to appear at trial?" asked McBride.

"Yea," said Ian.

"You don't have to appear in court," said McBride. "They can't force you to show up and testify. What do we care if he uses your deposition testimony to get Hope Kane off?"

Ian turned to McBride. "I have my reasons. I am not going to let Rose get her off, especially based on lies about what I said."

McBride shook his head. "Mr. Ramsey, there's no reason you should subject yourself to this. Who cares what happens to Hope Kane?"

"Who cares? I care. I care because that fuck Rose will make the world believe that I killed Hope's husband, and that I kidnapped her daughter. If I sit here and do nothing, everyone will believe his lies. I have to show up to set the record straight."

McBride nodded. "You're the client. You'll testify, but at least let me prepare you in advance this time."

Ian shook his head. "There's nothing to prepare. Rose thinks he's so fucking smart. He doesn't know who he's fucking with. I'm smarter than he is. I'm a fucking genius. Once I go up to that witness stand and tell my story, Rose will be dead in the water. I'm going to put a stop to all this bullshit once and for all."

69.

Palmer stared at Linda reading the letter. "What is he doing?" she asked.

"I don't know what he's doing," said Linda. "He wrote a letter to the court. He wants to move up the trial. He says he'll be ready next week. He wants to start trial on February 8."

"This makes no sense. First Rose begs the judge for an adjournment, only to ask that the trial date be moved up. Then Timothy Ryan gets me to offer up a plea deal, only to reject it. I just can't figure out what they are doing . . . they must have something up their sleeve."

Linda chuckled. "You must be joking. They have nothing."

Palmer shook her head. "But what about the allegations in the civil action about the attack on Annie Sharpe. Why would she lie about it? I know I've said this before, but you should seriously consider deposing her. We can get a stay of the civil action so that we can take the discovery we need."

Linda shook her head. "We don't need any more discovery. She works for Stern and Hobbs. No one's going to believe her story. She's biased. Besides, taking her deposition or seeking a stay of the civil action will signal that we're giving credibility to their little game. It really doesn't matter. We don't have time to notice and take her deposition because if Rose wants to go to trial on the 8th, then I'm going to go to trial on the 8th. The judge's going to grant Rose's request."

Palmer stood, knowing that Linda had made up her mind. She had a lot of respect for Linda, but she wondered if her prior successes had gotten to her head. Palmer had never interfered in any of Linda's cases, and Linda consistently pulled out a conviction. Now wasn't the time to start meddling in her case, especially with trial coming up in a week.

"Alright, Linda. I'll leave it in your good hands, but I have to tell you, Tom Rose has stirred things up, and he's gotten my attention. I'm not so sure this is a slam dunk of a case as we had thought."

"Heather, through all of this nonsense, the one thing that Mr. Rose has failed to explain is the simple fact that Hope was caught with the murder weapon with gun residue all over her. He can do all the song and dance he wants. She's going to get convicted, and there isn't a thing he can do about it."

"Very well," said Palmer as she headed out of Linda's office. She didn't see Milstein hovering by Linda's door and walked right into him.

"Jacob, what're you doing here?"

"Oh, nothing, nothing. I was just walking by and I heard you guys talking about the Kane case. I was just curious as to what was going on."

"Don't you have to be in court tomorrow on the Chang case?"

"I do, but this is all over the news. I was just curious."

Milstein looked over at Linda. "You have everything covered?"

Linda smiled. "Yes. I have it covered."

Palmer shook her head. "I think you should worry about your own cases," she said as she watched Milstein step into Linda's office. She turned back and watched Milstein sit down in Linda's office.

"So, what're you going to do about the mess Rose is creating?" Milstein asked.

"Nothing. I'm not going to do anything about it, because it's irrelevant to the case we have against Hope Kane. Now please leave me alone so I can prepare."

Milstein nodded and stepped out of the office. Heather watched him walk toward his office. Heather made her way to her office and dialed the number for Timothy Ryan. She waited a long while before he finally picked up.

"What happened?" she asked.

"I can't answer you."

"You beg me to offer up a plea deal, and she rejects it?"

"Heather, I thought this was a done deal. I can't explain why she wouldn't sign the deal."

Palmer chuckled. "Well, you should've asked your questions before running to me for a favor."

"Look, I thought this would get done, but things didn't work out. So now, you get to put on your case and get her locked away for a long time. Nothing's changed."

"I agree nothing's changed. I just don't like offering up a plea deal at the defendant's request, just to have it thrown back at my face."

"Sorry," said Ryan as he hung up.

Palmer leaned back in her chair as she placed her phone in the cradle. Ryan was right. Nothing had changed. The evidence against Hope Kane was overwhelming. But this was one case her office could not lose. With all the press the case was getting, she'd have egg on her face if Linda couldn't get a conviction. Palmer took in a deep breath and wiped the perspiration from her forehead.

70.

The taxi pulled up in front of his building on York Avenue. Tom stepped out and breathed in the cold February air.

He opened the door to his apartment and dropped his briefcase. The judge had granted his request to move up the trial date. He would be selecting a jury in three days, and then trial would begin two days after that. Tom felt the deep pain in his stomach again. The same pain that he fought through for the past two weeks, but it reached deeper this time. He opened his desk drawer and pulled out the pain killers. The thought of numbing the pain crossed his mind, but it would also blur his ability to think. He held the medicine in his hands for a few minutes. The pain was too great, but it would pass in a while. He needed to find a way to get through it.

Tom threw the bottle back in the drawer and put on his coat. He walked outside, hoping the cold air would take his mind off of the pain. Tom walked toward Lexington Avenue and stopped at the corner of 65th Street. The pain overtook him and he leaned against a lamp post and slid down to his knees. He took in a deep breath and then looked up. At that moment, he saw her. Melanie stood frozen, staring into Tom's eyes. Her boss Lance stood next to her with his arm around her. Tom didn't want her to see him this way. But it was too late. They had been together for too long for her to not have seen it in his eyes. She stood still, just staring. Tom gathered himself and pulled himself up. He turned away from her and headed back east. The pain had subsided. But his heart ached. He didn't know how to react to seeing her together with Lance. He tried to shake those thoughts out of his head. After all, none of it much mattered. This was the way it had to be.

71.

Tom sat on the metal chair, waiting for Hope. A few moments later, a guard stepped in with her. She stared at Tom as she walked in and sat down across from him.

"We are going to trial next week," Tom said in a low voice. Hope put on a surprised look.

"It's going to be a short trial. I have one witness. It'll be Ian Ramsey. I'm going to break him on the witness stand. I believe I can do it."

Hope looked down and shook her head.

"There's one thing you have to help me to understand," said Tom. "Why? Why would Ramsey go through all this trouble to put you in prison? He could've killed you that night he murdered your husband. Why would he keep you alive and try to frame you for his murder?"

Hope looked away.

"I know you're not going to answer me," said Tom in a soft voice. "But you can help me bring Mila home to you by finding a way to answer this question."

She didn't answer. Tom stood and started for the door. He turned back. "Hope, I believe I can break Ian Ramsey, but I need your help. I need you to help me understand why he didn't kill you that night."

Tom walked out to the parking lot and started for the Town Car. A voice startled him. He turned and saw Mike.

"What're you doing here?" asked Tom.

"I thought I'd check in to see what you were up to?"

Tom didn't respond. He opened the rear door of the Town Car and was about to get in when Mike walked up to him.

"Listen, we need to talk."

"Mike, I don't want you involved anymore. We talked about this already."

"I have some stuff to tell you," said Mike.

Tom nodded. "Okay."

"There's a diner up the street. Let's take a ride."

Tom nodded and followed Mike into his black Suburban. He saw Peterson sitting behind the wheel. They drove down Harris Road to Route 117 and headed into Bedford Hills. Peterson pulled into the small parking lot.

They walked to the rear of the restaurant. Mike and Peterson slid into an empty booth and Tom sat down across from them.

"Anything new with Hope?" asked Mike.

Tom shook his head. "No. I have a trial starting in five days. I need to get back to prepare."

"What? I thought you had another week," said Mike.

"I moved it up."

"Why?"

"Because Ramsey's on the run. The media's hot on the story, and I don't want to lose the momentum. More time will just work in Ramsey's favor. He'll have time to think, which is what I don't want him to do. I want him to continue to react to what I do, which is what he's been doing."

Mike nodded. "Okay, I see what you're trying to do. I have some good news for you. After you left, I got a call from my buddy, agent Brown at the FBI. Based on the last interview you gave to the media, the FBI's going to reopen the investigation on Mila."

Tom leaned closer toward Mike. "Go on."

"Bottom line, if we can find some evidence of where she might be, they'd be able to get a warrant to go look for her."

"How are we going to figure out where she is?" asked Tom.

"My guys have been hanging out in front of Ramsey's mansion. We've been trying to tap into their video security system. They have it coded pretty well, but we may get lucky. If we get in, we might be able to see everything their security cameras can see. If Mila's in that house, there's a chance we could see her eventually."

Tom furrowed his eyebrows. "Why are you doing this? I thought you wanted out."

"Don't confuse me being pissed off at you with having a change of heart. Besides, do any of us really believe Ramsey will keep his word and leave us alone? He's going to come after us no matter what, and the only way we're going to stop him is by putting his ass in jail."

Tom shook his head. "I'm not so sure that's a very smart decision," said Tom.

Mike laughed. "No one's ever accused me of being very smart."

72.

Edward walked down the long hallway and stopped in front of the corner office. He thought back to when he was in charge of both the corporate and litigation departments. It seemed like yesterday when others, including Timothy Ryan, waited by his own office, hoping to catch a moment of his time. Those days were long gone. Today, Edward was standing there because Ryan had called for him. After a few seconds, he heard Ryan's assistant's voice behind him. "You can go in, Mr. Miller."

Edward opened the door and saw Ryan and Mobley seated on the couch. Neither bothered to get up.

"Thank you for coming by, Edward," said Ryan. "Please, have a seat," he said, gesturing toward the chair across from them.

"We hear you dropped out of the Hope Kane matter," said Mobley.

Edward nodded. "I did."

"Why?" asked Ryan.

"It's a long story," said Edward. "What difference does it make? Tom's got things under control."

Ryan smiled. "I guess you're right, Edward. It really doesn't matter why you chose to drop the case."

"You wanted to see me," said Edward.

"Yes, we did," said Ryan. "We understand that Mr. Rose made a request to move up the trial."

"He did, and the judge granted the request. Trial's starting in less than a week."

"Well, that's a shame. It doesn't give us much time," said Ryan.

"Time for what?" asked Edward.

"There's something we'd like you to handle for the firm."

"And what would that be?"

"We want you to find a way to get rid of this case," said Ryan.

Edward chuckled. "It's Tom's case. He's the attorney of record. You've already tried to get him to push Hope toward a plea deal. It didn't work."

Ryan nodded. "I am painfully aware of that conversation. But we have a different approach."

Edward leaned back in his chair and crossed his legs. "Go on."

"We are going to be terminating Mr. Rose's employment," said Mobley.

"On what basis?"

"We don't need one," said Mobley. "He's an employee at will. We can terminate him at any time for any or no reason at all."

Edward leaned forward. "That's bullshit!"

"No, it's not," said Ryan. "And, we didn't ask you to come here to debate that decision."

Mobley cleared his throat. "Edward, Hope Kane is a client of Stern and Hobbs. She will need a lawyer to represent her after Tom's fired."

"That's where you come in," said Ryan. "We want you to take over the case and then make another push to get the plea deal done."

Edward shook his head. "You're going to fire our best associate just so you can get rid of this case? Why the hell do you care so much about this case?"

"Because the press coverage this case has generated has our clients breathing down our necks. Everyone knows the defense strategy is bogus, and our clients don't like to see their top tier law firm in the news for creating a circus in the courts."

"Why do they care what Tom does? He's not representing them," said Edward.

Ryan shook his head. "Come on, Edward. You know that's complete crap. The GCs of these companies hire us because we are considered to be the best. It covers their collective asses. If we lose a case, they can always tell the board that they tried their best by hiring the best. By Rose playing these games with the media, we come off looking like a fly by night operation with no controls. It destroys our pristine reputation that we spent decades trying to build up. No GC in his right mind would hire us, knowing that our lawyers are in the public eye making frivolous allegations to defend a known murderer."

"And if I say no?" asked Edward, looking into Ryan's eyes.

"You already know the answer to that Edward. You're already on the edge after what you did to that mirror. At this stage of your career, you need all the help you can get. Doing this will go a long way to telling the MC that it should reconsider its view of whether you can function as a productive partner."

Edward sat quietly for a long while. He stared into Ryan's eyes and then looked over at Mobley. "Fine. I'll do it."

"Good," said Ryan.

"Just one thing," said Edward as he stood. "I want to be the one to tell Tom about his termination."

"No," said Mobley. "That's the favorite part of my job."

Tom watched Bob Mobley staring at him. Two security guards waited for him. "I'm sorry, Mr. Rose, but we have to escort you out," said one of the guards. Helena stood behind them with her hands over her mouth. He could see the disbelief in her eyes. "Helena will pack up your personal items and ship them to your home."

Tom nodded and stood. He pulled on his coat and picked up his briefcase.

"I'm sorry, but we will need to search that," said the security guard. He took the briefcase and pulled out the Hope Kane files. "This'll have to stay."

"I have a trial starting. I need those files," said Tom.

"Our instructions are no files leave this office," said the guard.

"And you are no longer counsel to Hope Kane," said a voice from the hallway. Tom turned and saw Edward.

"I'm taking over the representation, Tom."

"But she's my client, Edward! I have a fucking trial coming up!"

Edward shook his head. "Hope Kane is a client of Stern and Hobbs. I'm sorry, but the client stays with the firm. You are not to make any further contact with her."

"Does she know you're doing this?"

"I'm heading up there now to tell her."

Tom stood, lost for words. Edward didn't say anything else. He turned and walked away.

73.

The sun started to set behind the tall buildings. Tom walked aimlessly around the city, thinking about what Edward had done. They had been friends for so long, yet in the end, none of it mattered. Edward had made his decision. Saving whatever was left of his job was more important than doing what everyone had thought was right. He wound up back at his office building. He stared at it for a while until he heard a voice.

"Edward told me," he heard her say. Tom turned to see Annie. "I know you wanted to help her," she said.

"What're you doing here?" Tom asked.

"Mike and I were looking for you. Edward left half an hour ago to go see Hope."

Tom looked away. "He's going to come after everyone," he said.

Annie didn't respond.

"We had him on the run. I was going to put him in jail for what he did, but now . . ." Tom shook his head. "Once Hope agrees to a plea deal, he'll seek his revenge." Tom turned to Annie. "I'm so sorry."

Annie shook her head. "No. I made my choices. No one forced me."

Tom looked up at her. "I don't know what I can do to keep you safe."

"What the hell's going on?" said a voice. Tom turned around to see Mike.

"I just heard the news. You were fired?"

Tom nodded. "Edward's on his way up to tell Hope. He's going to get her to agree to a plea deal."

"And what about us?" asked Mike. "We're going to spend the rest of our lives looking over our shoulders?"

Tom lowered his head and closed his eyes. There had to be an answer. But what?

"We have to make them reconsider what they're doing," said Mike.

Tom looked up. "What did you say?"

"I say we go back in there and make them change their mind."

Tom's heartbeat quickened. "No. We've got this all wrong. We don't have to change *their* mind. Stern and Hobbs doesn't get to decide who'll represent Hope. It's *her* decision."

Mike and Annie looked at each other and then turned back to Tom.

"We need to get to Hope before Edward gets her to sign the plea deal," said Tom. "You have your car?"

"Peterson's around the corner. Let's go."

The Suburban sped up Route 684. Tom repeatedly dialed Edward's number, but the calls bounced into his voicemail. He dialed the Bedford Hills Women's Prison. A woman answered.

"My name is Tom Rose. I'm Hope Kane's lawyer. I'm on my way up to meet with her. I need to make sure she doesn't meet with anyone else claiming to be her lawyer."

"I'm sorry, but Ms. Kane's already with her lawyer. Edward Miller. I believe you and he checked in here together the last time you were here."

"He's not her lawyer."

"Well, we can't get mixed up in these things. You should speak with Mr. Miller and work this out amongst yourselves. Thank you."

Tom heard her hang up. The Suburban raced up Harris Road and pulled into the lot. Tom saw Edward walking to his Mercedes. Tom jumped out of the car and ran toward Edward.

"Tom," said Edward as Tom rushed him.

Tom shoved him and watched him fall back against his car. "I can't believe you sold me out!" shouted Tom. "After all we've been through together."

Edward didn't respond.

"All you give a shit about is you! You never cared about her, me or anyone else!"

Edward stared into Tom's eyes for a few seconds. "Are you done?" he asked as he pulled out an envelope from his breast pocket and held it out toward Tom.

"What is this? You get her to sign the plea deal?"

"Just open it," said Edward.

Tom reached for the envelope and opened it. He unfolded the sheet of paper and read it.

> *I Hope Kane hereby terminate the legal representation provided by Stern and Hobbs, and hereby retain Thomas Rose to represent her in the criminal trial regarding the murder of Mark Kane and Mila Kane.*
>
> *Signed,*
> *Hope Kane*

Tom looked up at Edward. "I, I don't understand."

Edward smiled. "I gave her two pieces of paper. The plea deal and this one, and I asked her to sign one. She signed this one. Congratulations. You get to keep your client."

"I don't know what to say," said Tom, looking down.

"Don't say anything. Go and get ready for your trial."

"What about you? How are you going to explain this to Ryan?"

Edward smiled. "Don't worry. I've got it all figured out."

74.

"What do you mean she fired us?" Ryan shouted.

"Read it yourself," said Edward as he handed the envelope to Ryan.

"Who prepared this?"

"I did."

"Why?"

"She's the client. She has the right to decide who's going to represent her."

Edward could see Ryan seething. Edward pulled out the plea deal. "I handed this to her first to see if she'd sign it. I then handed her the letter you're holding. She chose to sign that one."

"You think this is funny?" Ryan asked.

"No, but I think your lack of foresight is what's amusing."

"My foresight?"

Edward nodded. "This was one area where you always had a serious deficit. But you were able to hide it from your partners and your clients through smoke and mirrors, by taking credit for the work of others. You were very good at surrounding yourself with talented associates who carried your load. But when you were left on your own, you fell right on your face."

Ryan chuckled. "Edward, you have no idea how much shit you're in. You're the one who fucked this thing up by not being able to control Tom. Don't make it seem like this is my fault."

"Did you really think she would have dumped Tom and hired us? He's the one kid who actually gives a shit about her. You think she cares

256

about a law firm name? And, do you really think Tom's the kind of a lawyer who'd just get up and walk away because you decided to fuck him?"

Edward could see Ryan's face turning red. "Remember Timothy, this is your fuckup. It was your idea to take on this case and to put Tom on it. You thought the world would turn just the way you spun it. You were too stupid to realize the world doesn't give a shit which way you want it to turn. It'll go about its business like it always has. Now, you are stuck with the consequences."

"Don't sound so happy, Edward. Remember, you're still a partner here. You really think the Management Committee will let you off the hook?"

Edward smiled and turned to walk away. He heard Ryan shouting, "It's not over Edward! You think I'm going to just stand here and let you fuck with me? There are other ways of making sure Tom doesn't tarnish this firm's reputation any further."

Edward turned back to him. "You can do what you want. I'm submitting my resignation today. And one more thing. Hope Kane's no longer a client of this firm. If you so much as mention her name to the prosecution or do anything at all to get in the way of this trial, I will go straight to the ethics board. Choose wisely."

Ryan sat frozen. Edward smiled. "Just think, all of this was your idea. If I were you, I'd pray that we put on a good show in court."

75.

Tom stared into the mirror. He wiped the sweat from his forehead and tried to take in a breath. The pain in his stomach drained him of all energy. He hunched over the sink and closed his eyes. He needed to get past this moment. The pain would subside soon, he told himself. He just had to make it through the trial. Just a few more days. He heard his doorbell. Tom tried to straighten up and take in some air. Then the nausea set in. He vomited into the sink and saw the blood. It was splattered all over the white tiles and mirror. It made his heart sink. He heard the doorbell again. "Please. Please give me a few more days," he said under his breath. He felt the pain subside. He rinsed his face and mouth with cold water. The doorbell rang again. Tom made his way out of the bathroom and opened the door. He saw Edward with Mike and Annie.

"You look like hell," said Edward.

Tom didn't answer. Edward picked up his litigation bag and walked in.

"What's going on?" asked Tom.

"You're starting trial tomorrow. I thought you may need your files."

"Why's there blood on your shirt?" asked Annie.

Tom looked down and saw the drops of red on his shirt. The pain started to come back and things became blurry. Tom reached for the wall to gain his balance. He fell to the floor. He tried to reach for something, but his arms wouldn't move. All he could see was darkness.

Edward saw the doctor walking toward him. He jumped to his feet to meet him. Mike and Annie followed. "How is he?" Edward asked.

The young doctor shook his head. "It's advanced all over. He's in his final stages."

Edward stood, holding out his hands in confusion.

"What do you mean final stages?" Annie asked.

The doctor looked puzzled. "You don't know?"

"Know what?" asked Edward.

"Maybe his primary physician should talk to you. He's on his way over now."

"Just tell me," said Edward. "Both his parents are dead. I'm the closest thing he's got to family."

The doctor stared at Edward for a while, then spoke in a low voice. "Mr. Rose has advanced stomach cancer. The cancer has spread everywhere. He's in stage four."

Edward stumbled back. Mike grabbed him before he fell. "What? How can that be?" Edward asked. "Is it treatable?"

"I'm sorry. He has very limited time."

"Why didn't he get treatment?" asked Edward.

"I don't know, but this thing's been all over his body for a while. Treatment wouldn't have done much. Mr. Rose apparently chose to live out his days, rather than going through treatments that ultimately wouldn't work."

76.

Tom opened his eyes and saw Edward hovering over him. Annie and Mike stood behind him. He could see Edward had been crying.

"Hey, how're you feeling?" asked Edward.

"I feel good," said Tom. "What happened?"

"You collapsed in your apartment. We had to call an ambulance."

"Tom," said a woman's voice. He turned toward the door and saw Melanie with tears in her eyes. She stood by the door and stared into his eyes.

"What are you doing here?" asked Tom. "I'm fine. It's probably just exhaustion."

"We all know, Tom," said Edward.

Tom turned to him. "What?"

"The doctor told us."

Edward wiped the tears with his hands and sat down.

"Why didn't you tell me?" asked Melanie as tears came streaming down her face. "Why?"

Tom turned to the window. He couldn't bear to watch her cry. He didn't want her to have to live through this moment. The last thing he wanted was for her to suffer the loss of someone she loved. He had hoped she'd fall in love with Lance; that she wouldn't feel the loss when his time came. All his efforts to ease the inevitable farewell had failed. He could no longer contain his emotions. His body shook as he tried to hold back his tears.

"You pushed me away so you can die alone," Melanie said through her tears. "You had no right. I love you, and you had no right to take away my right to love you until the very end."

Tom turned back to her. "I'm sorry," he said in a low voice. Melanie walked to the bed and leaned down. She hugged him and sobbed into his chest.

"Go on with your life," he said to her. "That'll be the best gift you can give me." Melanie nodded and stood. Tears ran down her face as she turned and left the room.

Tom watched Melanie leave just as he saw Dr. Klingman enter the room. He looked dejected.

Tom didn't let him say a word. "You did everything you could to help me," he told the doctor. "I chose to be here. You can do one more thing for me. You need to get me discharged."

"Have you lost your mind?" said Edward as he stood.

"You're in no shape to leave," said the doctor.

"I know I don't have much time, but I have to finish what I started."

"Tom, I really . . ."

Tom cut the doctor off. "We all know I will be gone in a matter of days. Nothing's going to change that. Let me do this my way. Don't make me lie here, waiting for that day to come."

"Why are you doing this?" asked Edward.

Tom smiled into his eyes. "I want to know that I made a difference in this lifetime. That's my dying wish."

Edward nodded and looked over at the doctor. Dr. Klingman stared at Tom for a long while. "I'll sign the papers to get you discharged," he finally said as he walked out.

77.

"The prosecutor isn't worried," said Dom. "They're confident with their proof. Rose's games aren't going to change the outcome. They feel good about their case and they're going to stick to the case they were going to put on."

Ian laughed nervously. "OK. I guess I should listen to them. They know what they're doing."

"Yea. Just sit back and enjoy the trial."

"I guess that's what I'll do. You know, Dom, this is our tax dollars at work."

Dom laughed. "When are you flying over?"

"Tonight."

78.

Tom stood in the marble hallway and watched as the crowd poured into the courtroom. Murder trials were a dime a dozen, but a silent murderer of her family who would soon meet her fate made for good drama. And, Tom's games with the media to accuse Ian Ramsey of the murder made this trial prime time entertainment.

He saw the prosecution team approaching. Linda walked up to him.

"I'm looking forward to seeing your house of cards come crumbling down," she said.

Tom stood quietly. She smiled and said, "Good luck. You're going to need it." She opened the large oak door and walked into the courtroom. He followed her in. He made his way through the crowded gallery and to counsel table. Edward looked up at him and smiled.

"What are you doing here?" asked Tom as he approached Edward.

"You probably don't remember me telling you that I'm your co-counsel since you pretty much passed out the moment we got to your apartment. Mike and Annie are over there if we need them."

Tom turned back and saw them seated in the front row. Behind them sat Ian Ramsey with McBride next to him. He also saw Timothy Ryan and Bob Mobley seated further back. And then he saw Melanie, staring into his eyes. She was crying. He lifted his hand to wave at her. She smiled with her eyes. A few moments later, two guards walked in with Hope. She wore a black dress – probably the dress she had on when they arrested her. The guards brought her to counsel table. She sat down and stared straight ahead without saying a word. Tom closed his eyes and took in a deep breath.

Please give me the strength, he said under his breath. He opened his eyes as he heard a loud banging against the rear door behind the judge's bench.

"All rise. The honorable Daniel Gonzalez now presiding," said the bailiff.

"Please be seated," said the judge. "Anything we need to take up before we invite the jury in?"

"No, your honor," said Linda.

"We are ready to proceed, your honor," said Tom.

"Well, I have something I want to address," said the judge. "Mr. Rose, you've been busy the past week."

Tom remained standing, without responding.

"I've read more about this case in the newspapers in the past week than I've read all year since the day she was arrested. If I were being cynical, I'd think you are trying to tamper with the jury. What do you have to say about that?"

Tom met the judge's eyes. "I have no interest in tampering with the jury, your honor."

"I'm warning you now, Mr. Rose. I don't have much patience with lawyers playing games. I had better not see you trying to try this case through the media."

"Understood, your honor."

"Very well. Bring in the jury," the judge said, turning to the bailiff.

The twelve jurors walked in through the side door and found their seats in the jury box. "Go ahead, Ms. Starr," said the judge.

Linda stood and started to pace back and forth in front of the jury box.

"Ladies and gentlemen of the jury. We are here today for the trial of Hope Kane for the murder of her husband Mark Kane – a husband and father who was brutally murdered on the evening of December 26, just over a year ago. We are also here on the murder of their three-year old daughter, Mila, who has disappeared from the face of the earth. The People of the State of New York will prove beyond a reasonable doubt that the defendant, Hope Kane, is responsible for both murders. The evidence will show that she spent the evening having dinner with Mark and Mila at a restaurant in Scarsdale. They then returned home and she killed her daughter, then shot Mark Kane twice – first in his forehead and then second in his heart. Evidence will show beyond a reasonable doubt that she pulled the trigger. When the authorities arrived, she was standing over her dead husband's body. She held the murder weapon, a Sig Sauer, 357 caliber pistol. We will prove beyond a reasonable doubt that the two bullets that killed Mark Kane came from that gun. We will show uncontroverted evidence that Hope Kane had gun residue all over her from her firing the murder weapon.

"Mila Kane, the second murdered victim in this horrific tragedy. Hope, Mark and Mila returned home from dinner on the night of December 26. We have not been able to locate Mila's body, but we do know that Mila was in that house that night. Evidence will show that she was with Hope and Mark at the restaurant, and that she sat in the back seat of their 2004 Toyota Camry as they drove home. There was no one else in that home. We don't know how she did it, but we don't have a doubt that she murdered her own daughter and hid her body.

"Once the prosecution lays out all of the evidence, I will ask you the jury to find Hope Kane guilty for the murder of Mark Kane and Mila Kane. You the jury have the power to make sure a person like Hope Kane is brought to justice for the horrors she has committed. A father and an innocent little girl are dead because this woman decided that they should no longer live. That's the kind of human being we are dealing with. The evidence will prove this beyond a reasonable doubt. She must pay the price for what she has done. Thank you."

Linda turned and stared at Tom for a few seconds. She then glared at Hope for a long while and then returned to the prosecution table.

"Mr. Rose?" said the judge as he looked over at Tom.

Tom stood. "Your honor, the defense will reserve the opening statement until its case in chief."

"Very well," said the judge, and then turned to Linda. "Please proceed, Ms. Starr."

Linda stood. "I would like to call to the stand, Ms. Louisa Faher."

A young woman stood from the gallery and walked toward the witness stand. She was a thin woman, about five feet tall. She didn't have much of a presence that could provide any degree of unearned credibility. Tom didn't remember seeing her the night he was at Capri. The bailiff swore her in and she sat down. Edward leaned over to Tom. "Predictable," he whispered. Tom nodded. Linda had an easy case to put on. Have the witnesses tell a simple, linear story from the moment Hope was seen together with Mark and Mila until her arrest. Finish off the case with testimony from Malachy O'Neal to testify about the forensics. It would be a short, simple presentation that any juror could follow.

"Ms. Faher, where were you employed on December 26, the night of the murder of Mr. Kane and Mila Kane?"

Tom stood. "Objection. Foundation." No evidence had been presented that Mila Kane had been murdered. Linda's question assumed that she in fact had been murdered. There was no way the judge could overrule Tom's objection.

The judge stared at Tom for a few seconds, then shook his head. "Sustained. Rephrase, Ms. Starr," he said.

"Ms. Faher, where were you employed on December 26?"

"I was employed at Capri."

"What was the nature of your employment?"

"I was a waitress."

"On the evening of December 26, did you see the defendant, Hope Kane, at Capri?"

"Yes."

"Under what circumstances did you see Ms. Kane?"

"I was their waitress. I served her."

"Was she alone?"

"No. She was with Mark and their daughter, Mila."

"You mentioned Mark and Mila by their first names. When did you learn their names?"

"They used to be regulars at the restaurant. It's a small restaurant and we get to know the regulars. I don't recall when I first learned their names, but it was some time ago."

"Approximately what time was the Kane family seated at their table?"

"I would say around 6 pm."

"How do you know that?"

"As I said, they're regulars. They almost always came in for dinner around the same time – around 6 pm."

"Do you know why they came to the restaurant around that time?"

"I don't know for certain. I presume it's because they had a young daughter who probably had a bedtime."

Tom considered objecting and moving to strike the testimony. Faher acknowledged that she didn't know why the Kanes came to the restaurant at a particular time. The testimony was based on pure speculation. But, he chose not to object. The testimony wasn't harmful, and he didn't want the jury to think he's trying to hide anything.

"What time did they leave the restaurant?"

"I believe around 7:30 pm."

"Did you watch them walk out together?"

"Yes."

"What did you do after they walked out of the restaurant?"

"I looked out of the window and saw Barry bring their car up. They got in and drove off."

"Who's Barry?"

"Barry's the valet. We have valet parking at the restaurant."

Linda turned to the judge. "Nothing further, your honor. I pass the witness," she said as she returned to her table and sat down.

"Cross examination, Mr. Rose?" asked the judge, looking at Tom.

"Yes, your honor," said Tom as he stood. He looked into Faher's eyes. He could see the discomfort. It was clear she wanted to help the prosecution. She saw Tom as an adversary.

"Ms. Faher, you testified that the Kane family were regulars at the Capri restaurant, do you recall that testimony?"

"Yes."

"About how many times have you personally served the Kane family as their waitress?"

Faher looked up at the ceiling, seemingly trying to count in her head. She looked at Tom after a long minute. "I can't recall an exact number."

Tom nodded. "Let's try it this way. You testified that they are regulars. How often did they dine at Capri?"

"I'd say about once a month."

"How many servers work at the restaurant?"

"We have five for the dinner shift."

"Including you?"

"Yes."

"When was the first time the Kane family started to dine at Capri?"

"It was a few years ago?"

"Would it be fair to say about four years ago?"

"Yes, that sounds about right."

"How long were you employed at Capri?"

"Seven years."

"So, you would remember when they started to become regulars?"

"Yes."

"Did the Kane family come to the restaurant about once a month from the very first time they started to dine at the restaurant?"

"Objection," said Linda as she stood. "Your honor, I've been patiently waiting, trying to see where Mr. Rose was going with all of his questioning, but I just don't see how any of this is relevant."

The judge turned to Tom. "Mr. Rose, I'm going to overrule the objection because I too am a little curious as to where you are going. So, I'll let you carry on, but you need to start showing me why all this questioning is relevant."

Tom nodded. "Yes your honor." He turned back to Faher. "Did the Kane family come to the restaurant about once a month from the very beginning?"

"I think that's right."

"When did they stop coming?"

"About a year ago. Since the night of December 26."

"So, would it be fair to say that they were regulars at the restaurant for about three years?"

"Yes."

"And, if we do some simple math, would it be fair to say that the Kane family went to the restaurant approximately 36 times from the first time they started going to the restaurant?"

"Give or take, but that sounds right."

"Now, you've testified that there are a total of five servers. Would it be fair to say that you would have waited on the Kane family about seven or eight times?"

"Oh, I think I served them more than that."

"Ms. Faher, all I did was simply divide 36 by five."

"That wouldn't be right."

"Objection," said Linda. "Again, on relevance. Also, there's no question pending."

The judge looked at Faher. "Sustained. Ms. Faher, please don't give testimony until counsel asks you a question."

"Yes. I'm sorry."

The judge turned to Tom. "Mr. Rose. Last warning. Get to the point."

Tom nodded and continued. "Ms. Faher, do you recall serving the Kane family more than eight times?"

"Yes."

"How do you know that?"

"Well, the Kane family had a table that they liked, which happened to be in the section of the restaurant that I was responsible for. The table is right by the window that overlooks Palm Avenue. They didn't always get the same table, but for the most part, they did. So, you can't just divide 36 by five. I would say I served them closer to fifteen or twenty times."

"In the fifteen or twenty or so times that you served the Kane family, did you have conversations with them?"

"Well, yes. We'd have small talk."

"And, the times that you spoke with them, were you able to get a sense of how Hope and Mark felt about each other?"

"Objection!" shouted Linda.

The judge turned to Linda. "What's the objection?"

270

"The question is vague and ambiguous. It also calls for speculation as to what the Kane family would have been feeling."

The judge rolled his eyes. "I think Ms. Faher can testify about her perception of the Kane family based on what she saw. But, Mr. Rose, maybe you can rephrase your question."

A cop out ruling, thought Tom. There was nothing wrong with the question, but the judge didn't feel like ruling. "Very well, your honor." Tom turned to Faher. "Think back to the first few times you saw the Kane family. Did they seem happy?"

Faher nodded. "Yes."

"How do you know that?"

"Just the way they interacted with each other. They would smile a lot. Mila was always so happy."

"Anything else? Did you ever see them holding hands together?"

"Yes."

Tom swallowed hard. The next question was the all-important one that'll serve as the foundation for his entire story.

"Ms. Faher, in the three years that you saw the Kane family, did Hope and Mark's demeanor toward each other change at any point?"

Faher shook her head. "I don't think so."

Perfect, thought Tom. "How about on the evening of December 26. Did Hope and Mark behave the same way as they had behaved the prior times they were in the restaurant?"

Faher looked up at the ceiling again for a few seconds and then turned back toward Tom. "Yes."

Tom smiled. He had gotten what he wanted. By first establishing the number of times Faher waited on the Kane family, he had created a foundation for her ability to testify about her perception on Hope's relationship

with Mark. "One final question. Ms. Faher, you testified that you personally had waited on the Kane family a number of times."

Faher nodded, "Yes."

"How did the Kane family pay for their meals?"

"Objection!" shouted Linda. "Relevance."

"Mr. Rose?" said the judge.

"This is my last question, judge. The relevance will become apparent
as the case proceeds."

"Go on," said the judge, looking at Faher.

"They paid with cash."

"Thank you, Ms. Faher. Nothing further, your honor."

The judge looked at Linda. "Any redirect?"

Linda stood. "No, your honor."

"Very good. It's already 12:30 pm. Let's take a lunch break. I want
everyone back by 1:30 to resume."

"All rise," said the bailiff as the judge disappeared out of the door
behind the bench. Tom looked at Linda as the courtroom started to empty.
She didn't look back at him. Tom noticed a slight bit of distress on her face.
He knew he didn't score any major points, but the testimony he got from
Faher left Linda wondering what he was going after. He guessed that Linda
thought this would be an easy conviction and didn't do a whole lot to prepare. Tom stood and looked at Hope. She stared back at him with tears in
her eyes. He wished he had the luxury to take his time with this trial, but he
knew that wasn't in the cards. He had to get to the end quickly. There was
no point in trying to throw roadblocks on the story Linda was going to tell.
People already knew that story. The only way he was going to convince the
jury was to tell his own story – a story that the jury would want to believe.
Faher was the start. Tom turned to Edward and saw him smiling.

79.

Linda sat at her desk, reviewing the outline she put together for the arresting officer, Mark Wilson. It was a short outline, largely based on the police report. After him, she was going to put on Malachy O'Neal. That too was going to be short. She thought about Tom's cross examination of Faher. That she didn't anticipate Tom's cross bothered her, but she was convinced it would have no effect on the jury. All he established was that Hope and Mark appeared happy with each other. So what? People do crazy things. No matter what testimony Tom may get from her witnesses, there were facts that he simply could not overcome. She was caught with the murder weapon in her hand. She had residue all over her from firing the weapon. The bullets that killed Mark Kane came from the Sig Sauer she was holding. That Hope and Mark were happy together at the restaurant did nothing to overcome these damning facts. A knock on her door made Linda look up.

"How are you feeling?" asked Palmer, stepping into Linda's office.

"I feel good."

"I sat in back and watched the trial."

Linda furrowed her eyebrows. It had been a long time since Palmer sat in on her trials.

"Oh. What did you think?"

Palmer sat down on the chair facing Linda's desk. "He scares me a little."

Linda smiled. "There's nothing he can do. You know the facts. There's nothing he can do to explain them away."

"Still," said Palmer with a worried expression. "How're you going to counter his tactic to blame the murder on Ian Ramsey? How were you planning on dealing with him on cross?"

Palmer made her feel like she was a rookie again. Linda had been doing her own trials without Palmer butting in for years. Now, it was as if Palmer was testing her, to see if she was able to handle the cross examination of Ian Ramsey. "I'm not going to have to worry about Ramsey. He's not going to say he had Mark killed. And, Rose's got no proof that Ramsey had anything to do with Hope."

"What about the tattoo? That the women who work at Shangri La Dream have the same tattoo as Hope?" asked Palmer.

"What about it? So what if she worked at a club that may have ties to Ramsey? They still have to put in some evidence that he is tied to Mark's murder. Also, what motive did he have to kill Mark? If he killed Mark, why not kill Hope too? Why keep her alive and deal with all this?"

Palmer nodded. "That sounds right."

"It *is* right," said Linda. "They can come up with whatever fantasy they want, but without evidence, it means nothing."

Dom leaned against the side of the building and watched the reporters take pictures of Ian walking out of the courtroom. Ian stepped up to Dom.

"Enjoying the show?" Ian asked.

Dom nodded. "Yea. It looks like it's going well. How do you feel?"

Ian put on a smile. "I feel great. Not only do we finally get to see her get convicted, but I get a front row seat. I couldn't have planned this any better."

"You ready to testify?" asked Dom.

Ian laughed. "I don't have to be ready. I'm gonna run circles around that asshole."

Dom nodded. Ian turned serious. "Do you remember what I told you to do after this is all over?" Ian asked.

"I do. I'll deliver his head on a platter."

80.

Linda paced in front of the jury box as Officer Wilson waited for the next question.

"Officer Wilson, what did you do when you received the call from the dispatcher?"

"Officer Cohen and I drove to Ms. Kane's home on Mulberry Street."

"What time was it when you arrived?"

"It was 8:10 in the evening."

"What did you do when you arrived?"

"Officer Cohen and I first looked around to make sure there wasn't anyone outside of the house."

"Why did you do that?"

"We were called to Ms. Kane's home because of reports from the neighbors hearing gunfire. We wanted to make sure there wasn't a potential threat outside of the home."

"What did you do next?"

"We walked to the front door and stood on each side of the door and we knocked. No one came to the door, so I reached down and turned the doorknob. It was unlocked. We pushed the door open."

"What did you see when you pushed the door open?"

"We saw Hope Kane standing with her back to the door. She had a gun in her right hand."

"Did you see anything else?"

"Yes. I saw the victim, Mark Kane, lying on his back in front of Ms. Kane."

"What did you do next?"

"We stepped into the house with our weapons drawn, and we asked Ms. Kane to drop her weapon."

"What did she do?"

"She stood for a few seconds without responding, and then she dropped the gun."

"What happened next?"

"I placed handcuffs on Ms. Kane's wrists and read her the Miranda rights, while Officer Cohen examined the victim's condition."

"What was the victim's condition?"

"He was already deceased. He had a bullet wound on his forehead and another bullet wound in his chest."

"What did you do next?"

"We called for an ambulance and then we examined the house. We found two bullet casings."

"And were those two bullets fired from the gun Ms. Kane was holding?"

Both the judge and Linda turned to Tom, expecting him to object. Tom sat without moving. Linda had not laid the proper foundation to have Officer Wilson testify as to whether Hope's gun had fired the two bullets. Officer Wilson is not an expert and would not have the necessary expertise to opine on the technical analysis that goes into identifying the gun that fired a particular bullet. But, Tom had seen the reports, and knew that there was no doubt that the two bullets came from Hope's gun. Tom's objection would have been sustained, but what would have been the point? Linda would just call her expert to opine that the bullets came from Linda's gun, and there wouldn't be anything Tom could do to undermine that testimony. Objecting now would just appear to the jury as if Tom were trying to run away from a damning piece of evidence. He would need to preserve his credibility for the story he was going to tell. It was that story that was going to win the trial, not the undeniable fact that the bullets came from Hope's gun. So, he just sat, staring at the judge.

The judge shook his head and turned to Officer Wilson. "Answer the question Officer Wilson," he said.

"Yes. The two bullets were fired from the gun Ms. Kane was holding."

"Thank you, Officer Wilson. I have nothing further," said Linda and sat down.

"Mr. Rose?" said the judge, looking over at Tom.

"Yes, just a few, your honor," said Tom as he stood. He looked over at the jury. They seemed to appreciate his comment that he only had a few questions. The look in their faces was clear. Why drag this out unnecessarily? She's guilty as hell, and there's no point in asking a hundred useless questions. We want to get back to our lives, so move it along.

Tom turned to Wilson. "Officer Wilson, you testified that you arrived at the scene at 8:10 pm, correct?"

"Yes sir."

"December 26 at 8:10 pm, that would have been pretty dark, correct?"

"Yes, it was dark."

"Were there streetlights in front of the house?"

"Yes, there are streetlights on Mulberry Street."

"That wasn't my question. Were there streetlights in front of the house?"

"No. There is no streetlight in front of the house. There is one light about six houses away."

"Was that one light sufficient to light up the area near Ms. Kane's house?"

"No. We had to use our flashlights to see around us."

"So, if there was someone present near the house, you would not have been able to see that person, correct?"

"Objection!" shouted Linda.

The judge turned to Linda. "What's the basis for the objection?"

"Relevance, your honor. He has not established that there was anyone outside of the house that's related to the murder."

Perfect, thought Tom. Her needless objection just focused the jury on the notion of someone else being present at the house. The judge turned to Tom. "Any response, Mr. Rose?"

Another gift, thought Tom. The judge should have had the attorneys step up to the bench to debate this to prevent the jury and the witness from hearing the back and forth. But by asking him to respond to Linda's objection, it gave Tom an opportunity to start telling his story to the jury while using the prosecution's witness. This apparently didn't trouble the judge. He figured the prosecution had an open and shut case. Why go through the trouble of making the lawyers step up for a sidebar when the outcome of the trial had already been determined.

"Your honor, the defense intends on putting on evidence that the murder of Mark Kane was committed by another individual. Whether or not the lighting provided Officer Wilson the ability to see anyone else near the Kane's home who could have been involved in the murder is relevant to the defense."

The judge nodded. "Objection overruled. You may answer the question, Officer Wilson."

"Could you repeat the question? I just don't recall what you asked," said Wilson.

"Yes, of course. If a person was standing outside of Ms. Kane's home on the night of the murder, was there sufficient lighting from the streetlight to have allowed you to see that person?"

"Unless our flashlight had shined on the person, I don't think so. It was very dark."

"When you and Officer Cohen entered Ms. Kane's home, you testified that you saw her standing in the house, holding a gun, is that correct?"

"Yes."

"Did you in fact see Ms. Kane pull the trigger?"

"No. Mr. Kane had already been shot before we arrived at the scene."

"So, in your mind, is it possible that someone else could have shot Mr. Kane and then placed the gun in Ms. Kane's hand?"

"Objection, your honor. Mr. Rose is asking the witness to speculate."

The judge looked over at Tom, and before Tom could say anything, he turned to the witness.

"Overruled. You may answer."

"I guess it's theoretically possible, since I did not witness Ms. Kane pulling the trigger."

Tom paused for a moment, allowing this testimony to sink in. "Officer Wilson, after you arrested Ms. Kane, did you conduct an investigation of the crime scene?"

"Yes, of course."

"What did you find in that investigation?"

"I'm not sure I understand your question. We found the victim, and Ms. Kane holding the murder weapon."

"Isn't it true you found two bullet casings at the Kane's home?"

"Yes."

"Could you describe for the jury what a bullet casing is?"

"It is the rear part of a bullet. When a gun is discharged, the front portion of the bullet goes through the barrel, and the casing, the rear portion, is discharged through a chamber in the gun."

"Where were the two casings found?"

"In the defendant's home."

"I wasn't clear, and I'm sorry. My question is, which specific locations were the casings found inside of her home."

"Well, one casing was found on the floor right next to Mark Kane's body and where Ms. Kane was standing. The second casing was found about ten feet away, near the front door."

"Would it be accurate to say that the bullet casing would generally land near the place where gun was discharged?"

"Yes."

"OK. Now, isn't it correct then that the fact that one of the casings was found near the front door would suggest that the gun was fired from someplace near the door?"

"Well, yes, that's right."

The fact that the gun was fired by the front door would support the theory that someone was hiding by the front door and shot Mark Kane when he entered the house. Of course, Tom had no proof that someone else was in the house that night to fire the first shot. He would have to get that proof from Ian Ramsey. For now, this was just a building block.

"Now, let's focus on the bullet casing found near the victim. Wouldn't the location of that casing suggest that that bullet was fired closer to the victim?"

Officer Wilson nodded. "Yes, that's right."

"Thank you, Officer Wilson," said Tom. "I have nothing further."

"Redirect, Ms. Starr?" asked the judge.

Linda stood. "Just a few questions," she said as she walked to the podium. "Officer Wilson, Mr. Rose just asked you a number of questions about the location of bullet casings and the distance from where the gun may have been fired, correct?"

Wilson nodded. "Yes."

"And when you arrived at Hope Kane's home, you testified you arrested Ms. Kane, correct?"

"Yes."

"Now, did the location of the bullet casings have any impact on your decision to arrest the defendant?" Linda asked as she turned toward Hope.

"It did not," said Wilson.

"Why not?"

"Because Ms. Kane was holding the murder weapon that had fired both bullets."

"That's all I have, your honor," said Linda as she returned to her seat.

"Mr. Rose?" said the judge.

Tom heard Edward whisper, "End it."

Tom nodded. He had gotten what he needed. There was no point in trying to refute the fact that the same gun had fired both bullets. It was a losing battle, and in any event, irrelevant to the story Tom was going to tell. "I have nothing further, your honor."

"You may step down, Officer Wilson," said the judge.

"How many more witnesses do you have, Ms. Starr?"

"I have just one additional witness, your honor, and the State will rest."

"It's now 4:30. Why don't we recess here and start up again first thing. Please be back here by 10."

"All rise," said the bailiff as the judge dismissed the jury and stepped off of the bench.

Tom sat down next to Hope. The pain in his stomach returned. He began coughing uncontrollably. He brought a tissue to his mouth and saw blood. A hand touched his arm. He turned and saw Hope resting her hand on his arm, staring at the blood. Tom shoved the tissue in his pocket. He spoke to her in a low voice.

"Tomorrow, I get to tell your side of the story. I am going to do whatever I can to save you and Mila, but you have to trust me. You are going to be surprised at what happens when I put my witness on, but you have to trust me. I know you want to protect Mila, but having her locked up in that shithole with that monster is no life. She needs to be with you, and I believe I can make that happen. Please, just trust me."

Hope stared into Tom's eyes. He could see the tears welling up. She put on a smile. It was the first time he saw her smile. Two guards approached her. "I will do everything in my power to find her," said Tom. Hope nodded as the two guards took her away.

81.

Edward leaned back against the leather chair in the large conference room. Mike had rented the room near the courthouse for the team to use as a war room. Edward saw Mike and Annie walk in. "Dinner should be coming in a few minutes," said Mike.

"Where's Tom?" asked Annie.

"He's in one of the offices preparing for tomorrow. We've made good progress so far. You think he can pull it off?" Edward asked as he put down his coffee on the conference table.

"I guess we'll see," said Mike. "I didn't think any of this shit would work, but he's theory's starting to come together."

"It's coming together because it's true," said Annie.

Edward chuckled. "There's a big difference between a story being true and convincing the jury to believe our story. That's the challenge."

"I'm confident the jury will believe us," said Annie.

Edward nodded. "Your lips to God's ears." He turned to Mike. "Any progress with your buddies at the FBI?"

"I was just going to tell Tom. They're sending a couple of agents to court tomorrow, particularly because Ramsey will be testifying. They obviously can't get a warrant because they don't know where to search. My buddy Brown promised me he'd be ready to get the warrant and go wherever Mila may be, but he'll only do it if Tom gets the testimony he needs to support the warrant."

"I guess that'll have to do," said Edward.

"Let me go check in on Tom," said Annie. A few seconds later, they heard her scream. Edward and Mike ran next door. They saw Tom lying on the floor with blood on his lips.

"Jesus," said Edward as they rushed over to him. "Call Klingman!" he shouted.

Dr. Klingman stepped out of the treatment room and walked over to Edward. "He doesn't have much time. He can go at any point. He barely has a pulse."

Annie sat on the chair, crying into her hands.

"I guess that's it," said Mike.

"No," said a voice. Edward turned and saw Tom standing by the door. "It's not over yet." He looked over at Dr. Klingman. "Doctor, give me whatever you can give me to keep me standing. Mike, any word from the FBI?"

"The FBI will send a couple of agents to court tomorrow. If you can get something out of Ramsey that can justify a warrant, they'll get it. But the key is we have to give them more than what we've got so far."

Tom nodded. "We'll get what we need."

82.

Linda sat down after completing her direct examination of Dr. Malachy O'Neal. Tom watched the jury hang on his every word. Linda masterfully walked Dr. O'Neal through his report. He testified about the first bullet hitting Mark's forehead, and the second bullet hitting his heart. The most damning testimony was the gun residue that they found all over Hope. He explained that when a gun is discharged, the residue from the gun powder is expected to be found on the person who fired the gun. He had found ample amounts of the residue on Hope. Linda also anticipated Tom's cross examination. She asked Dr. O'Neal about the angle of the bullet that went through Mark's heart. He was prepared well. He explained that the angles of the two bullets could easily be explained. The first bullet was fired at his forehead, and the second was fired as he hit the floor. He explained that it's not uncommon to find victims with bullets entering the body at different angles. Linda smiled at Tom as she passed the witness.

The one area of cross examination that he thought would help him was completely undermined by Linda's direct. A part of him wanted to just give up on cross examining Dr. O'Neal. His case was going to rise and fall based on Ian Ramsey, and Dr. O'Neal's testimony would not alter the outcome. But he couldn't just give up. Tom slowly stood and looked at the witness.

"Dr. O'Neal, would it be fair to conclude that the bullet that hit Mark's head was the first bullet that was fired?"

"Yes, that would be my opinion."

"What is the basis for that opinion?"

"It's really the angle of the second bullet that explains the first. Because the second bullet entered his body from below the heart, it's reasonable to conclude that the victim was lying down on his back. That leads me to conclude that the victim fell on his back after the first bullet hit his head."

"Why would the murderer fire the second bullet when the victim is already lying on his back?"

"Objection," said Linda as she stood. "Dr. O'Neal has not opined on Ms. Kane's intentions. Mr. Rose is inquiring about something that Dr. O'Neal has not provided any opinion on. He can't read Ms. Kane's mind."

"Mr. Rose?"

"He has opined on this topic because he's testified that it's common to see bullets entering the victim's body at different angles."

The judge took off his glasses and rubbed his eyes. He then looked up. "Mr. Rose, testifying about what he's seen in other victims is entirely different from testifying about what the murderer was thinking. Objection sustained."

Tom turned toward Edward. He could see Edward mouthing the word "finish." Tom nodded.

"I have nothing further, your honor."

"Any redirect?" asked the judge.

"No your honor," said Linda in a cheery voice. "The prosecution rests."

"Very well. It's almost twelve. Let's break here, and we can start with the defense after lunch at 1:30."

Tom sat down with a cup of coffee and emptied out his briefcase onto the conference table. The others had gone out to pick up lunch. Tom read through his notes and then tossed his memo pad on the table. He didn't like it. There was nothing convincing about the story. He walked to the large window and looked out at the parking lot. Snow began to fall. He focused on a random snowflake and followed it as it fell to the ground. The task became more difficult as the snow became heavier, and as each flake blended in with the others. Tom closed his eyes and thought through his opening statement. The rule was simple – say just enough to capture the jury's interest, but don't promise too much. If you're going to promise the moon and the stars, you'd better deliver, or you are dead. He shook his head. Those rules did not apply in the place where he was going. He had to make promises even though he had no evidence to back them up. He had to deliver on those promises by forcing Ramsey to make a mistake – a mistake that would make the jury believe Tom's story. It was an impossible task, and he knew it. But, he also knew that his story had the backing of the truth. He had to find a way to expose Ian for what he really was. Tom opened his eyes. He found a flake falling by the window. He followed it as it fell, knowing that it was just a matter of time before he'd lose it. At the last second when he could still see the flake, he closed his eyes again, and followed it in his mind. He opened his eyes and believed he saw the snow-flake, sitting on the thin layer of snow that had covered the parking lot.

"Do you want a sandwich?" he heard Annie ask. Tom turned and saw her walking into the conference room with a brown bag. Edward and Mike followed her in.

"I got a ham and cheese, roast beef, shrimp salad, and a pastrami," Annie said as she started to empty the brown bag.

"I'll just have some coffee," Tom said as he held up his mug.

"Are you ready?" Edward asked as he unwrapped a sandwich.

Tom nodded. "Yea. I'm ready." He looked up at Annie. "I don't think I'm going to put you on."

Annie looked surprised. "What? We discussed this. I'm all that you have."

Edward put down his sandwich. "She's your only witness who'll tes-tify about what Ramsey did to stop you. Without her, we have nothing."

"Annie's testimony won't make a difference. I don't want to take the focus off of Ramsey."

Edward nodded. "It's your call."

"I have to accomplish two things. I have to make the jury believe in the story I'm going to tell as part of my opening. And then, I have to make the jury believe Ian Ramsey's a liar. That is the only way we win this case. Annie's testimony will cloud the story. It'll just highlight the fact that we have no way of connecting the guy who attacked her to Ramsey. I don't want too many snowflakes."

Edward turned to Annie with a confused look. He turned back to Tom. "What did you say?"

Tom smiled. "Never mind. I'll meet you guys back at court."

83.

Tom looked in the eyes of each juror that walked into the courtroom. They didn't look back. It was as if they already knew they were going to find against Hope, and they didn't want to draw a connection to her lawyer.

"Mr. Rose?" said the judge. Tom looked back at the gallery and saw Ian Ramsey with McBride sitting two rows back. Then a figure caught his eye. He saw a man sitting in the back with short red hair. The man stared right back at Tom. "Mr. Rose?" said the judge again. Tom stood and took a step toward the podium. He felt a shooting pain in his stomach. He braced himself against the table and took in a deep breath. Sweat started to form on his forehead. He could see Hope staring at him with the corner of his eyes. Edward tapped his arm. "You OK?" he whispered. Tom took in another deep breath and felt the pain subsiding. He turned to Edward and nodded. Edward handed him the notes for the opening. Tom turned and walked to the podium, leaving Edward holding the notes.

"Thank you, your honor. Ladies and gentlemen of the jury. I am here today, trying to defend a woman who has already been tried and convicted by everyone who learned about her story. The police, who are tasked to protect the innocent, took Ms. Kane in handcuffs without for a moment wondering if they arrested the wrong person. The prosecution, who we ask to uphold justice was so busy worrying about another conviction that she never bothered to wonder if there was more to the Hope Kane story. And worst of all, Ms. Kane's own lawyers were too busy worrying about her guilt to even ask the question as to how they might help her find justice.

"I took on this case because I believe Hope Kane is entitled to justice, just the same as you and me. But this case has become more than a trial about justice. It has become a story about finding the truth about what really happened the night of December 26. I'm here today to tell you her story. And after you hear what I have to say, I'm not going to ask you to acquit her of murdering her husband and her daughter. I'm asking you for far more than just a finding of a reasonable doubt of her guilt. I'm here to ask you to find that she is innocent. And I make that request because she *is* innocent."

A murmur broke out in the courtroom. "Quiet in the courtroom," said the judge. A few seconds later, the crowd quieted down. "Go on, Mr. Rose."

"Imagine a world where you are given no choices, where the ones you love can be taken away from you at the whim of another person. Imagine a world where you have no one to run to for help." Tom stopped and looked at the judge. He turned to the jury and looked into the eyes of each of the twelve jurors. They stared back. They were listening.

"I will tell you the Hope Kane story. The story begins in Las Vegas, Nevada. Hope Kane was a dancer at a club called the Shangri La Dream. No. I misspoke. She was a prisoner at that club. Hope has a tattoo on her left arm. It's an innocent tattoo of a heart with the letters S and D inside of it. But, it's more than just a tattoo. It's a mark to show that she is the property of a man. A man named Ian Ramsey."

The courtroom broke out into a murmur again. The judge silenced the crowd. Hope stared at Tom in shock. Tom knew the mention of Ian Ramsey would capture everyone's interest – a man who everyone knew was a criminal, but who was too smart to have been caught.

"The victim here, Mark Kane, and Hope were madly in love with each other. One day, they found out that Hope was pregnant with their baby. And that baby was Mila. With that backdrop, this story should have had a happy ending. But that wasn't possible. It wasn't possible because Hope Kane was the property of Ian Ramsey. He had branded her with his mark, just the way he branded other women who work for him at the Shangri La Dream. So long as she was the property of Ian Ramsey, she and

Mark and their daughter Mila could never have a normal life; the kind of life that everyone wants to have."

Tom paused and turned back toward the gallery and his eyes met the piercing gaze of Ian. Tom turned back to the jury.

"Both Mark and Hope knew that the only way they could get away from the grips of Ian Ramsey was to run. To run as far away as they can. But running wasn't enough. They both knew Ramsey would come after them. So, they went to see someone who knows how to help people like Hope and Mark hide. They moved to New York and had Mila, and they lived a loving life. They were finally living the life that they wanted to live. A life they deserved to live."

Tom turned to Hope and saw that she was crying. He felt a rush of emotion overtake him. He swallowed hard and focused his thoughts. He turned back to the jury.

"Unfortunately, the story doesn't end there. You all know it doesn't end there. Ian Ramsey is not the sort of man who lets people take property that belongs to him. For three years after Mark and Hope escaped from his prison, he sent his men out to search for them. And one night, he found them. And that night was December 26, the night he had Mark Kane murdered."

The murmur in the courtroom grew louder. The pounding of the judge's gavel did nothing to quiet the crowd. Tom turned back to meet Ian's eyes. Tom could see the burning anger. He knew he struck a nerve. Ian was going to make a mistake. Tom was going to make sure the jury sees his mistake.

"Ladies and gentlemen of the jury," said Tom as the crowd finally started to quiet down. "Imagine you are Hope Kane. You are forced to watch Ramsey kill the one man you loved, and at the threat of killing your daughter, you are forced to take the blame for the murder of your own husband. That was the life Ramsey gave Hope Kane. And that's the reason she is here before you. To be judged for the murder she did not commit. I don't want you to find a reasonable doubt about her guilt. It's not good enough. After what she's been through. She is entitled to be found innocent of the atrocities committed by Ian Ramsey.

"During this trial, I will tell you the true Hope Kane story, and I will convince you to find Hope Kane innocent."

The crowd in the courtroom no longer even tried to whisper. Their voices echoed throughout the courtroom. Tom turned and walked back to counsel table. Hope had her tearful face covered with her two hands as her entire body shook. Edward nodded as Tom sat down.

"Quiet in the courtroom!" shouted the judge. After several moments, the crowd quieted down.

"One more outburst like that, I'm going to close this courtroom to the public! Is that understood?" said the judge in a firm voice. He turned to Tom.

"Mr. Rose, it's 3 pm. I have a commitment this afternoon at 4 pm, so unless you can complete your direct examination of your first witness in the next thirty minutes, I suggest we stop here and continue in the morning."

Tom stood. "Your honor, I do not believe I can finish my first witness in thirty minutes. I'm happy to start in the morning."

The judge nodded. "Very well. We can dismiss the jury, but Mr. Rose and Ms. Starr, I would like to have a brief conference in my chamber." The judge then left the bench.

His law clerk waited for Tom and Linda to escort them to the judge's chamber. The judge was seated behind a large wooden desk. He looked up when Tom and Linda stepped in.

"Please, have a seat."

Tom and Linda sat down on the two chairs facing the judge's desk. "Mr. Rose, that was a moving opening you gave just now."

Tom nodded, waiting for the judge to continue.

"I will tell you that you turned what I would consider an open and shut case into an intriguing case. You certainly have captured the audience's interest."

Tom didn't respond. He sensed something bad was coming.

"You've made a lot of promises to the jury, and you've also made a lot of accusations against a man who is not a defendant in this trial. When a lawyer in my courtroom makes the kind of promises and accusations you have made, I sure hell expect him to make good on those promises and accusations. I don't like my courtroom turning into a circus, and if you can't deliver, this will have been the biggest circus I would have witnessed. You think long and hard about how you are going to prove your case, but if you don't deliver, there will be a price to pay. Do you understand, Mr. Rose?"

Tom nodded. "I understand."

"Very good. I will see you both in the morning, and Mr. Rose, you better come with the goods."

Tom rejoined the team and headed out. He saw Melanie standing in the hallway. "How are you feeling?" she asked.

Tom didn't respond. He smiled into her eyes, grateful that he could look into them again. Edward motioned for Mike and Annie to follow him.

"I'm sorry," said Melanie.

"For what?"

"That you have to go through this."

Tom looked down. "No. I'm sorry that I have to put you through this."

"Don't. I would have stood by you to the end. I wouldn't have . . . I never would have left."

Tom smiled. "I know. I wanted you to be happy."

"I can't be happy without you," she said as her voice shook through her tears. "You can't push me away and think that I'd just forget about you. I needed to decide to be with you through all of this."

Tom looked down, not knowing what to say.

"I'm sorry I have to tell you this now, but I . . ." Melanie took in a deep breath. "I didn't know if I'd get a chance to tell you. I love you, and I will never forget you. You will always be a part of me. That will never change."

She took Tom into an embrace. Tom's heart tightened as he tried to hold back the tears. "Stop torturing yourself," she whispered into his ear. "You've already made people start to wonder about Hope's innocence." Melanie kissed his cheek. "Go and finish it."

Tom nodded. He watched Melanie walk away. And, in the distance, through the glass doors, he could see Lance waiting for her out on the street. He watched Melanie cover her face with her hands as Lance helped her into his car. "Take care of her," he whispered, and he walked toward his team waiting by the door.

84.

Linda's heart was pounding. She felt the perspiration on her back. She threw her briefcase on her desk and walked to the window. The deep breaths did nothing to slow her heartbeat. He has no evidence, she kept repeating to herself. But, a part of her feared that maybe he had something up his sleeve. But what? What could he possibly do? He only listed Ian Ramsey and Annie Sharpe as his witnesses. How could he prove anything with these witnesses? As a consultant with Stern, Annie was too biased to have any credibility with the jury. And Ian Ramsey would not be so dumb to testify to anything that would incriminate him.

"How are you doing?" she heard Palmer ask. Linda turned to her and tried to put on a smile.

"I'm OK."

"That was some opening."

Linda nodded. "People can say a lot of things to get the jury's attention. But it means nothing unless he has proof to back up his story. And we both know he doesn't have it."

"What witnesses is he planning on calling?"

"Ian Ramsey and Annie Sharpe."

"That's it?"

Linda nodded. "Yep. That's it. I'm not worried about the testimony of Sharpe who works for Tom Rose. And what could he possibly get from Ramsey? Saying anything that helps Hope will mean his own demise."

Palmer leaned against the door frame. "Sounds right, but Rose has surprised me already. What does he know that we don't know?"

"Nothing. The facts are what they are, and he can't change them."

"Right, but he's managed to tell a compelling story. You saw the reaction of the jury. If he can even get close to backing up his story, we're going to have a problem."

Linda forced a laugh. Deep inside, she understood what Palmer was saying. But there was no way she was going to lose this trial. "We are not going to have a problem," Linda said firmly. "I'm going to beat him. And I'm going to send Hope off to prison for a very long time."

"I was thinking, maybe we should consider a plea offer," said Palmer.

"What?"

"A plea offer."

Linda shook her head. "Absolutely not. They rejected the only plea offer we were willing to live with. Also, after that opening, it would look like we're running scared. He hasn't presented any evidence. Just false promises. Anyone can make a promise. I'm not going to run from him. I'm going to beat him."

"This isn't a fight between you and Tom Rose," said Palmer. "We have to think of the ramifications of not getting a conviction."

Linda put on a smile. "Heather, we *are* going to get a conviction. Don't worry. I know what I'm doing."

85.

Tom could barely keep his eyes open. The pain in his stomach and the nausea drained him of all energy. He leaned back against the headrest as the Suburban made its way to the hotel.

"You sure you don't want to take the medicine?" Edward asked.

Tom shook his head no. "The pain will pass," he said. "I need to keep my mind fresh."

"I know you feel you have to finish this, but . . ."

"I *am* going to finish this," said Tom, cutting Edward off.

"You've already done a lot," said Edward. "The media was all over us when you were in chambers. I think you are making them believers."

"They don't decide Hope's fate," said Tom.

"The point is, even if she's found guilty, you would've changed the mind of at least some people about what happened that night. Not everyone believes she's a murderer. That's something."

"Not enough."

Edward nodded. "You're right. Not enough," he said in a low voice.

The car pulled up to the hotel. Edward helped Tom out. "I can manage," said Tom.

"Do you want to discuss what we're going to do with Ramsey?"

Tom shook his head. "No. I know what I'm going to do." He looked over at Mike. "I believe Mila's in Ramsey's house. Be sure the FBI's in position to get into his house. It'll be the only chance we have to save Mila."

Mike nodded. "They'll be there, but what if she's not there? What makes you so sure she'll be in his house?"

"Because that's where Ramsey lives. He's a mad man who is playing some kind of a game with Hope. If the game involves a threat to kill Mila, I assume he keeps her close by."

"I'm not going to question your instincts," said Mike. "If we can get evidence tomorrow, I'll have the FBI in that house come hell or high water."

86.

"The defense would like to call Ian Ramsey to the witness stand," said Tom. Ian stood to make his way to the witness stand. Stuart McBride stepped up to the podium.

"Your honor, my name is Stuart McBride, counsel to Mr. Ramsey."

"Yes, Mr. McBride. Welcome."

"I just wanted to state for the record that Mr. Ramsey was served with a trial subpoena outside of this court's jurisdiction. He had no obligation to come here today, but he chose to appear to clear his name. Some outrageous allegations have been made by Mr. Rose in these proceedings, and Mr. Ramsey wanted to come here to show the court that he has nothing to hide."

The judge nodded, and then turned to Tom. "Let's proceed, Mr. Rose."

McBride looked disappointed at the judge's apparent disregard of his speech. He turned and found a seat on the row of chairs behind the prosecution's table.

Tom walked to the podium. He wanted to make Ian feel uneasy with unexpected questions. Tom knew he would be prepared for questions that relate to Hope Kane, but he wouldn't be prepared about his personal business dealings. Lawyers usually focus on the obvious, but generally don't bother with the minutiae. "Mr. Ramsey, what is your occupation?"

Ian sat in silence for a long while and then responded. "I don't have an occupation. I have shares in some companies."

"Where do you derive your income?"

"Objection," said McBride as he rose to his feet.

The judge glared at him. "Mr. McBride, let me remind you that you are not a party here. This is a fight between the State of New York and Ms. Hope Kane. I am not going to have you interrupt this trial with your objections to questions you may not like. In fact, you shouldn't even be sitting there. Please find a seat in the gallery."

"But, your honor. Counsel is asking unfair questions that have nothing to do with this case," said McBride.

"You don't seem to be hearing me, Mr. McBride. Whether a question is relevant or not will be decided by me, and if there is a problem with Mr. Rose's questioning, then I trust Ms. Starr will bring that to my attention. I don't need you interrupting this trial. And, if you interrupt this trial again, you will be removed from the courtroom. Do you understand?"

McBride nodded. "Yes, your honor." He picked up his briefcase and stepped into the gallery.

"Mr. Ramsey, answer the question," said the judge.

"I do not have regular income. I receive dividends from the companies I hold shares in."

"Your home address is 15 Pena Avenue in Las Vegas, is that correct?"

"Objection," said Linda as she stood.

"What's the basis for the objection?" asked the judge.

"Relevance, your honor."

The judge shook his head. "He appears to be laying a foundation with background information. Let's see where he goes. Overruled."

"Yes," said Ian.

"How many square feet of living space do you have at that house?"

"Objection, your honor," said Linda. "This is really going far afield."

"I agree," said the judge. "Where exactly are you going with this Mr. Rose?"

"Mr. Ramsey's house is critical to this case, and if your honor will indulge me, it will become apparent very shortly."

The judge nodded. "Alright, but please get to wherever you are trying to go, quickly."

"I don't know," said Ian.

"Is it more than five thousand square feet?"

Ian fidgeted in his seat. "Yes."

"Is it more than ten thousand square feet?"

"Yes."

"Twenty thousand?"

"Around there."

"How many bedrooms do you have?"

"A lot." The courtroom burst into a quiet laughter.

"How many is 'a lot'?"

"I believe I have eight bedrooms."

Tom smiled. "Now, who lives in this eight bedroom home of yours?"

"No one," said Ian.

Tom smiled at Ian. "Is it your testimony that not one person currently resides in any of the bedrooms in your home?"

"No," said Ian. "I live there."

Tom nodded. "OK. So, your prior testimony was incorrect. Let me try again. Anyone else live in that large house of yours?"

Ian fidgeted in his seat again. "Well, I do have a housekeeper who occupies one of the rooms. Uh, I had forgotten."

"Who occupies the other rooms?"

"No one."

"No one," Tom repeated. "We'll come back to this topic in a moment. Let's move on to a different topic. Mr. Ramsey, do you know who Hope Kane is?"

Tom noticed Ian sitting frozen, and then taking a quick glance over at Hope. He then answered, "I do not."

Tom turned back to see Hope, and he saw her staring at Ian with an intensity he had not noticed before.

"Mr. Ramsey, do you see Hope Kane sitting over there?" Tom asked, pointing at Hope.

Ian leaned back in his chair and stared at Hope for a few seconds before answering, "Yes."

"Have you ever met Hope Kane before this trial?"

Ian turned to Tom. "No."

"Are you sure?"

"Yes, I'm sure."

Tom felt the pain returning. He felt faint and wanted to sit. "Are you OK, Mr. Rose?" asked the judge. Tom couldn't respond. He heard Edward. "Your honor, Mr. Rose has a medical condition. Could we take a short break? Just five minutes?"

"Yes. Five minutes. Please let me know if Mr. Rose needs more time."

Edward helped Tom back to the table. Tom took in a breath and wiped the sweat from his forehead. He wiped his mouth and saw the thick blood against the white tissue. He looked up at Hope and saw that she was staring at him.

"I'll be OK," he whispered to her.

She didn't respond. Tom drank the water that Edward handed him. Tom looked over at Edward. "I'm ready," he said and stood. "Your honor, I'm ready to resume."

"Go ahead," said the judge.

Tom watched Ian sit up in the witness chair.

"Mr. Ramsey, I'm going to ask you one more question about Hope Kane."

The courtroom fell completely silent, watching Tom walk back over to counsel table. He picked up a manila folder and he held it up. "Mr. Ramsey, before I introduce this document into evidence, I will ask you a slightly different question. Have you ever met Hope Kane before this trial under the name Hannah Silver?"

Ian stared at the manila folder without responding. Tom knew exactly what he was thinking. What is in that folder? Is there a document in it that'll prove he knew Hannah Silver?

"Mr. Ramsey?" said Tom.

The silence was deafening. Even Linda sat frozen, waiting for Ian's response. Ian turned to Hope and stared at her for a few seconds. Tom saw her gripping Ian's eyes with her own and not letting go.

"I, uh, I may have met her before," Ian finally said, pulling away from Hope.

The mummer in the courtroom was deafening. The judge pounded his gavel to silence the room.

Tom put the manila folder down on the table. The manila folder had nothing in it. The trick worked. Tom turned to Hope and saw her glaring at Ramsey, with tears dripping down her cheeks. At this point, Tom knew he had gotten over a hurdle. Ian was too smart to get caught in a lie, and having already admitted that he knew Hannah Silver, there was no reason for him to lie about how or where he met her.

"And isn't it correct that Hannah Silver worked at the Shangri La Dream?"

"Yes."

"What is the Shangri La Dream, Mr. Ramsey?"

"It's a gentlemen's club."

304

"And how do you know that?"

"Because I'm a part owner of the club."

Tom smiled at Ian. He walked over to counsel table and pulled out the transcript of Ramsey's deposition.

"Mr. Ramsey, do you recall having your deposition taken by me last week in Las Vegas?"

"Yes."

"I'm going to read to you a portion of the transcription taken at that deposition. 'Question, Mr. Ramsey do you own Shangri La Dream? Answer, No I do not.'"

Tom put down the transcript. "Mr. Ramsey, do you recall me asking you that question, and you giving that answer?"

Ramsey fidgeted in his seat. His face turned beet red. "I, uh, I probably was a little confused. I own lots of companies."

Tom nodded. "OK. But today, as you sit here, you do remember that you are a part owner of Shangri La Dream, is that your testimony?"

Ian nodded. "Yes."

"What did Ms. Silver do at the club?"

"She was a dancer."

"And isn't there a special VIP room at the club?"

"Yes."

"Mr. Rose," said the judge. "It's now 12:15 pm. We've been going for a while now. Is this a good place for us to break for lunch?"

Tom didn't want to stop. He had Ian where he wanted him. He didn't want to give Ian time to prepare for what was to come.

"Your honor, I wouldn't want to interrupt this line of questioning."

"Well, how much longer do you have?"

"I believe I can wrap up this portion in about an hour."

The judge shook his head. "Mr. Rose, I'm not going to make the jury skip lunch. Since you seem to have a lot more, I'm going to break here. Let's meet back up at 1:45."

"Your honor, may I ask the court to instruct the witness that he remain under oath and he is not to discuss his testimony with anyone?" Tom asked.

The judge nodded. "Mr. Ramsey, you will remain under oath and you are not to discuss your testimony with anyone. Do you understand?"

Ian nodded. "Yes."

"Very well. See you folks back here at 1:45 sharp."

Tom noticed Ian give a piercing look at Hope and then quickly make for the exit. At that moment, it occurred to him that Ian's not coming back. He ran over to Mike Lynch. "Mike, where are the FBI agents?"

Mike looked around. "I don't see them."

"Ramsey's not coming back. If I were to guess, he's going to give the order to kill Mila and hide her body. He knows that's where this is headed. We need to keep Ramsey from getting to his phone so he can't call his guys. And, we need to get the FBI into Ramsey's house to look for Mila, now."

Mike nodded. He looked over at Peterson. "Go find a way to delay Ramsey. I'll call my guys at the FBI." Mike and Peterson ran out of the courtroom. Tom walked back to counsel table where Hope was still seated.

"Hope, I believe I can convince the jury of my story of what really happened, but there is one hurdle I can't get over. Why did Ramsey not kill you that night? He could have killed you just the way he killed Mark. Why? I need to be able to explain this part of the story, and I don't know how. I have a pretty good guess why you don't speak. I am not going to let him hurt Mila. I have people contacting the FBI right now, and we are going to get Mila out of Ramsey's home. But now, you have to help me get you out of prison."

Hope slowly turned her head to look into Tom's eyes. Tom saw two guards approaching. He held up his hand. "I need a minute, guys. Please." The guards nodded and took a few steps back.

"Hope, I need for you to testify and to tell the world what really happened."

Hope stared blankly at Tom. A moment later, the guards returned to take her back to the holding cell.

Peterson ran after Ian and put his hand on his arm. "You are being summoned back to the courtroom," said Peterson.

"Excuse me?" said McBride, who stood next to Ian.

"The judge asked me to come get you. He wants to tell everyone something."

McBride rolled his eyes. "Let's go," he said to Ian. Ian walked over to the marshal to retrieve his cell phone.

"I'm sorry," said Peterson to McBride. "The judge ordered everyone to come back immediately." He could see Ian getting his phone from the marshal and walk out of the building.

"Good day," said McBride as he walked toward Ian.

Mike stood in front of the glass doors as he waited for agent Brown to pick up. He could see Ian walking toward the door. "Brown here."

Mike covered his mouth and started to walk away from Ian. "Jack, it's Mike Lynch."

"What's up?"

"Listen, we made significant progress here. Ramsey just admitted that he knew Hope Kane and that her prior name was Hannah Silver. We just broke for lunch. Tom Rose's got him where he wants him, and he's concerned Ramsey's not coming back. And that means he's figured out that Tom knows about Mila. He's going to kill her and hide her body unless we get her out of there."

"And how do we know he's going to kill her?"

"Stop asking questions. We can't take the risk. You gotta get to Ramsey's house and get her out."

"How do I know she's there?"

Mike didn't know the answer. He had his guys hack into a part of Ramsey's security system, but saw no sign of her. Other than what Tom said, he had nothing. He had to say something to convince Brown to take action. "Tom got it from Hope Kane."

"You sure?"

"Stop wasting time!"

"How much time do I have?"

"Not much. I see that asshole powering up his phone. He makes his call, she's as good as dead."

"Damn it, Mike. There's no fucking way I can get a warrant in time. You stall him. I'm on my way to the house."

Mike ended the call and walked toward Ian. Ian was bringing the phone to his ear when Mike bumped into his hand. When the phone fell to the ground, Mike fell on it and crushed it with his knee.

"What the fuck!" yelled Ian.

"Sorry man," said Mike. "I wasn't paying attention. I'll pay for a new phone."

Ian turned to McBride. "Give me your phone," he said, holding his hand out. Mike stepped in between McBride and Ian. "Hey, I said I was sorry. Why don't you tell me what the phone cost and I'll pay for it."

Ian pushed Mike out of the way. Mike got in his face and shoved him back. "Who the hell do you think you are!" he shouted at Ian.

Two marshals came running out to break up what looked like a fight. They pulled Ian and Mike apart. "What's going on here?" one of them asked.

"He punched me," said Mike. "I accidentally bumped into him, and he punched me for no reason."

"That's a fucking lie!" shouted Ian. "I didn't touch him."

"Both of you come with me," said one of the marshals.

"Bullshit!" said Ian as he tried to walk away. The marshal grabbed his arm. "You are on court premises and you don't get to ignore what I tell you. Come with me!"

Mike stared at the marshal pulling Ian back into the courthouse. He had bought a little time for Brown to get to Mila. Tom, you'd better be right, he said under his breath.

The judge returned to the bench and the jury was seated. Tom sat at counsel table with Edward and Hope. The judge looked confused. "Where's the witness?"

"He left, your honor," said Tom, rising to his feet.

"What do you mean he left?"

"I don't know, your honor. I saw him walk out of the courtroom during a break, and we can't find him."

Tom turned to Linda. She just sat and said nothing. The judge looked stunned. "I guess we'll have to bring him back another day."

Tom shook his head. "There is no other day. We'll never find him again, and God only knows what he's going to do to Mila."

"Objection!" shouted Linda as she rose to her feet. "Your honor, counsel is improperly tainting the jury with that statement."

"Mr. Rose, I don't appreciate your tactics," the judge said, glaring at Tom. "You keep this up, and I'm going to have to declare a mistrial, and we'll have to do this all over again!" He turned to the bailiff. "See if you can find Mr. Ramsey," he said. Tom saw the bailiff talk to two court officers who quickly stepped out of the courtroom.

Tom sank down into his chair and covered his face. He turned to Hope, knowing it was over. "I'm sorry," he said, looking into her eyes. He saw Hope rising to her feet. She started for the witness stand. The entire courtroom fell silent.

"What is this?" asked the judge.

Hope stared into Tom's eyes and then nodded. Tom turned to the judge. "I would like to call my next witness. Hope Kane, formerly known as Hannah Silver."

Linda stood. "Your honor, I object. Ms. Kane hasn't spoken in over a year. She is not listed as a witness for the defense. This is a complete ambush."

"If the defendant wants to testify, I'm not going to deprive her," said the judge. "Swear in the witness."

The bailiff stepped to her. "Do you swear to tell the truth, the whole truth, and nothing but the truth, so help me God?"

Hope continued to stare at Tom. She spoke in a delicate voice. "I do."

Tom swallowed hard. He had no idea how to start, but he knew this had to be perfect.

"Ms. Kane, do you know Ian Ramsey?"

"Yes."

"When did you meet him?"

A tear flowed down her beautiful face. She swallowed and spoke through her tears. "I was eighteen when I left home and wound up in Las Vegas. I stepped off of a bus and tried to make a life. I got a job waiting tables. Then, I ran into Tony. Tony Remo. He worked for Ian Ramsey. He told me he had a job for me that paid a lot of money. He took me to the Shangri La Dream and introduced me to Ian Ramsey.

"He offered me a lot of money to dance in the VIP room. He put a tattoo on me, like the other girls who dance there. After two years, I met Steve Wolfe. He handled the money at the club. He worked for Ian. We fell in love. I had never known love before. And we were happy. We spent every possible moment together, and we promised each other that we'd be together forever. But then, Ian found out about us. I always knew Ian wanted me, just like the way he had other girls go to his house to please him. One day, he sent Sean Boles to tell me that I had to go and see him. I didn't have the option to say no."

Hope closed her eyes as the tears came flowing out of her eyes. Everyone in the courtroom looked stunned as they waited for her to continue.

Hope took the tissue the bailiff handed her. She looked up at Tom. "I spent that night with Ian Ramsey."

Tom saw Hope's gaze move toward the rear of the courtroom. He turned to see the two court officers on each side of Ian, walking toward Tom.

"Mr. Rose, how would you like to proceed?" asked the judge.

"I would like to finish my examination of Ms. Kane," he said.

The judge nodded. "I don't want Mr. Ramsey out of my sight," he said. "He's not to leave this courtroom while we finish this examination."

The two guards escorted Ian to the front row of the gallery and sat him down.

Tom turned back to Hope. "Continue, Ms. Kane."

Hope stared directly at Ian. "That night, he told me he loved me. He didn't want me to dance anymore. He wanted me to live in his mansion with him. But I couldn't. I was in love with Steve. And Ian knew that. What Ian didn't know was that I was pregnant with Steve's baby. If Ian had found out, he would have killed both of us. We knew we couldn't stay. I went to see a man. He knew how to change our identities and help us hide from Ian. I became Hope Kane, and Steve became Mark. We took as much money as we could from the club and we ran as far away as we could."

Hope looked down, getting lost in her thoughts. "We found a perfect home. There was a room for our baby, Mila." Hope tried to speak through her tears. "She was so beautiful. So happy. I wanted for her to have everything I didn't have."

Hope stopped and then took in a deep breath. She looked up. "It was a day after Christmas. The tree was still up. Mila played with her toy kitchen set and Mark made a fire. I sat and watched them."

Tom turned back and saw Ian. He sat with a stunned look. "Continue, Ms. Kane," Tom said.

"That night, we had dinner at Capri." Tom saw her staring directly into Ian's eyes. "When we arrived at our home from dinner, Mila was sleeping already. Mark carried her into the house. When I came in through the door, Ian was waiting by the door. He was with another man. A man he called Dom." She looked out toward the gallery as if she was looking for someone. Hope turned back to Tom. "Ian covered my mouth so I couldn't scream. Mark came back to the living room after putting Mila down, and Dom shot him."

Hope glared at Ian as she gritted her teeth. "Ian then released his hand. Dom ran into Mila's room and came back with her. Ian told me he was going to take Mila. He said Mila would die unless I did exactly as he wanted. He put the gun in my hand and made me shoot Mark who was already lying dead on the floor. He told me I could never speak again. He told me I had to suffer in silence. That I had to be held responsible for Mark's murder – for murdering the man I loved. And if I ever spoke, he would kill Mila. He told me that this was the price I had to pay for betraying him. He told me that this was his revenge. He told me he loved me, and for my betrayal, I would have to be held responsible for the murder of the man who stole me from him. For the rest of my life."

The courtroom went into a frenzy. The judge repeatedly hit his gavel. After several minutes, the courtroom quieted down.

"Ms. Kane, do you know where Mr. Ramsey would have kept Mila?"

Hope looked into Ian's eyes. "The night he took her, he told me he'll keep her close by where he can check in on her."

Tom turned and walked back to Mike who was sitting behind counsel table. "You heard her."

Mike ran toward the two FBI agents. The agents stood and ran out of the courtroom.

Agent Brown sat in the black car with three other agents. They were a block away from Ian's house. His phone rang. He closed his phone and looked at his partner. "It's a go," said Brown.

"We don't have the warrant yet."

"Fuck the warrant. We can't wait."

The car sped up to Ian's house. Brown shot out the camera on top of the wall, and the car went crashing through the iron gates. The car pulled up to the mansion and the four agents jumped out. Brown's partner shot out the lock on the door and ran in. Two men rushed into the foyer holding guns. The agents pointed their guns at them and told them to freeze. They quickly dropped their weapons. Two agents cuffed them. Brown pointed his gun at the head of one of the men. "Tell me where she is or you die." Brown then looked over at the other man. "After him, it's your turn."

"What's your name?" Brown asked.

"Tony Remo."

"So Tony, how's it going to be?"

"I'll take you to her," said Remo. "Let's go," said Brown and allowed Remo to take them down the stairs to the basement.

"What's the other guy's name?"

"Sean Boles."

"You guys work for Ramsey?"

"Yes."

"You know that fuck's going to go to jail for a real long time, don't you?"

Remo didn't respond. "Here," he said as they approached a closed door down a long hallway. Brown tried to open the door, but it was locked. He saw a keypad next to the door.

"What's the code asshole?"

"1226."

"Cute," said Brown. "The date when Ramsey kidnapped her."

Brown punched in the code and the door unlocked. He opened it. He saw her sitting in a corner with her face buried in her lap.

He turned to Remo and Boles. "I should shoot you both dead right now for this, but I'll let you off easy. You both are going to testify that you called me to tip me off about her. You help us put Ramsey in jail, I will make sure you are not charged with kidnapping."

"But Ramsey will kill us if we do that," said Remo.

"Then you'd better help us put that fuck away for a real long time."

Hope lowered her face and began to sob. Everyone in the courtroom remained silent. The wooden doors swung open and Mike ran in with a group of men. Two men walked up to Ian. "You are being arrested for the kidnapping of Mila Kane," one of the men said as another man placed cuffs on his wrists.

Tom saw Mike smiling. "Brown got Mila," he said. "They found her locked up in a room. She's safe."

Tom turned to Hope. "Hope, you heard him. Mila is safe. The FBI got her out. She is safe."

Hope stood and ran over to Tom to hug him as the tears streamed down her face. "Thank you," she said. "My girl. My little Mila," she kept repeating.

The judge looked over at Linda Starr. "Do you have anything to say?"

Linda remained seated and stared off into the distance. She looked frozen, unable to respond to the judge.

"The State dismisses all charges," said a voice from the gallery. Tom turned and saw Palmer. "District Attorney Heather Palmer, your honor. The State dismisses all charges against Ms. Kane."

McBride stood. "Your honor, this is all a complete lie."

"I would keep quiet, if I were you, Mr. McBride. I'm sure the FBI's going to want to know how much of this you knew."

Two agents approached McBride and placed cuffs on his wrists.

"Mr. Rose?" said the judge.

Tom nodded and then turned to the jury. "Ladies and gentlemen of the jury, I really don't care if the State drops all its charges. Our system had convicted Hope Kane without a trial, and she has spent over a year of her life in hell, because the prosecution decided to become the puppets of Ian Ramsey. Today, she will be reunited with her daughter, and tomorrow, she and Mila will properly mourn the death of the man they love. They say time heals all, but they say that only because people forget. Hope and Mila will never forget what Ian Ramsey did to them, and they will never forget that we are all responsible for the torture they had to live through. No. The State dropping all charges today isn't good enough. I want the jury to find that Hope Kane is innocent. It won't change the past or diminish the wrongs that we committed, but it would be a statement to the world that we were wrong."

The judge turned to the jury. "Do you wish to deliberate?"

All of the jurors looked at each other. A woman stood. "There is nothing to deliberate. I find her innocent." One by one, all the other jurors stood to state that Hope Kane was innocent.

At that moment, Tom felt the pain in his stomach fade. His entire body felt numb and he thought he was floating in air. He could no longer hear anyone's voice in the courtroom. He turned toward the gallery. He saw the stunned look of the crowd. He saw Ryan and Mobley arguing with each other. And then he saw Melanie. She was crying as she walked slowly toward him. She mouthed the words "I love you," as she stared into his eyes. Tom turned to his left and saw Edward. His eyes were filled with tears as he gave him a slow nod. Tom felt someone next to him. He saw Hope Kane bringing him into an embrace. She said something, but he couldn't hear her. Tom closed his eyes for the final time and fell to the floor.

87.

Edward stood next to Hope. The arrival board said the plane had landed. Her heartbeat quickened. It had been over a year since she last saw Mila. Mila's fourth birthday had passed with Hope not being able to hold her in her arms. What did she do on her birthday? Did anyone have a cake for her? What if she doesn't remember me? Will she remember that I am her mother? Hope's mind couldn't stay focused. Her heart raced. She felt a hand on her shoulder.

"Everything will be OK," said Edward, smiling into her eyes.

Hope nodded. "It's been so long."

"She'll remember you, just the way you'll remember her."

Hope nodded. She wanted to believe him, but his words did nothing to calm her nerves. She saw the gate open and passengers walk out. Hope waited impatiently, bringing her two hands together as in a prayer and then to her lips. Then she saw her. A man held Mila's hand as they walked out of the gate. Mila looked around for a few seconds and then her eyes met Hope's. Mila screamed, "Mommy!" as she ran toward Hope.

Hope fell to her knees as Mila ran into her arms. "I missed you so, my baby," whispered Hope as she cried into her daughter's shoulder.

"I love you, mommy," said Mila. "Don't leave me again."

Hope held Mila tight. "I will never leave you again," she whispered into Mila's ear.

"Do you promise?" she asked.

"Yes, I promise."

88.

The rain fell gently as Hope held Mila's hand and followed the crowd of people. She saw Edward, Mike and Annie standing together. Hope walked up to Edward and then at the mahogany coffin. The crowd stood quietly and waited for the minister to finish his prayer. He asked if anyone had anything to say. "I do," said Edward.

"Tom Rose was my friend. And then he became my conscience. And most of all, he lived a life that meant something to me and to those he touched. He reminded us of the difference between right and wrong, of what it is like to overcome the impossible and to push yourself to the limit to do what you believe in. When we first learned about his cancer after he collapsed in his apartment, we begged him to walk away, that he had done enough. He looked into my eyes and told me, I want to make a difference. I want my life to have meant something. He told me that he wanted to save a life. That was his last wish. As I stand here, my friend Tom, you saved more than a life. You saved many, many lives, including mine.

"I will miss you my friend," said Edward as he allowed the tears to drip down his cheeks.

Hope kneeled down and hugged Mila. "Who is this?" asked Mila.

"He was an angel who brought you to me," said Hope through her tears.

A woman walked up to her. "You are Hope Kane?" she asked.

Hope nodded as she looked up at her.

"I'm Melanie Mann. I was going to be his wife," she said as she started to cry.

Hope couldn't contain her tears. She stood and brought Melanie into an embrace. "I'm so sorry."

"I will miss him," said Melanie. "But, you allowed him to live the life he deserved to live. Thank you."

Hope watched Melanie walk away. She noticed the rain had let up and a ray of sun shine through a small opening in the clouds. She stared at the beam of light. "Thank you," she said.

THE END.

[T]o know even one life has breathed easier because you have lived. This is to have succeeded

-Emerson